CW01429854

A CO[UNTRY]

SCANDAL

Sasha Morgan

First published in the United Kingdom in 2018 by
Aria, an imprint of Head of Zeus Ltd

A CIP catalogue record for this book is available from
the British Library.

ISBN 9781035907236

Aria
c/o Head of Zeus
First Floor East
5–8 Hardwick Street
London EC1R 4RG

Megan Taylor inherits her grandmother's country cottage in the village of Treweham and decides to make a fresh start there, taking a job at the local country pub.

When Megan meets Tobias, the attraction is clear, but she is determined to resist his charms, put off by his reputation and that of his best friends - the rakish Seamus Fox, son of a millionaire race horse trainer and dastardly jockey Dylan Delany. But Tobias is a hard man to resist…

For my dad, who enjoyed a flutter on the horses.

'C'mon my son!'

Cast of Characters

Tobias Cavendish-Blake – the new custodian of Treweham Hall with a wild-child reputation.

Megan Taylor – bequeathed her gran's cottage in Treweham and decides to make a new start after her boyfriend cheats on her.

Dylan Delany – Champion Jockey and lovable rogue, unable to resist any temptation.

Flora – stable girl at Treweham Hall, falls madly for Dylan's charm.

Ted – old gentleman living next door to Megan.

Seamus Fox – childhood friend of Tobias and Dylan, with a matching reputation.

Nick Fletcher – local vet who has a rather curious side to him. Archenemy of Tobias.

Sebastian Cavendish-Blake – gay younger brother of Tobias, quite dramatic.

Finula – local barmaid, becomes a good friend of Megan's.

Dermot – Finula's father, landlord of The Templar.

Gary Belcher – lottery winner from the North with a happy-go-lucky attitude.

Tracy Belcher – Gary's wife, with a quiet, caring side to her.

Lady Cavendish-Blake (Beatrice) – Tobias and Sebastian's rather cosseted mother.

Aunt Celia – sister to Lady Cavendish-Blake, a no-nonsense, tell-it-like-it-is old tartar.

Sean Fox – race-horse trainer and bullying father to Seamus.

Adam – Megan's cheating boyfriend, with a self-regarding attitude.

Chris Taylor – Megan's older brother.

Mr and Mrs Taylor – Megan's parents.

Carrie – Tobias' late fiancée.

Jennifer Goldsmith – Adam's very efficient secretary.

Samantha Tait – rich wife with horses, takes a shine to Dylan.

Sadie Stringfellow – a kiss-and-tell opportunist, who also takes a shine to Dylan.

Sharon – Tracy Belcher's jealous friend.

Wifrid – Aunt Celia's holiday companion.

Kate – Megan's old friend from the office.

Marcus Devlin – Irish TV producer with an eye on Finula.

Chapter 1

It was day break. A rosy, warm sunrise glowed over the valley. Galloping through the early morning mist, Tobias Cavendish-Blake finally slowed his horse to survey the sight before him. Treweham Hall stood proud and majestic against the smooth, rolling hills. The imposing building was made of sandstone with four corner turrets and sturdy buttresses that gave it a castle-like appearance. Gothic windows with stained glass twinkled in the sunlight. He sighed heavily: would it always remain so resilient, the fortress of his family?

That seemed dubious, going through the estate accounts. His father, the late Lord Richard Cavendish-Blake, had looked after the place well – too well. All the contingency funds had haemorrhaged, bled completely dry relentlessly maintaining the upkeep of the Hall. The outgoings far outweighed the incomings. The payroll of the staff alone made Tobias' eyes water, not to mention the colossal energy bills. Tobias had suggested shutting down the many vast unused rooms, but his mother wouldn't hear of it. Lady Cavendish-Blake had been sheltered by her late husband, leaving her totally oblivious to the fact that her home was a money pit and the current state of affairs could only be described as dire. As the new custodian, it was down to Tobias to keep the place running. He was responsible not only for the staff, but the village tenants too. Feeling the burden weighing down on his broad shoulders, he realised it was time to grow up. Time to settle down. The future meant kissing goodbye to the wild parties for which he was notorious.

His thoughts turned back to his thirtieth birthday bash, making him wince. It hadn't been so much a party, more a two-week brawl around Europe with a few friends, including his oldest childhood chum, Seamus Fox, son of a millionaire racehorse trainer. The two of them together had been a lethal combination, each egging the other on, the more daring and outrageous the exploits the better, resulting in the occasional brush with the tabloids. The picture of him and Seamus plastered over the front page of a newspaper showing them tumbling out of a St Tropez nightclub, legless (and trouserless) with a beauty on each arm, was one he couldn't forget. His father wouldn't let him. They'd been dubbed 'the Heir and the Fox'. Ironically, Tobias wasn't a natural wild child, the opposite in fact.

His one true love, Carrie, had been a local girl from the village. They'd always been close. Even when he had been sent to Eton they'd written, phoned and constantly made arrangements to meet. When Tobias had turned twenty-one he had proposed, claiming she was the only thing he wanted. Both families had been happy with the arrangement. Carrie's parents were glad that being married to Tobias meant she would stay in the village close to them and obviously be well looked after. Tobias' parents were just plain relieved he wanted to settle down with a sensible, local girl, instead of turning to drink and drugs like so many of his peers. Then one year after their spectacular engagement celebration, Carrie had been hit by a drunken driver and killed instantly. Tobias had been inconsolable; not even the Fox could calm him. He turned his back on society and locked himself away, refusing to talk or open up to anyone. His mother had been sick with worry, every attempt to reach him futile. Then, as if overnight, he completely changed. After twelve months of grieving, Tobias stopped being angry with the world and everyone in it and decided to rip the hell out of it instead. He forced himself to live life to the max, which meant spending his considerable allowance on any substance necessary to get the highs he craved, not to mention a string of stunning girlfriends who were more than happy to be showcased on the arm of a lord.

*

But now those days were over. Treweham Hall needed him and life had to be different. Even Seamus had grown up and settled down with Tatum, a red-haired beauty, with a red-hot temper, to boot. If anyone could tame the Fox, Tatum could; and he adored her for it, along with their two daughters, whom he worshipped. Tobias envied them. Deep down that's what he wanted, too, but how? Instead he would have to face some difficult choices alone. The one and only love of his life was gone for ever. She was lying in the village graveyard next to his own family crypt.

Chapter 2

Adam narrowed his eyes and settled further back into his office chair. His secretary was sporting a pale, see-through blouse today, revealing a black, lacy bra, along with a short, tight pencil skirt. He leant forward slightly, certain he couldn't see a visible panty line, so he assumed she must be wearing a G-string. He admired her long brown legs, slim ankles and red-painted toenails, revealed by stiletto sandals. She was playing a game and they both knew it.

At first he'd been quite shocked at her behaviour, brushing past him so her breasts gently stroked his arm, bending over his desk to expose a more than generous glimpse of ample cleavage, dressing more provocatively by the day as the dresses and skirts got shorter and tighter, the neckline lower, the material more transparent. Her body language was open, the innuendos grew a little more risqué, and she was definitely giving him the green light. He'd gone from being shocked to amused, to burning-hot curious as to what was under that damn sexy outfit. Now she was standing to the side of him by the filing cabinet. She dropped a file and slowly picked it up, revealing two pink nipples peeking out from the black lace cups. He watched her pert buttocks bend over, making the skirt ride further up her endlessly long legs. 'Clumsy me,' she smirked, seeing the lust in his eyes, then licked her lips.

He got up and sidled behind her, playfully slapping her bottom. 'Ready for some *dic*-tation, Moneypenny?' he asked. She giggled, liking the nickname. Good job, seeing as he couldn't for the life of him remember her name. Was it Fay or Kay? Or maybe May? Well, he couldn't remember everything, could he, with his high-powered new job as a partner? Recalling the name of his temporary secretary wasn't at the top of his list of priorities. She certainly helped to pass the long, stressful days, though. His hands reached round to cup her large breasts, which felt firm and heavy. More giggles.

'Adam, we can't. What if someone comes in?'

'But that's what makes it so exciting,' he whispered thickly in her ear, as his thumbs slowly circled her nipples, transforming them to hard buttons. She let out a sigh of pleasure, and he sniggered; that's how much she wanted him to stop. His hands slid to her waist, then down again over her hips and thighs and began slowly to hitch the skirt up, uncovering two smooth, brown cheeks, one of which was decorated with a red love heart tattoo. He was wrong about the G-string, though – she wasn't wearing any knickers at all.

He laughed under his breath. 'Well, someone came prepared, didn't they?'

She sighed again. He gently pushed her legs apart and explored between them. He gasped at how warm and ready she was. The gasp was returned, but it seemed to come from the doorway…

'Megan!' He shot up. 'I can explain…' he began, with his hands up his secretary's skirt.

Walking straight backed, with her head held high, Megan Taylor weaved through the busy office, ignoring the smirks and sniggers that followed her. Did everyone know but her? She hurtled out of the building, tears stinging her face. Traffic whizzed by, headlights illuminating puddles of rain as the passing cars threatened to drench her. Walking home wasn't an option. She dug out her mobile and rang the voice of reason, who would always offer the comfort and reassurance she badly needed.

'Dad, can you come and get me?' she choked.

*

Adam and her relationship had been good in the beginning, she reflected, once she was sitting silently in her dad's passenger seat. Luckily he could read his daughter well enough to know just what to say and, more importantly, when not to say anything. On first meeting Adam, Megan had been struck by his boyish good looks and charm. She liked the way his copper hair flopped into his blue twinkly eyes, the way his full mouth smiled mischievously, his ability to make her laugh with his quirky sense of humour, but all that seemed gradually to vanish over the months and was slowly replaced with an air of confidence bordering on contempt, assuming he could take his girlfriend for granted. So what if he appreciated other girls, there was no harm in looking, was there? Well, yes, there was, conceded his friends when they could see how blatantly he flirted with them in front of Megan. Even they were perplexed at why she tolerated him. Well, not any more. His lovemaking had gone from tender and caring to an almost mechanical, cold act, which had left Megan feeling lost and lonely. It was over. Thankfully she hadn't properly moved into his flat, so there was no need to call and retrieve her possessions, just a few bits and pieces that she could do without, or at least replace easily enough; she thought of her Ed Sheeran CDs, her *Bridget Jones* DVD, her collection of Jane Austen books and Cath Kidston toiletries, which all looked so out of place in Adam's modern, black and white apartment, with chrome fittings and wooden flooring.

Her dad cast a sideways glance. 'You all right love?'

'No,' she sobbed, 'I can't face having to work with him.'

'Hmm,' he replied by way of agreement. She could just imagine the gossip this would cause. The girls in her admin team often told Megan to dump Adam, but funnily enough it didn't deter them from fluttering their eyelashes at him every time he entered their office. It didn't help either that Adam was particularly good at his job as a solicitor. He had a way with words and knew exactly how to pitch his spiel and work his charm. Whether it be with a senior partner of the firm, or a rich client, he always extracted everything he wanted from them. As a result he was the golden boy, inevitably going places. Whereas Megan wasn't going anywhere, she conceded. She was one of the many faceless admin staff that quietly went about their business. In fact, it was a miracle to her that Adam had even noticed her in the first place.

It had been a rainy Monday morning and Megan had forgotten her umbrella. She was rushing to the office, dodging the puddles, when suddenly the huge canopy of a golf brolly had covered her head. Sharply turning round, she was greeted by the most beautiful blue eyes and engaging smile.

'Here, let me,' Adam had said easily, walking alongside her. 'We work in the same building, don't we?'

'Y… yes,' stammered Megan, not quite believing the office heart-throb was actually talking to her. Droplets of rain ran down her cheeks, and she quickly wiped them away. He smiled again. That big, confident grin was beginning to melt her. Reaching the stone front steps to the solicitors' office building, he casually held out his hand to guide her in, and for a second he touched her arm and it sent electric pulses through her.

'Would you like to go for a drink after work?' he simply asked, whilst pulling down his umbrella and opening the large glass door for her. Megan couldn't believe it. The delayed reaction caused him to look quizzically at her, but still with an air of assurance.

'Er… yes, thanks,' Megan had finally replied.

'Great. I'll meet you here at six o'clock then,' and with a final winning smile he took the lift to the second floor, where his office was and where a one-shot skinny latte was waiting for him on his desk.

All that seemed a lifetime ago now, Megan sadly reflected. It was impossible to believe that the Adam she had just caught fondling his secretary had been the handsome, charming man that had gallantly offered cover that bleak morning.

Turning to her dad, she noticed that his eyes were tired and swollen. 'Dad?'

He put one hand over her clenched ones. 'I'm sorry, love, I know this is bad timing, but it's Gran.'

'Gran?' she interrupted urgently. 'What's happened?'

'She passed away, love, early this morning.'

A dull, sickening force hit Megan full in the stomach. *No, not Gran.*

Chapter 3

Tobias knocked back the malt whisky in one. Feeling the hot liquid shoot through his system, he ducked down under the bubbles and shut out the world and its worries. Under the warm water he relaxed momentarily before resurfacing, pushing his long black hair away from his face. He rubbed the dampness out of his greenish hazel eyes, laid back in the roll-top bath and contemplated.

He would have to talk to his mother after dinner: she had to know the position they were in. After the initial grief of her husband's death, Beatrice had carried on as before, spending money like it was going out of fashion. Tobias shook his head – no wonder they were in this state. His father had totally indulged her, never giving her reason to stop and think just how much she was getting through. Luxuries were everyday things to Beatrice. The grand flower displays gracing the Hall, the running of her Mercedes and Daimler, her regular foreign holidays, designer clothes, the exquisite antiques she collected as well as the impressive art work – it all had to stop. This wasn't going to be easy.

Tobias grimaced and poured himself another malt from the bottle propped up by the bath. Having given himself a few more minutes to soak, he stood up, letting the water run off his muscular torso and down his long, lean legs. He wrapped a towel loosely round his hips and made his way into the master bedroom. It was tastefully decorated with pale walls and heavy tapestry drapes, and a large four-poster bed stood in the middle of the room.

There was a knock on the bedroom door. Entering, the butler hesitated on seeing Tobias dressed only in a towel round his slim hips, revealing a dark hint of hair. He coughed and averted his gaze. 'Excuse me, Lord Cav—'

'Henry, how many times? Call me Tobias. You have known me since I was three years old.'

'Yes, sir. Sorry, sir, it's just that the late Lord Cavendish-Blake always insisted—'

'Well, the current one doesn't,' cut in Tobias.

Henry handed over a freshly pressed dinner suit. Tonight was to be a formal affair with guests representing his mother's charities. It struck Tobias as rather paradoxical, believing charity should begin at home. Instead, his mother headed up various charitable organisations, and Tobias feared Treweham Hall could well be the next charity case if he didn't put plans in place immediately.

'Sir, Mr Fox rang earlier.'

'Did he indeed, and what does the old Fox want now?' replied Tobias with a smile, dropping his towel and stepping into boxer shorts.

'Er... asked if you would be available tomorrow, sir.'

'And am I, Henry?' Tobias slid his pressed black trousers over firm, shapely thighs.

'I... believe you have an engagement with English Heritage, sir.'

'Ah, yes, so I do.' Now his biceps were inserted into a crisp white shirt, he began buttoning the front over his wide, dark chest. 'Could you assist?' Tobias looked directly at Henry, sticking his arms out. 'Cuff links.'

'Ah, certainly, sir.'

Once dressed and prepared, Tobias braced himself to face the evening. This was going to demand some effort, but, as he was learning fast, when duty called he must respond.

*

Dinner had been a long drawn-out affair. Finally the last of the visitors had left, leaving Tobias alone with his mother. He tried to be as sensitive and diplomatic as he could, but the message had to hit home: the family were in grave financial difficulties. Beatrice sat and listened, dumbfounded, and a tear trickled down her pale, powdered cheek.

'I had no idea,' she eventually whimpered.

Tobias took a deep breath; it killed him to see her like this. 'I will do everything possible to keep us afloat, but we'll all have to make drastic sacrifices, Mother,' he warned gently.

'Yes, yes, of course. I'll cancel my Caribbean cruise?' she offered, arching a hopeful eyebrow.

'That's a start. We really need to draw in the purse strings and expand where we can to generate income.'

'But how?' replied a confused Beatrice.

'We'll have to sell some of the paintings, I'm afraid.'

'Oh, but not the Turner? That was a present from Daddy,' she pleaded.

Tobias held back the retort they were all bloody presents from Daddy, which is why they were in this fucking mess. His patience was wearing thin.

'I'm sorry, Mother, the Turner's the most valuable.'

She looked down to her gold court shoes and chewed a quivering lip. 'You mentioned expanding…'

'We'll need to invest more in the land. At the moment our vegetable gardens and orchards only provide produce for local businesses. We have to grow, develop new products, market them, brand them with the Treweham Hall name, give them a logo, our coat of arms, perhaps. I propose we renovate the old stable block into a farm and craft shop, maybe a country café, too.' Beatrice looked horrified. 'I believe the Prince of Wales has done something similar at Highgrove,' Tobias added quickly, thinking on his feet. That seemed to appease her.

'Has he really? Well, putting it like that...' Her gaze was distant, considering, then her shoulders straightened and she forced her chin out. 'Yes, it's what Daddy would have wanted, to battle on through adversity.'

The corners of Tobias' mouth twitched. 'The family is renowned for its fighting spirit,' he encouraged.

'Absolutely, darling, absolutely.' Then, pausing, she turned to face him. 'But not the Turner.'

Chapter 4

Megan was functioning on autopilot, dully going through the motions and trying her utmost to be strong for her mum. Megan had always had a close relationship with her gran, being the only granddaughter, and had played a central role in her life. The quietly spoken old lady had had a gentle air about her and was aptly named Grace. Megan pictured her gran's cosy cottage deep in the Cotswolds, with its crackling open fire. Often she would sit and watch its flames dance whilst listening to Gran humming peacefully to the radio in the kitchen. Megan remembered being tucked up in the bedroom under the eaves, being read bedtime stories. She had loved staying at Gran's. It made a refreshing change to be in the heart of the lush countryside, in sharp contrast to the suburbs of the Midlands. It had been a magical hideaway to her as a youngster, where she and Gran would walk along the leafy lanes, through the verdant forests that smelt of wild, earthy garlic, and pick bluebells. Megan smiled, remembering toasting bread on a long fork by the open fire and stacking chopped wood by the front door for it to season. As she grew up, the pull of staying there grew stronger, the cottage acting as a bolt hole in which she could hunker down and pour out her troubles to Gran, who would always listen patiently, nod her head at the right times and then offer sensible advice, which Megan undoubtedly took.

She only once brought Adam to see her gran, cringing at the impatient way he had been desperate to leave, obviously never intending to stay long as he drank his coffee quickly and started to drum his fingers edgily on his knees. They were staying at a nearby country inn for the weekend and Megan couldn't resist calling at Gran's on the way. Adam, begrudgingly appeased her, but made it patently obvious he considered it an inconvenience. Grace easily saw behind the false smiles and niceties, as for once his charm hadn't worked. After that embarrassing meeting, Megan never took him back and in turn her gran never asked after or even mentioned Adam.

Grace's funeral was desperately sad, yet so poignant. She had lived a long and eventful life, which her family were determined to celebrate. Her ninety-three years had seen her survive a world war in which she had been a land girl. Gran often regaled them with stories of the scrapes she and a close-knit group of girls had had living in their land hut. Megan recalled the sepia photographs of them huddled together on haystacks, laughing, wearing overalls and polka-dot headscarves. Soon after the war she had married Michael, Megan's granddad. There they had stood, outside on the registry office steps, Granddad in uniform and Grace elegant in a turquoise satin tea dress. Megan's mum had been born very shortly after, a honeymoon baby, they would proudly announce. Little Molly was their absolute joy. Gran had a habit of hoarding, which interested Megan; she enjoyed searching the memorabilia that evidenced her gran's life. Grace had had a spell in a cotton mill, in a grocery store, on a farm and, later in life, had trained to be a corsetière. Megan recollected the full-length mirror she used to measure her ladies and often wondered what else it had seen: Granddad in his smart, one and only navy-blue suit standing proudly with his daughter on his arm, ready to give her away on her wedding day; Mum looking radiant in white lace, full of happiness, yet maybe a touch apprehensive at leaving her childhood home and her parents. Perhaps that's why Mum married rather later than average for her generation, thought Megan, such was her reluctance to part from her doting parents. A fire at the brewery where Granddad worked had tragically cut short his life. The raging flames that had been started so carelessly by a discarded cigarette had soared through the hops store and surged mercilessly through to the brewing room, catching the busy working men unawares until it was too late to escape. The rampant fire had not only robbed five men's families of their husbands and fathers, but had also devoured their bodies, leaving the bereft without even graves to visit. Megan vaguely remembered the memorial service, clutching her mum's hand and staring in bewilderment at all the crying people wearing black.

Now here she was again, only this time she was also dressed in black, staring into her fine bone-china tea cup. Gran would have approved of the small country hotel that was hosting her funeral tea.

She suddenly became aware of her brother talking. 'Megan, they want a word with us.' He gently tapped her arm.

'Oh, right.' She blinked back the tears that threatened and quickly followed Chris into a small anteroom where her parents and an official-looking man in a dark suit were sitting beside a bureau. Megan assumed, from the papers that lay scattered in front of him, that he was the solicitor overseeing her gran's will. He had obviously spoken to her parents before summoning her and Chris.

'Please, do all take a seat.' He ushered them towards the table and chairs. Once they were all seated he cleared his throat. 'I act as the executor for Grace and I'm here today to explain her will and its contents. Your mother and father were already aware of what Grace wanted for her family, in fact they had previously discussed it together at length, so I am able to inform you both today of exactly what has been agreed.' He coughed rather piously. 'Christopher, you are to inherit her shares, to the value of £150,000.'

Chris's jaw dropped. 'But I never thought she had...' he stammered.

'She didn't want you to know, Chris,' Mum interrupted quietly, then glanced towards the solicitor to continue.

'Megan, you are to inherit Bluebell Cottage.'

'We'd rather you both have everything. Me and your mum don't need it and Gran wanted to give you two the best start she could,' Dad explained.

Megan stared in disbelief. Bluebell Cottage, the beautiful, cosy little safe haven that had acted as a refuge throughout her childhood, was now hers. Megan's eyes swam until slowly the tears began to tumble down her pale cheeks. It was Gran's last gesture of love, providing a fresh base, a new future, away from Adam and the office, with all its whispers and gossip and a job that she had gradually grown to hate. Megan glimpsed freedom, the tightening in her chest slowly released and she began breathing deeper. Hesitation mingled with excitement, as she dared to dream about the beginning of a new chapter in her life. A fresh start in the village of Treweham.

Chapter 5

'Mr Fox and Mr Delany to see you, sir,' announced Henry to Tobias, who was busy perusing paperwork behind his desk. Seeing his old friends made a welcome break from all the depressing figures stretched out before him.

'And what brings you two here?' he smirked, then added, 'Thank you, Henry, that'll be all.' Henry nodded and left the study. Tobias got up to join the two men. Seeing these close friends he'd known since childhood lifted his spirits. They'd never changed, in their ways or looks: Seamus, with his swept-back copper-red hair, freckles and ready grin; Dylan with his dark gypsy looks, black curls and piercing blue eyes. Together they had made a formidable force, forever challenging the authorities of their public schools, earning them early reputations, which had carried on into adulthood.

'Good to see you, Tobias.' Dylan Delany slapped him on the back.

'Surveying the estate?' enquired Seamus Fox with a raised eyebrow.

'What's left of it,' answered Tobias drily. His eyes fixed on the brandy sitting on the sideboard. 'Fancy a drink?' It was 11o'clock in the morning.

'Why not?' Seamus sat down on the sofa and stretched his legs out, whilst Dylan sat in the Chesterfield chair, rubbing his hands together.

'Yeah, never too early for a snorter.'

Tobias collected cut-glass tumblers from the side and poured three generous brandies, handing two to his friends. He plonked himself next to Seamus Fox. 'Cheers,' he saluted them, and downed it in one. Seamus frowned, sensing all was not well with his best friend.

'What's wrong, Tobias?'

Tobias looked gloomy for a moment then stated flatly, 'We're broke. The estate's fucked.' A short silence followed, until Dylan spoke.

'Listen, I can lend you—' He was interrupted by Tobias' harsh laugh. Though Dylan Delany was Champion Jockey, not even his money would touch the colossal funding that the Hall desperately needed. It wasn't thousands, it was millions.

'Thanks, Dylan, but there's a Third World-size debt to clear. I can't believe my father has got us into such a state.'

Seamus frowned again. 'But it all looks fine, everything as it always was.' He was commenting, of course, on all the plush surroundings and well-tended grounds, the staff quietly going about their duties. To all intents and purposes it did look like business as usual, but Tobias knew full well what lay beneath the façade.

'That's because he borrowed so much money to keep the Hall ticking over. My business alone can't support it.' He shook his head in despair. Tobias had started his own company years ago, buying old, dilapidated buildings, renovating and selling them at astronomical prices. Freshly renovated barns with a modern twist – skylights, mezzanine balconies, streamlined, sleek fittings – were all the rage in areas such as the Cotswolds, as were the crumbling historical houses that were transformed into high-class apartments. It amazed Tobias just how quickly and expensively these properties sold. But even the profits that he had stacked up could hardly touch the debts Treweham Hall was accumulating. He paused, then turned to Dylan. 'But thanks for the offer anyway.'

Dylan looked troubled. He hated to see his old mate like this, so glum, a far cry from the lovable rogue he knew so well. Seamus was racking his brains to find a solution to his friend's dilemma.

'What can you sell to raise emergency funds?' He, too, had thought of giving Tobias support. His family owned a racehorse training yard, with stables of top thoroughbreds earning them thousands. However, he knew Tobias too well to offer him money. It wasn't the way he operated. Beneath the playboy exterior that the media had been so keen to portray lay a gentleman at heart.

'Paintings. I've arranged for five pieces to be auctioned, which should raise immediate cash.'

Seamus nodded in acknowledgment.

'I'm due a race soon,' Dylan chipped in. 'A substantial wager would bring in the bacon.'

Tobias grinned. 'What if you lose?'

'I never do, not when it matters,' replied Dylan with confidence and a wink. Dylan's ocean-blue eyes twinkled with mischief. He was fiercely competitive and his athletic physique made him the hugely successful jockey he was. His ancestry dated back to Romany travellers, and he attributed his gift of the gab to this, as well as his success with the ladies. Dylan Delany was a real catch, everyone knew that, but the trouble was he refused to be caught. He weaved his way through various relationships, ducking and diving, avoiding any commitment. The more unobtainable he became, the more he was desired.

Dylan had a reputation and it took some upholding. He couldn't help it if he loved women. He genuinely did like their company. He appreciated their femininity, the way they dressed so elegantly, their fragrance, their beautiful shiny, long hair, or sassy short hair, for that matter – he liked both. He was a sucker for any damsel – he was only human, after all. But deep down Dylan was a decent man and hated to see one of his close friends in any kind of trouble. Seamus was equally protective of his best friend.

'True,' agreed Seamus, 'but it's too much of a risk in the current climate.'

Dylan looked at him. 'Says the Fox for whom I've made a fortune.'

'True again,' said Seamus with a laugh. Fox was a fitting name for him, with his ginger hair and sly, cunning wit.

'Sometimes I feel like selling the whole bloody place, lock, stock and barrel to some rich American... throw in the title, too,' moaned Tobias.

'Surely it's not that bad,' sighed Seamus. He'd grown to love Tobias' home, spending many a childhood summer there, and he smiled wistfully remembering the scrapes they'd got into. He'd also grown to love the family, who always made him feel so welcome. In later years Treweham Hall had acted as a temporary retreat when he had fallen out with his father. Sean Fox was a formidable force. He had a driving ambition where his horses were concerned, and ran his stables with a cast-iron fist. Although he loved both his sons, he wouldn't tolerate any form of subordination and treated them as he would any other member of staff, strictly but fairly. A young Seamus didn't agree with his father's authoritarian methods and his defiance had got him booted out of the Fox household. The Cavendish-Blakes came to the rescue, giving him the full use of the Gate House on their estate. This had proved to be the perfect solution, especially to Seamus' mother, whose desperate pleas to bring Seamus home had been totally ignored by her hardened husband.

'Do you remember my stay in the Gate House?' Seamus chuckled.

'No, I remember when you *lived* in the Gate House,' retorted Tobias.

'Well, yes, perhaps I did rather outstay my welcome.'

'You were there for two years, Fox.'

Then suddenly Tobias' face lit up with a flash of inspiration. 'The Gate House! That's it.'

'What?' replied Seamus and Dylan in unison.

'Combine my business with the estate. Renovate the Gate House and sell it. It could fetch a fortune.'

'Bloody hell, you're right,' agreed Seamus.

'Sounds like a plan to me,' said Dylan. He'd always loved the Treweham Hall estate and its many places they had played in as youngsters. It was here, right in the old stables, that he had first developed his love of horses. After encountering the Cavendish-Blakes' thoroughbreds, he had been bitten by the bug and had longed for a career involving these magnificent animals. His grit, pure determination and natural competitive streak had led him to the world of horseracing. On impulse, he longed to go back to where it had all started.

'Do you mind if I take a look at the stables?' He also couldn't resist sizing up other people's horses. Plus there was a rather nice blonde he'd noticed earlier, sweeping up in the yard. Not waiting for a response, Dylan stood up and left the room, leaving Tobias and Seamus looking at each other in amusement.

As luck would have it she was still there tending to the horses when he jumped over the fence and made his way to the stables. She recognised him immediately. 'Hello, Mr Delany,' she gushed.

'Please, call me Dylan,' he smiled, giving her the full benefit of his white teeth and gleaming eyes. She blushed.

Embarrassed, she blustered, 'Would you like a ride? Erm, my name's Flora.' He looked at her pert bottom in tight jodhpurs, and cleavage spilling out of a partially unbuttoned check shirt.

'I'd love a ride,' he answered, looking her full in the face. Flora gazed back in admiration; Dylan had been her hero since Pony Club. Now, at twenty, she was working in the stables as a groom and loving every minute, especially with the chance of meeting Lord Cavendish-Blake's close friend the one and only

Dylan Delany. And he was here! He moved closer and asked quietly, 'Anyone in those stables?'

The penny dropped. Startled yet thrilled, she slowly shook her head.

'No,' she replied huskily. He pulled the band out of her hair, making it tumble over her face. She pulled it back hastily. 'But I'm expecting Lord Cavendish-Blake to arrive any moment.'

Dylan, however, knew better. 'Not for some time yet. He's busy at the moment.' Flora turned her head sharply towards the Hall, as if willing Lord Cavendish-Blake to suddenly appear, and her hair swung over her face again in a silky blond wave.

He found it incredibly sexy. He could just about see her eyes through the blond waves, her pupils had dilated and she was breathing deeply, making her chest heave up and down. He was home and dry.

'Could you show me inside the stables?' he whispered in her ear, gently licking her lobe. Flora's sensations swam, totally mesmerised, yet she tried to hesitate.

'I'm not sure, what if…' But Dylan gently took her hand and guided her inside.

It was dark and warm. Hay bales were piled up against the walls. He took two and placed them on the floor. Turning to her, he slowly began unbuttoning the rest of her shirt, sighing with delight at the creamy breasts bursting out of a red silk bra.

He dipped his head and kissed one, his tongue seeking the nipple and flicking it hard, making her gasp. His hands found their way inside her jodhpurs and stroked the pert bum he had so admired earlier.

'Now, about that ride…'

Chapter 6

Megan's Fiat Panda had actually made the journey all the way to the Cotswolds, much to her surprise. Packed to bursting with her belongings, complete with a roof rack creaking with the weight of suitcases, the little car had chugged along gently until it reached its destination, Treweham village. Staring at the stone cottage, with its pretty front garden packed with daffodils, Megan still couldn't believe all this was actually hers. Her heart longed for Gran to come scurrying out of the front porch and up the cobbled pathway to greet her. But no, everything stood still, except for the soft, gentle sway of the conifer trees and the overgrown pampas grass. The trickle of the nearby stream and a wood pigeon calling in the distance were the only sounds. Taking a deep breath, Megan got out of the car, reached her suitcases down from the roof rack and began to heave them up to the front door.

She had been given a key to the cottage, but on impulse she bent down to the flowerpot standing at the side of the porch, bursting with purple, white and yellow crocuses. As always, a spare key was buried underneath it, amongst the gravel and soil. A lump suddenly appeared in Megan's throat that she couldn't swallow. The key still had the familiar key ring attached to it, a copper heart, all tarnished and worn now from years of being hidden under the terracotta pot. Megan turned the key and slowly opened the door. The hinges creaked and the place smelt slightly of damp.

Everything was just as she remembered it: the tiny kitchen with the white ceramic butler sink, brass taps and wooden draining board, the stone floor and oak table and chairs, the Welsh dresser displaying various pieces of crockery, the cosy inglenook fireplace in the lounge, the floral wallpaper that was now blotched with damp patches, the steep, narrow staircase with squeaky wooden boards.

Upstairs, her gran's bedroom was exactly as she'd left it, with her patchwork quilt cover neatly spread over the bed, patiently waiting to be pulled back and to keep its occupant warm, the French-polished dressing table stood at the side with photo frames containing pictures of Megan and Christopher, and bottles of perfume. Megan walked towards it, picked up a round, lilac bottle and sprayed it into the cold air. A comforting memory seared through her immediately: Parma violets, the smell of Gran. Her knees buckled and she quickly sat on the edge of the bed, taking steady breaths. After a few moments her eyes searched the room, and she smiled when they rested on the cast-iron fireplace, then stopped when she noticed the pile of ash at the bottom of the grate. Ashes to ashes, dust to dust. A chill hovered over her momentarily. This was ludicrous, Megan chastised herself. There was no need to feel uneasy here. This had been Gran's home, and now it was hers. This was a safe place, away from everything that had caused her pain. The only communication she had had from the office was a phone call from Kate, whom she had worked alongside and had grown close to. Megan had told her she wasn't coming back, despite Kate's pleas for her to return. Megan hadn't needed to ask if she was the subject of office gossip – she knew damn well she would be. Kate had kept her word and not told a soul where Megan was, especially Adam, who had come sniffing round her for information. She allowed herself a moment to picture Adam, slouched in his chair, hands behind his head, swivelling behind his desk, oozing confidence that once she had fallen for. She shuddered, then with determination hauled herself up and made her way back down to the kitchen. She could almost hear Gran's voice saying, 'It will all seem much better after a cup of tea.'

'Yes, Gran, I'll put the kettle on,' she said aloud.

Chapter 7

In a little terraced house tucked away in the back streets of an industrial town in Lancashire, Gary Belcher was settling down for the evening. He'd had a very long and tiring day at the supermarket and his hands were red raw from stacking the freezer cabinets. Although he was only in his mid-twenties, and in good shape, his body still ached. He'd done a double shift and was knackered. His crew-cut hair was wet with sweat and he longed for a hot bath to ease his aching muscles, but had opted for a quick shower, knowing how much it cost to heat the water. Tracy, his wife, was still working at the care home, but would be back soon. As it was Saturday he'd treated them to a curry on the way home, just one portion, but they'd share it along with some oven chips and bread to spread the meal out. He opened a can of lager and swigged it back. After gulping the last drop he burped loudly and reached for the remote control.

Flicking through the channels, he rolled his eyes at the talent competitions that dominated Saturday night TV. Call that singing? He could do better down at the club. He smiled to himself, remembering how he had serenaded Tracy on their wedding day. It had

34

been a small but intimate affair in the local church, then a big booze-up in the hall next door. Tracy and her sister had decorated it with bunting and balloons, and used two wallpaper pasting tables covered with pink plastic tablecloths on which to lay out the buffet. Later a couple of his mates from the club had set up a karaoke machine and Gary had set the ball rolling with his rendition of 'Lady in Red', which he changed to 'Lady in White', gaining him a collective 'Ah' from the wedding party. Tracy had been bowled over. She'd never heard him sing before. He could just picture her now, looking slim and tanned in the off-white meringue dress she had snapped up in a charity shop, her long, blond hair all done up by Sharon from 'Cut Above' on the corner. She looked beautiful and he'd never felt so proud or happy as he serenaded her, meaning every single word.

He turned the television off, then pulled out his phone from his pocket to check the lottery numbers, as he routinely did on a Saturday night. Six figures stared at him. He screwed his eyes, shook his head then looked again. He'd recognise those numbers anywhere: 27 his age, 25 Tracy's age, 11 the number of the house, 2 because they'd got married on 2nd February, 30 the age Tracy wanted children and 13 as it had always been a lucky number for him. And tonight, if his eyes weren't deceiving him, he had been bloody lucky, absolutely fucking lucky… Surely not? He sat up straight and gaped at the six numbers lit across the screen. Yes, there they were, plain as day, numbers 27, 25, 11, 2, 30 and 13. He sat still, frozen on the settee.

He heard the door bang shut, then Tracy's voice call out. 'Hi, Gaz, I'm home!' He was motionless, all he could hear was the pounding of his heart in his chest, boom, boom, boom.

'Gary? Are you all right, love?' asked Tracy, full of concern at seeing her husband still as a statue, perched on the edge of the settee. *Oh my God, he's had a stroke.* She dashed towards him. 'Gaz! Talk to me!' She slapped his face in panic. This seemed to shake him out of his reverie. He gave her a lopsided smile. Had he been drinking? She looked around her and noticed only one can of lager on the coffee table.

'Trace, we've done it, we've bloody done it, love,' he whispered hoarsely.

'Done what, love?' she asked gently. Something was definitely wrong. He wasn't himself at all. She stroked his face tenderly. 'Gary, you're shaking, love. What's the matter?' He pointed to his phone. Frowning, she turned to look and then she too saw the numbers, each one holding some small significance to them. Now they held so much more. Those six numbers held their destiny, their fate, their future. She faced her husband and they gazed into each other's eyes before screaming and jumping in the air. 'We've won the lottery, Gaz!'

'I know, I know Trace, we've won the fucking lottery!'

Chapter 8

Megan woke the next morning with the sun piercing through the gap in the floral curtains. She had chosen to sleep in her old room, snug under the eaves, rather than in the main bedroom, and after a moment's disorientation she smiled at the comforting surroundings. This had always been her favourite room in the cottage, and it held so many fond memories. Glancing at the patchwork quilt on the bed she was reminded of how she and Gran had painstakingly matched up the small squares and carefully sewed them together on the old Singer sewing machine.

That gave Megan an idea. The sewing machine would come in very handy now that she had decided to completely refurbish her new home. Whilst she loved everything about Bluebell Cottage, Megan wanted to put her own mark on it, though still keeping the traditional look. New curtains would be a good place to start, along with freshly painted walls to replace the damp, curling wallpaper. Megan was filled with a bright optimism. It was amazing what a good night's sleep could do.

Flinging back the sheets, she scrambled in the bedside cabinet for paper and a pen. A 'to do' list was in order whilst she was feeling so positive. Number one, 'Get a job'. Although she did have some savings, they wouldn't last for ever and she had to do something. Local would be best. On her arrival in the village she had noticed a sign outside The Templar asking for part-time bar staff. Although she'd never worked behind a bar, it would be good to work so close by.

Ideally she wanted to work from home. Since leaving her old office job she had visions of fulfilling her dream to make a living as an artist. She had studied art at college but, instead of continuing on to university, she had opted to get a job and stay at home. Maybe she had inherited her mum's reluctance to fly the nest. Her dad had always said it was such a waste of talent. Her portfolio was bursting with paintings, from the buzz of street life in vibrant cities, with their bright lights and towering buildings, to the rolling velvet hills and swaying cornfields of the countryside. Megan longed to paint, but she had hardly touched her brushes since... well, since she had met Adam, actually. She missed the smell of the paint, mixing the colours into misty sea turquoises, fresh verdant greens and pale pastel shades. Deciding there and then to resurrect her talent, she wrote number two on her list, 'Start painting again'.

Maybe she could combine both action points? Get paid to paint, start commissioned work. The more she thought about it, the more appealing the prospect became. She'd get business cards made, advertise in magazines, print flyers… Excitement tinged inside her as the idea began to flourish. She would need to fetch her portfolio from Mum and Dad's so that she would be able to display samples of her work where she could. Perhaps the local tearoom would be a good place to start. A shiver of anticipation rushed through Megan as she imagined the quaint little café showing off her paintings, with a card and price tag discreetly lodged in the corner of the frame. It would be a good idea to paint nearby locations, capturing the essence of the village with its old-fashioned post box, its beautiful fifteenth-century church, its bubbling brook and, in high summer, its poppy fields. On impulse, Megan decided the first thing she'd paint would be Bluebell Cottage and dedicate it to Gran.

Spurred on by her master plan, she jumped out of bed; there was a lot to do today. First stop was The Templar, so she dressed smartly in black trousers and a fitted short-sleeved white blouse, wanting to make a good impression.

*

Entering the pub Megan was greeted by a cheery, 'Hello there!' from a red-headed girl serving behind the bar. Megan guessed they were a similar age, judging by her pale, smooth skin covered in freckles and her skinny jeans and crop top.

'Hello,' Megan replied with a smile, making her way towards the bar.

'All moved in?'

Megan grinned, she was accustomed to village life, having spent so much time with Gran, but it would take a little adjustment, having neighbours who knew your every move 24/7.

'Yes, thanks. I'm Megan, by the way.' She held her hand out.

'Finula. Pleased to meet you.' She gripped Megan's hand in a firm, confident shake, making her silver bangles jingle.

'I've come about the part-time job advertised.'

'Great, have you any experience of bar work?'

'Not exactly, but I'm a quick learner.'

'Right,' laughed Finula, 'let's see how you pull a pint then.'

Megan, rising to the challenge, joined Finula behind the bar.

'OK, so slowly does it, tilting the glass.' Finula had obviously pulled many a pint, making it look so easy as the amber fluid gradually made its way up the glass. 'Now your turn.' She handed Megan a pint glass. Licking her lips in concentration Megan pulled back the hand pump, which hissed and a slight spray of beer squirted in their faces, making them giggle. After several attempts and much chuckling, Megan was getting the knack of it.

'We do bar snacks and there's also the restaurant, so we'd need you to wait on the tables, too,' Finula informed Megan.

'That's fine, no problem.' Megan looked towards the room where the restaurant tables were neatly dotted about in cream linen tablecloths with tall-backed leather chairs. It all looked very elegant; a good contrast to the real traditional bar area with its stone floor and wooden benches. 'It's lovely, Finula. You must love working here.'

'It is a friendly environment. I do a lot of the catering. All our food is sourced locally. The vegetables are from Treweham Hall.'

'Really?' Megan pictured the impressive manor, with virginia creeper and wisteria growing up its majestic stone walls. She'd always admired it and had often wondered what the Cavendish-Blake family would be like, hidden away in such a vast, imposing home.

'Sure, the Cavendish-Blakes are keen to support the village. So, when can you start?' asked Finula.

'What, that's it?' Megan asked, startled. 'Don't you have to ask anybody first?'

'Well, only the landlord and he's my dad. To tell you the truth, we're desperate and so far you're the only one that's showed any interest. Anyway, you seem keen enough so why not? And Dad usually does what I tell him,' Finula smirked.

'Yes, that's usually the way, isn't it, Fin?' called a loud Irish voice from the side of the room.

'Ah, here he is, the man himself. Dad meet Megan, our new barmaid.'

'Is she indeed?' quipped the larger-than-life chap. He had thick silver hair and sideburns, reminding Megan of an Irish Pa Larkin. 'Hello, Megan, I'm Dermot.' He nodded towards the pint glasses filled with ale. 'Got the hang of it?'

'Think so. I'm honest and reliable, too,' Megan added with a winning smile.

'To be sure you are, Megan,' laughed Dermot. 'Tell you what, you supply a reference and I'll give you a month's trial, lass. When can you start?'

'Er... tomorrow?'

'Tomorrow it is then. Come at lunchtime on the first day, when it's not too busy If you cope with that you can do some evenings as well.'

'Thanks.' Megan was elated. 'And thanks too, Finula.'

Finula beamed, it was about time she worked with someone closer to her age instead of the middle-aged housewives in the village. Something told her Megan would prove to be just the tonic this pub needed.

Chapter 9

As he opened the door the smell of damp hit Tobias immediately. Cobwebs hung from almost every crevice. He scrutinised the interior of the Gate House with a critical eye. Outside it was clear what work was to be done. The Cotswolds stone needed sandblasting, ridding the walls of the murky stains that defaced the original honey glow. The gardens needed landscaping, fencing mended and stained; the roof needed replacement tiles and the outhouse needed to be renovated into a double garage. All straightforward jobs that he could fix, no problem.

It was the inside that was the problem. This being a listed building, he was restricted to a certain degree, but even that wasn't the issue. It was the memories it harboured that caused Tobias to stand still, take stock and for the thousandth time torture himself with what could have been. He and Carrie had been promised the Gate House for a wedding present. They had planned to live there after their marriage. Carrie had been ecstatic when Tobias' parents had announced their intention to give them their own home on the estate. Together they had made plans for their love nest, and Tobias remembered Carrie going from room to room, deciding on the décor and furnishings. He had watched her, smiling, drinking in the sense of utter happiness she made him feel, deep down to his core.

He gulped and his eyes misted over. Cursing, he forced himself to get a grip. *Pull yourself together, man, it's been ten years.* A whole decade since she had been cruelly snatched away that fateful night. Even now, Tobias just couldn't comprehend how Carrie had vanished from his life, a life that should have been shared with her. Would they have had children by now? Probably. He allowed himself to picture Fox playing with his two little girls, piggybacks on the lawn, squealing with delight, his wife, Tatum, watching with laughter and adoration. Tobias physically doubled over, feeling like he'd been punched in the stomach. It was so unjust, brutally unfair; and it was never ending. Never had anyone come close to Carrie. True, he'd had plenty of girlfriends, rich, celebs, models, but they were just bed companions, playthings that helped pass the time. They weren't soul mates he could open up to. Some had tried to delve inside that incredibly sharp and complex mind of his, but to no avail. He was a closed book. His eyes started to fill again. He would not cry. He *would not* cry. How could there be any tears left? Counselling had been suggested, but Tobias had refused. Nothing and nobody could mend him, of that he was convinced.

Now, with a big sigh and an iron will he forced himself to begin his list of renovations. All the wooden floors needed sanding down and varnishing, as did the doors. The skirting boards and architraves needed a fresh lick of paint. The kitchen needed ripping out and replacing with more modern, yet traditional units, alongside maybe an Aga to keep that country feel. The boot room he'd convert to a utility room. The main bathroom was actually quite quaint with its claw-foot bath and big brass taps, but he'd need to put in a shower, plus knock through into one of the bedrooms to create another en suite for the master bedroom. He made a list in a notebook and put it in his jacket pocket. Rubbing his hands together, he decided to light the wood burner in the lounge. A log basket holding dried wood and matches stood at the side. Soon the room was filled with warmth.

Tobias sat on the rug watching the amber flames flicker and dance. His thoughts gravitated back to the past like a magnet. This house held such happy memories. He chuckled to himself at the parties he and Fox had thrown here. Not just wild, crazy ones where endless young men drank themselves stupid on cocktails until the early dawn, playing strip poker with girls they'd coaxed back from the village, but intimate dinners with Carrie and close friends, sharing secrets and ambitions for the future. He watched the fire crackle a little more, then took out his notebook again and decided to draft an advert for the sale of the property to give to the estate manager. It wouldn't take long with his good team of workers to complete the renovations. After several minutes he'd composed a rough draft.

Set on the edge of the Treweham Hall estate and surrounded by beautiful parkland, this grade II listed Gate House's delights are traditional, comprising five bedrooms with mullion windows and open fires. The kitchen and bathroom boast modern restorations, along with the additional en suite to the master bedroom.

Price? Chewing his pen, he pondered. Probably around £850,000 to £900,000, considering the location and surrounding gardens. With the renovations he'd try his luck at £999,000 – just under a million. Previous experience as a property developer told him to aim high. More often than not there was someone who was prepared to pay the asking price.

His thoughts were interrupted by his mobile phone. 'Aunt Celia' glared up from the screen. This should be interesting, he smirked to himself. Celia was the polar opposite of her sister, Beatrice, being razor sharp, intuitive and extremely observant. She both shocked and entertained Tobias in equal amounts. Although demanding at times and frustrating to the limit, she was ceaseless fun and remained his favourite aunt.

'Aunt Celia, how are you?' he asked with mirth, knowing what was to follow.

'Ruddy awful. Back's playing up, the cat's got the shits and your mother's just told me you've cancelled our Caribbean cruise.'

'We can't afford it, Celia,' he stated flatly.

'So finally someone's taking the finances in hand. Your father never did have any business acumen.'

With that he couldn't argue, so he didn't try.

'Well, I've decided. I've had enough of it in this poky institute, and since you've cancelled my holiday I'm coming to visit.' That 'poky institute' was in fact a top-class retirement community set in stunning grounds. Another expense. It was worth every penny keeping her there, under lock and key, as opposed to running riot in his home.

'Splendid. Sebastian will be delighted.' She actually scared the hell out of his younger brother.

'Huh,' she puffed into his ear. 'I'll let you know when.' Then bang went the phone. Conversation apparently over. Shaking his head, Tobias got up and made his way back to the Hall, in desperate need of a large brandy.

Chapter 10

The next few days working at The Templar proved to be busy for Megan. Although she enjoyed waiting on and talking to the locals, she came home in the evenings absolutely tired out. She wasn't used to being on her feet all day, having only ever worked behind a desk. Wandering home from the pub slowly in the early evening dusk, Megan promised herself a luxurious, hot bubble bath and an early night. Seeing the charming row of stone cottages with their lantern porch lights glowing homely in the twilight gave Megan a reassuring warmness. It was amazing how soon Treweham had become her home and she genuinely couldn't envisage living anywhere else now.

She noticed her next-door neighbour's side gate was open. Frowning, she wondered why, aware that Zac, her neighbour's black Labrador, slept in his kennel in the back garden. Old Ted always made sure Zac was secure and locked in. Sure enough, there was the dog ambling along the roadside, sniffing the flowerbeds, intermittently cocking his leg. Where was Ted?

Running across the road, Megan gently took hold of a vaguely surprised Zac. 'Come on, old boy, you shouldn't be outside here on your own.' She patted Zac's head, slowly led him back into his garden and locked the side gate behind them.

'Ted!'

There was no answer. Megan saw the back door was ajar, so she gently pushed it open and shouted again for her neighbour. Still there was no answer. Megan entered the cottage. All was still and quiet, except for the faint crackle of the radio.

'Are you there, Ted?' Megan made her way into the sitting room. Ted was slumped in the armchair by the fire. 'Ted!' Megan rushed to him and eased his shoulders up. His face was pale and moist, but he was still breathing, just, in shallow little gasps. 'Ted, I'm ringing for an ambulance, stay with me,' she pleaded whilst reaching for the mobile lodged in her jeans pocket. She punched out 999, was put through immediately and gave all the necessary details. Megan grasped Ted's hand and squeezed it hard. 'Please stay with me,' she whispered. The ticking of the mantelpiece clock emphasised how slowly the time was passing. Zac whimpered in the kitchen, sensing something was wrong.

'Come here, Zac!' she called out. Zac wandered in slowly, his head bent and he whimpered again. 'It'll be all right, Zac,' she reassured, hoping she was right. Zac sat next to her and licked her hand, which was clutching Ted's.

At last the ambulance arrived. Two paramedics rushed in and assessed Ted. 'I just found him here, slumped in his chair about twenty minutes ago,' Megan started to ramble, now that shock had set in. One of the paramedics put something delicately into Ted's mouth. Then they carefully lifted him onto a stretcher and carried him out to the ambulance, Megan following.

'We've managed to stabilise him,' one of the paramedics said over his shoulder, whilst opening the ambulance doors. 'We need to get him to the hospital as soon as possible. Can you inform his family?'

'Yes, of course,' Megan hovered on the road, not really knowing who that would be. She watched Ted being bundled into the ambulance. Within seconds the blue lights were flashing and the ambulance sped off. She went to stand motionless in the middle of the road, watching it go.

Suddenly a loud horn sounded, making Megan jump with fright. She just managed to turn in time to see a sports car swerve, marginally missing her. Her heart pounded in her chest as she took gasps of air. She squinted her eyes to make out the car's registration plate, TOB 1. The lunatic! Megan started to tremble, her shock levels peaking with all that had happened, and tears began to spill down her face.

'Are you all right?' a soft voice spoke somewhere behind her. She turned round to see through her tears a blurry figure standing in front of her. The figure was a young man in combat pants and a white T-shirt. He put an arm loosely round her shoulders and guided her off the road.

'It nearly killed me…' stammered Megan.

'I know, I saw. He's a bloody idiot,' the man stated flatly. Together they made their way back down the lane to the cottages. 'I'm Nick, by the way. I live up the track,' he signalled back towards a dirt track, off the main road. Then he frowned when Megan led them into Ted's cottage. 'This is old Ted's cottage.'

'Yes,' Megan paused, 'I've just found Ted slumped in his armchair and called an ambulance. I live next door.'

'Oh, no.' Nick's face contorted with emotion.

'I'm Megan.' She offered her hand, which was still shaking. Nick held it, making her feel safe and warm.

'Pleased to meet you, Megan.'

Zac suddenly barked, startling them both. 'I'll look after Zac. We'd better lock up here.' Megan bent down to stroke a bewildered face with questioning brown eyes.

'Poor chap, he's wondering what's going on.' Nick joined Megan to stroke him. 'He's been with Ted since he was six weeks old. I remember giving him his first set of injections. I'm the local vet,' he said by way of explanation. Then he straightened up. 'I'll check the windows are closed upstairs.'

Nick made his way to the stairs whilst Megan put the fire guard up to the fire. The embers were still warm, which hopefully meant Ted hadn't collapsed too long ago, and she'd found him in good time. Once the cottage was locked up the three of them went next door to Megan's.

'Come in, Nick. Would you like a coffee?' she asked, pushing the front door hard as it had been sticking.

Nick smiled wryly, 'I think you need something a little stronger than coffee.'

'Probably,' agreed Megan, 'but the strongest I've got is wine.'

'Wine it is then.'

Soon they were both sitting outside on the new wrought-iron furniture Megan had bought for the courtyard garden, with Zac snug at Megan's feet.

'Looks like you've made a friend there.' Nick pointed towards the sleeping dog.

'Yes, he's lovely.' Megan looked up to the inky, dark sky scattered with star dust. The mild evening air was filled with the daffodils' heady, sweet scent. 'Cheers,' Megan handed Nick a glass of sparkling white wine.

'Cheers.' Nick took the glass and gave a hard sigh. 'As far as I know, Ted doesn't have any family, I don't think there's anybody to notify about his collapse. I'll go and visit him in the morning.'

'My gran was a close friend. She said Ted had made her feel welcome when she first moved here.'

'How long ago was that?'

'About twenty years, not long after my granddad died. She wanted a fresh start, somewhere new, to avoid constant memories, I suppose.'

'How are you finding Treweham?' Nick smiled, his head tilted to one side. He brushed his long, brown fringe away from his face. Megan noticed how blue his eyes were, and how they seemed to hold a touch of humour, as if he suspected this little village wouldn't be enough for her. He rested his elbows on the wrought-iron table. His arms were brown and very muscular. His chest would be too, she suspected, judging by the tight white T-shirt. Megan swallowed.

'In truth, it feels like I'm meant to be here somehow, like… well, like home.' Then stopping, she changed the subject completely, 'Nick, who was driving the car? You said "he's" an idiot.'

'There's only one person it could be with the car registration TOB 1,' Nick replied in a voice dripping with scorn. Realisation hit her.

'Tobi? Tobias Cavendish-Blake?'

Nick nodded his head slowly, his face showing complete distaste. 'Got it in one.'

Chapter 11

'Big smiles for the camera!' called the news reporter. 'That's it, Gary, put your arm round Tracy and hold the winning ticket in the air. Yes, that's it!' Gary and Tracy embraced, giggling with excitement. After several more shots were taken, the reporter approached them to ask a few questions. 'So, how does it feel to be millionaires?' she beamed, holding a microphone in Gary's face.

'Well… bit of a shock to be honest, but… well, we're getting used to the idea, aren't we, Trace?' He nudged her with a wink.

'Too right we are,' Tracy gushed. 'We still can't believe something like this has happened to us.'

'So what plans have you got for the three million you've won?'

'Not sure, like I said, it's not properly sunk in yet,' answered Gary firmly. Tracy looked sideways at him with a slight frown.

'Well, whatever you decide to do, we wish you all the best.' The reporter shook hands with both of them.

The next day there they were: front-page news in the local newspaper.

Gary and Tracy Belcher – local lottery winners!

Tracy was pleased with the photograph, thinking how good her hair extensions looked, while Gary's visit to the dentist had given him that real winning smile. The uneven, yellowing front teeth had now been fixed and polished, making them perfect shiny white ones, which were displayed quite a lot lately, as he couldn't stop smiling. He'd resigned from his job, obviously – who would want to keep stacking freezers in a supermarket five days a week with three million in the bank? Tracy, too, had left the care home, but missed her old friends dreadfully.

'Gary, why did you go all cagey when the reporter asked if we had any plans?'

He looked wary, then sat down, indicating she sit next to him. 'Listen, Tracy, I've been thinking.' This sounded serious she thought and sat still. 'We've got to move.'

'But—'

'No, hear me out. Everyone round here knows us, knows how much money we have.'

'So?'

'So, Trace, things have changed. It makes things more complicated now. Before we were just Gaz and Trace, a working couple like everyone else round here, but now… well, now I'm beginning to feel a bit used, taken for granted.'

'How do you mean?'

'Take for example the other night at the club. Everyone automatically assumes it's my round, permanently. It's like I'm only there to pay for everything, not because it's me, Gary.' Tracy looked crestfallen, but she knew exactly how he felt.

'I know, I felt similar when Sharon asked me outright for a few grand, bold as brass, like she had every right to.'

'I think we should move. Somewhere nobody knows us.'

'But what about our parents?' Tracy looked horror-stricken, having always been close to her mum.

'We'll see them right, of course, but we need to get away, Trace.'

She understood now, and nodded in agreement.

At first they searched close to home, a radius of a few miles. After narrowing down a few properties they liked the look of, Gary contacted the necessary estate agents. But news travelled fast and soon they realised that going public and appearing in the papers had been a bad decision. Each estate agent was bending over backwards to assist the new lottery winners, knowing full well how much commission they'd be coining in.

'It's no good Trace, we're going to have to look further afield. Everyone knows us in this area. I don't feel like I'm me anymore.'

Tracy dully agreed. Her phone had never stopped ringing with 'old friends' suddenly wanting to keep in touch. Sharon, her best mate, had continued to ask for money and routinely supposed that Tracy would fund the shopping sprees and lunches she constantly organised. Tracy, too, had become unsettled. She had loved her job in the care home, had really felt needed. She *had been* needed. Her kindness and attention to the elderly were a credit to her, and she had a genuine gift for making people feel wanted and cared for. Not for the first time she sadly thought of the group of old people that would be wondering where she was. Would they understand what had happened? Would they think she'd abandoned them? A lump formed in her throat. She pictured Alf, sitting by the bay window, patiently waiting for her to come in the morning. Often she would help him with his breakfast and make sure he took his pills with a cup of tea. Who was seeing to Alf now? A tear ran down her face. Now they were having to leave their family. Now they were beginning to realise just who their friends were. Being ousted from your own home wasn't a pleasant experience, even though you had pots of money to buy another one. This tiny terrace was their first house. They'd been so excited to get the keys and build a home. Tracy had made it theirs with the dozens of photographs framed, depicting their childhood romance, wedding day, honeymoon and family occasions. Focusing on those happy memories changed her mood. It also gave her an idea.

'Gary?'

'Hmm?' He was on his laptop, continuing the property search.

'Do you remember our honeymoon?'

He gave a short laugh. 'Course I do, why d'ya ask?'

'Just thinking…' She stared out of the front window. Children were playing noisily in the street. No garden for them to release energy, just a busy street and back yard.

'What?' Gary looked puzzled. She had his full attention now.

'How would you like to go back?'

'You mean to the Cotswolds?' He remembered the lush, green hills and quaint villages they'd visited on their mini tour. His old Fiesta had just about managed the trip down there and together they had explored the charming tearooms, the black-and-white Tudor building trails, the historic halls and old-world village pubs. Both he and Tracy had loved it, being a far cry from the built-up sights of Preston, with its tall old factory chimneys and smoky, grey skies. They had adored the cosy rented cottage, which had proved to be an ideal base in one of the central small villages. Each evening, after a fun-packed day visiting the surrounding area, they'd browse the internet using local information to decide where to go next. Tracy had been enchanted by the beautiful stone cottages with trailing roses and wisteria growing up the walls. Gary had enjoyed the camaraderie in the local pubs, where they had always been made welcome. One landlord, when told it was their honeymoon, gave them a bottle of champagne and toasted them a long and happy marriage, blessed with healthy children. That was another consideration – children. Did he really want his kids playing out on the roadside like round here? Or would he sooner see himself kicking a football with them in a large, secluded garden, safe from traffic and smog? In his mind's eye, he could see Trace at the gates of a small, country school, not waiting with the many mums outside the railings of their nearby primary. After a few moments' thought they looked at each other.

'Are you thinking what I'm thinking?' Tracy asked.

'Yeah, let's go for it.'

'But what about our parents? We'd be far away from them.'

'It's not that far, Trace, and besides, we'd get somewhere big enough to have them stay. Plus, we'll get a decent car, so we can always come back whenever we want.' Tracy nodded in agreement: yes, that all made sense.

'OK, let's do a search.' Gary typed 'properties, sale, Cotswolds' into the laptop and a display of houses filled the screen. He whistled at some of them, not just the grand scale of the properties, but the prices, too. Then a name leaped out at him. It was where they had rented the honeymoon cottage.

'Look, Trace!' She quickly leant forward to see the screen.

'Treweham! That's where we stayed!' She clapped her hands in delight.

'The Gate House, set on the edge of the Treweham Hall estate and surrounded by beautiful parkland…'

They were completely in awe of what they had discovered and truly thought fate was playing a hand. Often on their honeymoon they had joked about living is such an idyllic place. Now it looked like their dreams may come true.

Chapter 12

Flora lay wantonly, sated with utter pleasure in the haystack. The combined sensations of Dylan's stubble rubbing against her pale, soft cheek, the smell of his aftershave and the excitement of his hands caressing her bare breasts made her cry out his name with desire.

He slowly made his way down her long, shapely legs, till he reached a sleek, blond triangle of pubic hair. He nuzzled his face down to taste her, making her hips bolt upwards, so he steadied them with his two hands, whilst letting his tongue gently glide into her. 'Dylan!' she cried again, making him intensify his rhythm. Then his mouth gradually traced his way back up her body, his lips kissing her flat stomach, her firm breasts, until he covered her mouth to stop her from any more screaming. He didn't want the whole of Treweham Hall knowing what he was up to with their stable girl.

His hand was on her thigh, pushing her legs further apart. She felt him at the very core of her and then he was deep inside her with a single thrust. Flora gasped, but he didn't stop, grinding deeper and deeper. Her body ached with lust. It had been a full week since she had seen him last. She heard him grunt and felt him pulse as he released himself. Taking a few steady breaths, he rolled off her and lay by her side.

Since he had introduced himself at the stables a few weeks ago they had met quite regularly. Despite the ten-year age gap, they had plenty in common: horses. Together they had ridden the Treweham Hall estate, through its forests, over the wild-flower meadows and alongside the crystal-clear rivers, always to return to the stables where Dylan had coaxed Flora into loosening her inhibitions.

'I can't stay long. I'm supposed to be meeting Seamus and Tobias at The Templar.'

'Oh, right...' Flora's voice held disappointment, which tugged at Dylan's guilty conscience.

'But I'll be back soon, promise.' He kissed her hard on the lips.

'When?' she persisted, her voice hopeful.

'Soon, don't worry.' He got up and dressed himself, as Flora did the same. Turning, he kissed her again. 'Until next time.' He winked and left the stables, whistling. Flora admired his perfect muscular body and dark, curly mane of hair. The famous Dylan Delany – he was so gorgeous and he was all hers.

*

'No way, that doesn't sound at all like Tobias.' Finula was busy sprinkling freshly baked custard tarts with nutmeg.

'But it was his number plate – who else could it have been?' insisted Megan, her mouth watering at the scent of Finula's latest creations.

'I don't know, but there's got to be some explanation, honestly. Tobias is a top bloke. He wouldn't nearly run someone over and not stop. Especially with his history—'

'Any chance of some service here?' Dermot called through to the kitchen. It had been a hectic afternoon with many locals and tourists making the most of the beautiful spring weather. Relaxed couples sat outside sunning themselves, sipping cool lager, children ran and squealed in the beer garden, and Zac lay panting by the back door of the pub kitchen with a bowl of water.

'Coming!' called Megan, and scooped up two plates of prawn salad. Scurrying through to deliver the meals, she noticed how full the place was getting.

'Over here, please, Meg!' shouted a red-faced and harassed Dermot. Megan hurried behind the bar.

'Next, please.' She scanned the small crowd at the bar waiting to be served. Out of the corner of her eye she saw Nick sitting at one of the tables in the corner with a friend. He looked comfortable, laughing with a guy with blond hair, arms animated in conversation. He noticed her looking and waved. She waved back smiling.

'When you're ready,' said a voice tinged with humour. Quickly turning, Megan stared slap bang into two green eyes, flecked with amber. They belonged to a face with a strong jaw line and full lips, which were smirking ever so slightly at her.

'Sorry,' Megan mumbled, blushing as she reached for a pint glass, 'what can I get you?'

'A large malt, please.' He grinned as she looked at the pint glass and swiftly swapped it for a smaller spirit glass.

'There you go.' She placed it in front of him. 'Anything else?'

'One for yourself.' He smiled, nodding his head slightly. The light caught his hair, all black and glossy. He reminded her of a young Oliver Tobias, whom she recalled from her mum's old videos, all swarthy and with a distinct presence. He frowned slightly; obviously she was staring again. Flushed, she thanked him and quickly started serving another customer. Whilst doing so, Megan noticed the man acknowledge the blond-haired friend of Nick's, then go outside to join two men sitting at the tables on the grass verge. One of the men looked familiar to Megan, but she couldn't place him.

At the table, shaking, Tobias put down his glass. My God, he thought, for a moment back there he'd seen a ghost. Carrie's ghost. That girl behind the bar bore a startling resemblance to Carrie and it completely jolted him as he had entered the pub. The fact she'd been distracted had given him time to study her face. She had the same cheekbones, almond-shaped eyes and her hair was dark, albeit slightly shorter in a bob, rather than long like Carrie's had been. It was uncanny and it unnerved him.

'You all right, Tobias?' Dylan asked, noticing his hand quiver when he knocked back his drink. Tobias didn't answer. His gaze was fixed on the girl that had come out to collect glasses. Dylan's eyes followed Tobias' stare. As did Seamus.

'Holy shit,' muttered Seamus, seeing for himself the double of his best friend's dead fiancée. Megan couldn't help but notice how all three men were staring at her. She looked down to see if something was wrong. Had she spilt something? Had her top come down? No, everything was in place. One of the men, the one with ginger hair, spoke to the other two then got up and made his way back into the pub. She now recalled the other man. She'd seen him on the TV; he was a jockey. Megan wondered if they lived round here or if they were visitors.

Finally, by late afternoon, when everyone had finished eating, drinking and basking in the sun and trickled home to sleep off their lazy afternoons,

Megan and Finula sat by the bar drinking well-deserved pints of cider.

'Ah, that tastes good,' Finula gasped. Her cheeks were rosy from working in the steamy kitchen. She wiped the auburn curls plastered to her forehead.

Megan didn't know how she did it, producing so many delicious meals with such ease and efficiency. When she said as much Finula just shrugged. 'It's what I love doing. I've always got a buzz from creating dishes that people appreciate. I enjoy watching their reaction when it first hits the taste buds. A bit like your paintings, I suppose.'

Megan had never really thought of it like that.

'Yes, it probably is. It's good to see people's faces light up when they like what they see.' Megan hadn't had much time to invest in her painting as originally planned but she'd shown Finula her portfolio one evening. Impressed, Finula had offered to display some pictures in The Templar. A few pieces had been sold, which encouraged Megan to concentrate more on her art work. Drinking the cold cider, she closed her eyes, letting the cool liquid hit the back of her dried throat, glad that not only had her shift in the pub finished for the day, but she was taking the next few days off, too. Perhaps now was the best time to set up the easel and start mixing colours again.

'Before you go, would you mind delivering this to the Hall?' Finula dug into her apron pocket and pulled out a piece of paper containing a long list of vegetables and fruit. 'Just pop round the back to the gardens. There's usually someone about in the greenhouses. Tell them I've sent you from The Templar.'

'Oh, right.' Megan had never set foot in Treweham Hall and was a touch apprehensive about 'just popping round the back'. Taking the list, she asked, 'Are you sure? I mean, won't they mind a stranger strolling through their grounds?'

Finula laughed. 'You're not a stranger strolling through their grounds, you're a local, working in the village pub, delivering our fresh vegetable requirements. Seriously, Megan, you need to change your attitude towards the Cavendish-Blakes. They don't lord it up like you seem to think.'

'I don't think that. I'm sure they are nice people, even though their son's a maniac driver,' she added flatly.

'And,' Finula pointed her finger accusingly, 'you've got that wrong, too.'

Megan walked down the stone-walled pathways, over the little hump-backed bridge covering the babbling brook, through the village green with its cricket pavilion and past the old church with its ancient graveyard. Next to it stood Treweham Hall.

Taking a deep breath, she checked her back pocket for the list and made her way through the enormous iron gates. The Hall really was magnificent with its sandstone edifice, large mullion windows, stone columns and decorative cornice. The gardens were well manicured, arrayed with daffodils and fresh spring foliage. Megan followed the gravel path to the side of the Hall, which led round the back to the grounds. She was still a little uneasy and half expected to be held at gun point by some gamekeeper in tweeds. Typically, despite Finula's assurances, there was no one in sight. Hesitating she decided to look into the greenhouses, hoping to see someone pottering about, but no, they were closed shut and empty of any gardeners. What now? The list definitely had to be delivered as the pub had completely run out of vegetables. There was only one thing for it: she'd have to call at the Hall. Slowly, she walked towards the rose archway, and through that she could see the huge wooden back door of the main building. Hammering on the door with its rustic fox-head knocker, she waited with baited breath. After a few seconds she hammered again. Still no response. Then, just as she was about to leave, she heard a slam and the hinges creaked as the door swung open. Those green eyes flecked with amber stared into hers again.

Recognising her immediately, Tobias smiled lazily. 'Hello again.'

Chapter 13

'Hah!' Finula threw her head back and barked out a laugh. She was sitting in Megan's back garden in denim shorts and a black top, large dark sunglasses covering her freckled face. 'Serves you right,' she finished with a sense of righteousness as she slid her flip-flops off, wriggling bright purple toenails.

'Trust you to send me when there was nobody about,' Megan replied with a touch of exasperation, although seeing Finula's reaction when relaying the events of a few days ago she was beginning to see the funny side.

'Yes, and instead of getting the gardener, you got the Lord of the Manor himself,' joked Finula. 'He isn't so bad, is he?'

'Well, no, I must admit, he does have rather a nice smile,' Megan conceded.

'And the rest,' replied Finula drily, and sipped her elderberry juice. 'Hmm, this is good, Megan.'

Megan had found a few bottles in her gran's pantry and had a jug of it chilling on the garden table.

'I know. Gran always used to make it for me. It really takes me back, smelling the cloves and cinnamon. Your arms are burning.'

'Oh bugger, that's what pale skin does for you. I'm not made for the sun.'

'Here, put some of this on them.' Megan handed her the suntan lotion discarded at her feet.

'It's all right for you, all beautifully bronzed.' She eyed Megan with envy. Megan had developed a slight tan in the last few days. She'd been lucky with the weather, which had been unusually warm and sunny, whilst she'd been spending time at home. Her brunette bob had developed highlights and she oozed a healthy glow. Compared to how she had felt a few short months ago, it was a relief to feel as happy and relaxed as she did. All the fresh country air made her sleep well at night. Walking Zac through the leafy lanes of Treweham and working hard at The Templar had kept her fit – that and keeping busy renovating the cottage. That morning she had stripped the wallpaper from the sitting room, leaving the walls grey and chipped. Deciding to have them freshly plastered, she had searched the internet for a local tradesman, but couldn't find anyone.

'Don't suppose you know a good plasterer, do you?'

'No, but I know someone who will.'

'Who?'

'Tobias.' Finula smirked. 'Seriously, he owns a property business, buys houses and renovates them. He'll have all kinds of tradesmen working for him.'

'Really? I didn't realise he had his own business, besides obviously helping to run the estate.'

'Since his dad died last year, he pretty much runs the whole thing.'

'Busy man, then.' She considered how much responsibility he must have for his age – he couldn't be more than thirty.

'Does he have a wife to help him?'

Finula's mouth twitched. 'No, Megan, he's single.' She looked directly at Megan.

'Just asking.' Megan held her hands up defensively.

'Yeah, course you were. He was engaged once, a long time ago.'

'What happened?' Megan was more than curious.

'Very sad.' Finula shook her head. 'She was killed in a car accident, drunk driver ploughed into her.'

'Oh my God!' Megan covered her mouth with her hand. 'That's awful, poor man.'

'Yes,' Finula said gravely, 'which is why Tobias is *the* last person to have nearly driven into you.' Megan pondered Finula's last remark. Given Tobias' history she couldn't help but agree with her friend's chilling words. But how could Nick imply he was capable of doing this? As if she had conjured him with her thought, she heard his voice calling from the side passage.

'Anyone home?'

'Round the back!' called Megan.

Nick appeared and made his way over to them. 'Just thought I'd call and see how you and Zac are.' He looked at Finula, who was suddenly getting up from her deck chair. 'Don't go on my behalf.'

'I'm not,' Finula replied dully. Megan sensed a degree of awkwardness as she glanced from one to the other. 'Time to go, hon, see you tomorrow.' Finula kissed Megan on her cheek and flip-flopped out of the garden, completely ignoring Nick. Megan frowned and looked at Nick questioningly.

He raised his eyebrows. 'Oh dear, hope I haven't ruined your afternoon.' He plonked himself in the empty deck chair.

'Do I detect a little tension between you and Finula?' Megan poured him a drink of elderberry and handed it to him.

'Thanks. Yes, I'm afraid you did.'

'Why?' Megan was puzzled.

'Well, let's just say I didn't want what Finula did.'

'Sorry?'

'Me and Finula, we used to date.'

'Really? She never mentioned it.' Megan was totally taken by surprise that Finula had never told her.

'Well, she probably wants to forget the whole thing. I think she was feeling rather bruised at the time.' He took a sip and looked around the garden.

Changing the topic completely, he asked where Zac was.

'He's inside snoozing.' She eyed Nick carefully. His arms were crossed and he repeatedly tapped his foot against the chair leg. Was she imagining it, or did Nick look a touch uncomfortable?

'I went to visit Ted,' Nick said, sitting back in the deck chair, finally relaxing.

'Oh, how is he?'

'Better. Not sure if he'll manage on his own, though.' Nick looked genuinely concerned. His eyes clouded over, looking into the distance. Despite Finula's obvious dislike of him, Megan could see a real compassionate side to Nick. He was a vet – surely that must mean he *was* a caring person? She studied his face. He had a flawless tanned complexion; obviously his work kept him outdoors a lot.

He noticed her looking at him and smiled. 'Like what you see?' he asked, giving her a cheeky grin. Megan laughed, a little embarrassed. If she did, she wasn't about to admit it.

Chapter 14

Dylan swung his Jeep into The Templar car park. He'd booked in for a few days before the races at Newmarket. Racing was as much a mental sport as it was a physical one and he always followed the same pattern before a big race meeting. He would take time out in a hotel, or somewhere away from home to focus his mind. Although his house was nearby on the edge of Treweham village, it was too much of a distraction, with family and friends popping in and the phone constantly ringing. People knew where he was and felt free to visit any time. Normally that wouldn't bother him, but before a race it was different.

He knew he had to apply himself and look after his body properly. This included a strict diet and exercise regime. He had private coaching at the gym to maximise the strength in the key muscles in his legs, lower body and core area. He knew how upper strength body was crucial to control his horse better. Regular cardio exercises kept him lean and light, while his stringent, low-fat food intake ensured the ideal weight before weighing in for a race. Dylan was constantly checking the scales before racing; he took it very seriously, almost to the point of paranoia.

However, it was this meticulous routine that had put Dylan where he was, Champion Jockey. Racing was a game of starts and probabilities, but in Dylan's eyes it was also about commitment and the absolute burning desire to win at all costs. Basically, Dylan Delany worked hard and played hard. He was a winner in both disciplines.

Carrying his cases through the pub, he was greeted by Finula. 'Ah, Finula, you look stunning as ever.'

'Whatever. Right, you're in room four as requested, rear of house. Do you want a hand with those?' She looked at his cases.

'No. I wouldn't expect a delicate thing like you to carry my luggage. You could show me to my room, though.'

'You know where it is, Dylan,' she replied drily.

'Well… perhaps keep me company—'

'Hands off my daughter, Delany,' that firm, Irish voice of Dermot's thundered behind him, making Dylan jump.

'Ah, Dermot, good to see you,' he tried to smooth the situation over, but Dermot was having none of it as he picked up one of the cases and nodded towards the stairs.

'This way, Delany. *I'll* show you to your room.'

Finula stifled a giggle as she watched Dylan hastily follow behind. He'd never change, she thought, always the same silver-tongued charmer. At first she'd been flattered by his attention, until quickly realising he was like that with all females. Now she just rolled her eyes and let him get on with it. Dermot, however, would not tolerate anyone flirting with his daughter, especially someone like Delany, whom he classed as an overconfident Casanova. Sure, he was a good jockey, which was to his credit, but Dermot knew he used his position unscrupulously with women and didn't approve, taking particular exception when this included his own daughter. It amused Finula no end the way her dad terrified Dylan, making him act so jumpy and out of character. Moments later Dermot returned to the kitchen where Finula was preparing that evening's vegetables. Giving her a piece of paper, he spoke with sarcasm.

'These are his lordship's requirements.'

Finula took the paper. She'd been expecting this, understanding his routine from previous visits. The list contained the meals he required over the next few days – chicken and vegetable risotto, noodles with beef and green beans and salmon and boiled rice. All low calories. She knew he'd be drinking nothing but water, so had left two bottles in his room, rather than the usual tea, coffee and shortbread. Once you cut through all the shallow flattery and saw past the false bravado, Dylan was actually a nice guy. It was just a case of not taking him too seriously. Finula had got used to the banter between Dylan, Seamus and Tobias as they were regulars at The Templar. All the locals in the pub had wanted to watch Dylan racing, so Finula had organised a large-screen viewing. Dermot had begrudgingly agreed to it, as it was good for business and brought the village together.

Dylan lay on his bed, with his hands behind his head in contemplation. He'd dearly love a crack at that feisty redhead Finula, but there was little chance of that with her father constantly watching over her like a guard dog. He smiled to himself, wondering what kind of father he'd make. Probably more protective than Dermot. He knew what kind of men were out there – he was one of them. What was the saying? You can't kid a kidder. The thought of him with children was an unfamiliar one. Never once had he considered settling down and starting a family, but why not? Most of the jockeys he knew had wives and children. He puzzled himself with his train of thought. What could have prompted it?

There was a knock at the door. 'Come in!' he called.

'I've just come with some more bottled water.' Dylan looked at the dark-haired beauty and sat up immediately.

'Thanks. Could you leave them on the table?' He couldn't resist adding, 'You're new here, aren't you? What's your name?'

The girl smiled. 'Yes. I'm Megan.'

Dylan moved towards her, looking her up and down with appreciation. Wasn't this the girl that had turned Tobias' head? He could see why.

'I'm Dylan, pleased to meet you.' He held his hand out. She shyly shook it.

Chapter 15

It had been two weeks since Megan had taken in Zac. Together they had forged a strong friendship. Basically the black Labrador followed her everywhere. Dermot had allowed Megan to bring him to work and most mornings they would trot along the lane, side by side to The Templar, where Zac would settle by the open fireplace waiting patiently for Megan to finish her shift, whilst being stroked and patted by the customers. He was proving to be quite an attraction and Zac relished the attention.

That bright April morning Megan was busy helping Finula prepare the lunches, chopping vegetables, slicing fruit and washing salads. She couldn't help but notice how quiet Finula was, missing the usual chatty banter they shared.

'Finula, is there something wrong?'

'No, not really.' She bent down to open the oven door and a hot wave of air blew back at her. Squinting, she checked the baked potatoes were browning nicely. Megan's thoughts turned to what Nick had told her the other day about him and Finula. Suspecting Finula's mood was to do with Nick, she decided to broach the subject.

'Fin, why didn't you tell me you and Nick had been an item?'

Finula turned sharply. 'We've never been an item.'

'Oh, but he said—'

'Yeah, I'm sure he says quite a lot,' interrupted Finula hotly, 'and most of it's crap.'

Taken aback by her tone Megan decided not to push any further. Obviously the two shared some history and it wasn't her business. What was unsettling was the effect Nick had had on Finula. She'd never seen her so agitated.

Realising how sharp she'd sounded, Finula wanted to ease the awkward silence. 'Found yourself a plasterer yet?'

'Not yet.'

'Do you want me to ask Tobias, see if he can recommend anyone?' Not wanting to offend, seeing as Finula was obviously trying to help, Megan agreed. Inside she was reluctant, but then again, she really did want the walls plastered, eager to get at least one room finished. The last few days had gone so quickly. She'd visited Ted in hospital. Megan had been touched when he genuinely seemed pleased by her visit and he'd smiled sweetly when she had given him a bottle of her gran's elderberry juice. She had assured him that Zac was absolutely fine and missing him. Ted had chuckled. Then, looking rather serious, he had told her that he didn't want to return to his cottage.

'Oh, Ted.' A lump had formed in Megan's throat. The thought that he would no longer be her next-door neighbour had saddened her, although she completely understood his dilemma.

'It's the old ticker, you see.' He gently thumped his chest with a shaky fist. 'Not sure I'd feel safe on my own now.' His watery eyes blinked. 'They're putting me in a home.' He coughed and looked out of the hospital window.

Megan wanted to cry. Swallowing, she cleared her throat. 'Don't worry about Zac. I'll have him.'

The old man's face lit up. 'Would you?'

'Of course. To be honest I was dreading having to give him back.' They both laughed.

'Thanks, Megan. You're a good lass.' Ted's eyelids twitched and he closed his eyes. He was tired and it was time for her to leave.

'Bye, Ted,' she whispered, and placed her hand over his frail, pale one, in which a blue vein bulged from the drip he was attached to. She checked his chest was still rising and falling, then quietly left the ward.

'You're needed at the bar, Meg!' Dermot broke her thoughts, making her jump. Quickly she washed her hands, removed her apron and hurried behind the bar, leaving Finula with her own thoughts, whatever they might be.

As on most days, the hours passed in a flurry of serving drinks, taking food orders and scurrying back and forth from the kitchen. Late in the afternoon Megan collected Zac, who was lying by the large inglenook fireplace, tail wagging when he saw Megan had come for him.

'Come on, old boy, time to go home.' Zac got up and leant into her legs for a stroke. He really was a lovable dog, she thought fondly, scrunching under his ears, which he loved.

Together they leisurely wandered home. Megan pushed hard on the front door of her cottage, which was still sticking – another job to sort out. She made herself a sandwich and sat at the kitchen table, flicking through various interiors magazines, looking for inspiration for her own revamp. The chintz floral curtains she'd been admiring reminded her to go and retrieve Gran's sewing machine from the loft.

She finished her sandwich and headed for the attic opening in the hall. She used the long pole, which stood in the hall corner, to unhook the latch to the loft hatch. Stepping back, she waited for the folding ladder to whizz down to the ground. Coughing as the dust settled, she climbed up the ladder and put on the light switch just by the side of the entrance. She smiled as she recognised all the attic's contents, an archive of family memorabilia, each telling a tale of its own. Her doll's cot, which had been Mum's, with its chipped red paint and dusty covers, ancient brown suitcases packed with goodness knows what – old clothes, she suspected. The old-fashioned hairdryer, which had a nozzle and bonnet, made Megan giggle at the memories of using it. Yellow, mouldering newspapers and magazines lay scattered randomly. Then something she hadn't seen before caught her eye. A vintage tin box lay in the middle of the attic floor. Frowning, Megan climbed fully into the loft and reached down for it. It was a rusty, old lilac tin with Parma violets engraved on the lid, and had obviously contained Gran's perfume years ago. Just as she picked it up, Megan heard a crack, and she saw that her foot had gone through the plaster between the roof joists. Hell, she'd been so engrossed with her find, she'd let her foot sink into the floor. Great, now an indent of her footprint would show on the sitting-room ceiling – another damn job.

Cursing, she took the tin and, forgetting the sewing machine, started to climb slowly back down the ladder, only to hear someone knocking on the front door. This would be Finula, no doubt, wanting to talk after their conversation earlier.

'Come in, it's open!' Megan called, still climbing down the ladder. On hearing several attempts at

Finula pushing the door, Megan shouted, 'Harder! The door's sticking!'

As she reached the final rung on the ladder, clasping the tin box, the door thrust open with force, making her lose balance and topple in surprise. 'Ahh!' She landed on her bottom, startled to see those mocking green eyes staring down at her.

Chapter 16

'Oh, it's you.' Megan struggled to move.

'Are you all right?' Tobias bent down and helped her to stand. His strong arms eased her up. He smelt fresh, with a tinge of sandalwood, and again she admired his glossy black hair.

'Fine, thanks.' She patted the dust off her jeans, looking hot and flushed.

'Finula tells me you need a plasterer,' he smiled, putting his hands inside his navy quilted jacket.

'Yes, I've stripped the walls in there,' she pointed towards the sitting-room door, 'and half the plaster came off. Not to mention the ceiling.' He frowned. 'I've just put my foot through it, up there,' she added drily, pointing towards the loft.

'Ah, let's have a look.' Tobias made his way through to the sitting room, his tall frame and broad shoulders dwarfing the small cottage. Gazing round, he took in the grey, crumbling walls. Then he turned his head upwards towards the ceiling to see the clear outline of her footprint. 'Oh dear.' He turned to grin at Megan.

'I know, I was engrossed and stepped off the joist.'

'What with?'

'This.' She held up the lilac tin.

'What's in it?'

'I don't know. I just found it lying in the middle of the attic floor. It was as though it was put there deliberately.'

'So you were meant to find it?'

'Maybe.' They both looked at it curiously. Megan went to the nearby table and put it down. The lid was rusty, but she forced it off. She could feel Tobias behind her. The back of her neck tingled. 'Photographs...' she quickly flicked through them, 'and letters, too.' She unfolded one of them. 'They must have been written years ago.' The paper was thin and yellowed with age. The letters were written in fountain pen, neatly with defined loops. Old sepia pictures depicting images of a young couple laughing, linked arm in arm, looked back at her. Each photo told its own story: a trip to the seaside, trouser legs rolled up, paddling in the shallow pools with the sun shining in their eyes; another of them leaning against a mossy tree trunk, surrounded by bluebells. A carving of the initials 'G & E' appeared behind them, deep in the tree. Happiness exuded from the two of them so that it was almost tangible. Megan instantly recognised one of the photos. It was Gran sitting on a haystack, dressed in her land girl overalls and polka-dot headscarf. The last picture was of a young soldier in uniform looking very smart, but solemn. On the back was written, '*To my darling*

Gracie, love always, E.' Megan drew in a jagged breath, not sure what to make of it all.

'You OK?' Tobias asked gently. He was still standing patiently behind her and didn't want to pry. At the same time he didn't want to appear indifferent when this was obviously a big deal to her.

'I think so. Just puzzled.' She finally handed him the last picture. 'Read the back.'

'*To my darling Gracie, love always, E.*' He turned it round to look at the image of the soldier, staring gravely ahead to face the monstrosities of war at such a young age. 'Is this your granddad?'

'No.'

'Obviously sweethearts before she met him.' Then looking closer at the face of the soldier, he narrowed his eyes, then looked at Megan, then back at the photo. There was a poignant pause.

'Perhaps it's better if I left you to read them alone.' Tobias tactfully backed away.

'No, it's fine. I'll put them away.' Megan quickly got a grip on herself.

'Sure?'

'Yes, really.' Putting the letter back in the tin, she sat down by the table. 'I'll read them later.' She stared into space, not quite knowing what she'd just uncovered.

'Fancy a drink?'

Megan shook her head, 'Yes, sorry, I'll put the kettle on.'

'I'll do it, you stay there. You look rather pale.'

'I think I'm in shock,' she agreed.

Moments later Tobias entered the sitting room with two strong, black coffees. 'This'll put some colour in your cheeks.' He pulled a silver hip flask from his jacket pocket and emptied its contents into the two mugs. Winking, he handed her one.

'What's in that?' she laughed.

'Just a hot toddy. It'll do you good.'

Megan knocked back a mouthful and nearly choked. The potent liquor stung the back of her throat, then ran warmly down her body, soothing before finally hitting her stomach.

'It certainly has a kick to it,' she gasped.

Tobias was grinning. 'Yes, it tends to hit the spot.' She started to giggle. Her nerves had been jolted and the alcohol was taking effect quickly. Tobias gazed around the room. 'So, should I get my man on the job?'

'Your man?' She chuckled at the expression.

'Plasterer. Remember, that's why I'm here?' he stared, bemused at Megan's shoulders shaking with laughter. 'What's so funny?'

'Oh, nothing, it's me. I'm not used to hot toddies,' she wiped her eyes, 'and one way or another it's been quite a day.'

'I know.' Tobias looked straight into her face, suddenly serious. 'Listen, don't worry about the walls, or the ceiling. I'll sort it.'

'Are you sure?' The relief to have a helping hand was enormous.

'Absolutely,' Tobias replied.

'Thank you so much.'

'Not a problem.'

'I'll return the favour.'

'I'm sure you will.' The corners of his mouth twitched.

'I mean, obviously I'll pay—'

'We'll come to some arrangement.'

Megan shook her head, 'Are you laughing at me?'

'Not at all.' His eyes widened innocently. 'There is something you could do for me, though.'

'What's that?' Megan asked uneasily.

'I've noticed your paintings in the pub. They're good.'

'Thanks.' She really was beginning to warm to him.

'I'd like you to paint the Hall.'

'Really?' Megan was surprised. Usually she painted landscapes and wasn't sure she'd be able to paint such a grand building.

Sensing her hesitation, he continued, 'Someone with your talent could do it justice.'

'Well…' Taken aback by the compliment, Megan was wavering further.

'That's settled then,' Tobias cut in. 'I'll mend your house and you paint mine.'

Why not? She wanted to get back into painting, a fresh challenge could be just what she needed, plus she'd be saving her hard-earned cash into the bargain.

'OK, you're on.' Megan held out her hand in agreement. He shook it. His hand felt firm and warm, reassuring. Or maybe that was the effect of the hot toddy, she thought wryly.

Chapter 17

6 Jan 1945

Dearest Gracie,

Just received your letter and how I would have loved to have been there sitting with you against our oak tree. Instead, I am writing this by candlelight in one of the worst storms we have had this year. It is raining, thundering, and lightning, and I expect this tent to go down soon. I am glad I don't have to go out tonight – my heart goes out to those infantry soldiers out there in holes filled with water. The mud is knee-deep, even in this tent. Enough of my complaints.

Darling, I have but one wish and that is to get back on the other side of the Channel to you. How about throwing me a rope?

My sweet, I will close this letter, as the wind is coming up again, and the candle is about to blow out.

All my love,

E.

Megan was sitting up in bed reading the first letter from the Parma violet tin. It was such a lot to take in and she couldn't quite face reading any more. She looked through the photographs again, taking particular interest in the one of 'E' in his soldier's uniform. She cast her mind back to Tobias' reaction when she had shown it him. Had he been thinking the same as she? Because right now, it felt like she was looking at herself. 'E' had the same almond-shaped eyes, the same button nose, sprinkled with freckles, the full lips and jaw line. Even their ears were the same, small and compact. With an uneasy feeling starting to brood, Megan decided to try to get some sleep.

*

True to his word, Tobias had arranged for the plasterer to call at Bluebell Cottage early the next morning. Megan rubbed her eyes and let him in.

'Looks like your door's—'

'Sticking. Yes, I know,' Megan interrupted the rather portly-looking workman wearing white overalls and a cheery smile. Far too jovial for this time in the morning, she thought whilst showing him into the sitting room and pointing out the ceiling with her footprint in the middle of it.

'No problem, love, just you leave it to me. It'll be perfect by the time you come home.'

'Will it?' Megan was surprised, not daring to think that her return from work would welcome freshly plastered walls and ceiling.

'Course,' he winked. 'You won't recognise the place.'

'Oh, thanks,' she beamed, fatigue suddenly replaced with a little more zest.

She decided to walk past Treweham Hall on her way to the pub, to weigh up exactly what she had agreed to paint. In the early morning mist it stood proud and resilient. The pale pink sky made a splendid backdrop as rosy sun rays highlighted the fresh green of the virginia creeper elegantly draping the creamy stone. Across the silvery haze of the grounds, swallows flew and dipped, and she heard a wood pigeon call, and then the shuffling of hoofs.

Megan turned her gaze towards the stables to the right of the hall. Her heart stopped. There he was, Tobias, looking magnificent in jodhpurs, slowly leading his horse through to the courtyard. Quickly Megan hid behind a tree so he couldn't see her spying on him. She saw him gently reassure and pat the horse before he swung one leg over to land directly in the saddle. His jodhpurs certainly showcased his powerful physique, Megan noticed in awe, not to mention the black T-shirt hugging his broad shoulders and biceps. As if sensing he was being watched, Tobias suddenly looked up. Megan jerked her head back behind the tree trunk and held her breath. Daring to stare through the branches, she saw him canter straight backed out into the dewy morning. She just hoped she'd be able to paint the hall without too much distraction.

*

'You're early,' Finula was busy cooking breakfast for the pub's overnight visitors.

'I know, making way for the plasterer,' Megan replied, taking off her jacket and donning an apron. 'Thanks, by the way, for asking Tobias.'

'No problem.' There was a pause and Megan still sensed a slight awkwardness between them.

'Finula, I know it's none of my business about Nick,' she watched Finula's back tense whilst she was frying eggs, 'and I'm sorry if I've upset you in any way. I promise not to pry in future.' She saw Finula's shoulders relax a little.

'No, Megan, it's me who should be sorry for snapping at you.' She turned to face her. 'Just be careful.' Megan frowned. 'Of Nick.' Then she turned back and carried on cooking.

Well, what was that about? Megan still couldn't fathom it out. Both Nick and Finula seemed perfectly nice, rounded people, so why couldn't they see eye to eye? What had gone so wrong between them?

Deciding it really wasn't her problem, or her concern, Megan put it firmly to the back of her mind.

'Finula, do you think I could have a few less shifts just now? I know it's short notice,' she asked warily.

Finula shrugged. 'Don't see why not. We've no guests for the next few days, apart from Dylan. Just check with Dad. Why? Got anything planned?'

'Hmm, Tobias has asked me to paint Treweham Hall.'

Finula whisked round, face animated. 'Really?'

'Yes,' laughed Megan.

'Well, good for you! Just think, this could be the start of your new career as an artist.' Megan was touched by Finula's enthusiasm and, fingers crossed, there could be some truth in what she said. Two other paintings that had been displayed in the pub had sold already.

'Now that would be a dream come true.' Megan stared wistfully into the distance.

Finula grinned. 'Sorry to put a dampener on things, but could you deliver these breakfasts, please?' She held out two perfectly cooked full English breakfasts.

'Yeah, sure,' Megan smiled, and scurried into the dining area with them.

*

Megan finished her shift late in the afternoon and after Dermot had very kindly granted her some leave, she set off for home with a spring in her step. Feeling the anticipation build at the prospect of painting again was exciting as well as daunting. For the hundredth time she hoped that agreeing to paint Treweham Hall was the right decision. What could go wrong? Well, for a start, Tobias might hate it, causing embarrassment all around. *Stop it,* she heard her Gran's voice in her head. *Have conviction in yourself.*

She opened the door, very easily. Puzzled, she looked at the bottom of the door and noticed it had been planed. Tobias must have arranged that, too. How thoughtful. She felt a little warmer inside. Once through the door she rushed to the sitting room to see the freshly plastered walls and a perfect ceiling, without the footprint. A great sigh of contentment escaped her. What a difference! It all looked so clean and spacious. She really must thank Tobias without delay for all he'd done.

As if he had read her mind she saw him through the window strolling up the footpath. His jodhpurs had been replaced with black jeans, but he still wore the figure hugging T-shirt from this morning. Megan opened the door with a huge grin.

'Thank you so much! Come in and look.'

Tobias smiled at her gusto. As they entered the sitting room Megan saw again how he dwarfed the place, standing astride, arms folded, face in concentration inspecting the work done. After a few minutes he looked at her, pleased with what he'd seen.

'Yes, he's done a good job.'

Megan laughed. 'It's brilliant. Thanks again, Tobias, especially for sorting it so quickly.'

'My pleasure,' he nodded. 'So when do you start my painting?' he added playfully.

'How about tomorrow morning?' she chipped back.

'Tomorrow morning sounds fine. About eight o'clock?'

Megan gulped. He was keen, wasn't he? Seeing the look on her face, Tobias went on, 'That way you can join me in my early morning ride.'

'Oh… I see.' A strand of hair fell into her eyes. Tobias instinctively touched her face and pushed it behind her ear. His eyes bore into hers. It felt strangely intimate and left her speechless.

'Do you ride?' he asked eventually, breaking the spell.

'No,' she whispered huskily.

'Then I'll teach you,' he grinned. 'We'll ride the grounds and then I'll show you around the hall, before you start to paint.'

'Good idea, I'd like that,' she agreed, appreciating the opportunity to get a feel for the place.

'That's settled then.' He turned to go.

Megan halted him. 'Tobias?' He stopped and faced her. 'You did see me this morning, didn't you?'

'How could I? You were hiding behind a tree, Megan.' His lips twitched, then he turned on his heel and went, leaving Megan once again rather flushed. She watched him out of the sitting-room window stride down the footpath. Then she saw Nick at the garden gate, waiting for him to pass. Tobias stopped momentarily, then practically barged past him. Did Nick seem to be hiding a smirk? She went to open the front door.

'Hi, Nick.' He was holding a small case.

'A duty visit.' He held out the case. 'Worming tablets for Zac. His records tell me he's due for a booster vaccination, too.'

'Ah, right. Sorry, I should have thought about that.'

'Not at all.' Nick shook his head. 'You weren't to know. I can give him his booster now and leave the tablets with you.'

'Fine, thanks. Come in.'

Zac ran to Nick, wagging his tail. Nick bent down and stroked him. Megan smiled at how good Nick was with him.

'Right, old boy, let's get you sorted.' Nick opened his case and pulled out a syringe. Very carefully he injected the vaccine into Zac's neck. Megan watched his gentle hands administer the needle: Zac hadn't flinched. 'There, all done.' He patted the dog's head and stood up. 'That's him seen to for another six months. You need to give Zac his worming tablet with his next meal.'

'Will do,' Megan smiled. 'And thanks again. I dread to think what would have happened to him if I hadn't taken him in.'

Nick looked hurt. '*I* would have had him, Megan.' His eyes looked searchingly into hers, as if she had insulted him.

'Sorry, Nick, of course you would have,' she replied. 'Would you like a cup of tea?'

'Yes, thanks. It's been a long day, the surgery was packed full and one of the vets is still on maternity leave, so we're short staffed at the moment.'

'It must be such a satisfying job, though, helping all those sick animals?'

He laughed. 'Yes, but it's not giving me much free time at the moment. Sometimes it's just good to spend time doing what you want, with someone you want.' He stared directly at her. Megan paused. Nick's eyes slowly looked her up and down. She felt like he was mentally undressing her and she found herself blushing slightly. Coughing, she carried on making the tea and passed him his cup. His fingers touched hers in taking it. Again, his eyes caught hers.

He puzzled Megan. There was something about him she couldn't define.

Chapter 18

Picking up her sketch pad and jute bag containing paints, brushes and pencils, Megan made her way, bleary-eyed, up the path. She'd decided to wear leggings as the best substitute for jodhpurs, along with her fitted navy-blue quilted jacket, which was about as horsy as she could muster. Deciding the bag was too heavy to carry on foot, she plonked everything on the back seat of the car. She once again admired the early morning sun and the dewy, moist air. What a difference from queuing in the town traffic smog. It really did feel a lifetime ago that she was working in the office. She shuddered at the thought and started up the car. Moments later she slowly drove up the gravel driveway of Treweham Hall and parked at the side of the stables.

Tobias was leading a horse out and waved her over. Megan gulped again as she approached Tobias, resplendent in his jodhpurs.

'Meet Juke, he's strong, but very amiable.'

Megan sized up the animal, who looked magnificent with his chestnut coat shimmering in the early sun. She patted him gingerly.

'Don't look so timid, Megan. He'll not harm you. He has the gentlest nature of all our horses.'

'He's lovely.' She touched him again, firmly this time, earning herself a neigh.

'There you go, rule number one: always let your horse know who's boss.'

Megan nodded. 'Will do.'

Tobias narrowed his eyes and looked her up and down. Feeling a little unnerved, Megan frowned.

'Just calculating how to adjust the stirrups. Here…' He took the stirrup iron and, lifting her hand, placed it under her armpit and measured her arm. 'The stirrups should hang at the same length as your arm,' he explained. Tobias had a firm, warm grip, making Megan's heart flutter uncontrollably.

'Oh, I see,' she answered feebly as he fiddled with the straps.

'Right, ready to mount?' he asked her, eyebrows raised. Was that a smirk playing round his lips?

'Er…' Megan glanced at the huge bulk next to her and swallowed. Sensing the hesitation, Tobias reassured her, putting his hand on her shoulder.

'Here, just put your left foot into the stirrup, lift your right leg over and land softly.'

With a heave and sheer determination, she comfortably straddled Juke and sat upright, feeling quite pleased with herself. Tobias threaded the reins through her fingers, his touch sending little shivers down her spine. Willing herself to concentrate, she took a deep breath and watched him climb with ease onto his horse. The figure-hugging jodhpurs outlined the hard muscles of his thighs and his groin, making her blush slightly. He was born to do this. She considered her childhood, weaving her bike through the bustling streets. Whilst she had been whizzing through the mayhem of urban suburbs, he would have been cantering calmly through the tranquil grounds of the estate. What a difference.

'OK?' He looked puzzled, obviously wondering what she was thinking.

'Yep, let's go,' she answered decisively, shoulders back.

'To ask him to walk on, make a clucking sound and squeeze his sides slightly with both legs.' He showed her and Megan copied. Soon they were gently walking side by side. Megan was surprised at how much she was enjoying herself.

'Ready to trot?'

'Let's go.'

'Squeeze with both legs again, then rise up slightly and stand in the stirrup for one step, and then go back down. Let the horse's pace lift you, go with the flow.'

Megan concentrated hard and did as she was instructed. She soon got into the swing of it, softly swaying up and down. Tobias followed her closely and she was all too aware of his eyes burning into her back.

'You're doing really well, Megan!' he called from behind, whilst admiring her pert bum bobbing up and down. He could feel himself getting aroused.

'Thanks!' She was beginning to feel exhilarated as the wind rushed past and the morning sun rested its warm rays on them.

'Slow down!' Tobias' voice edged with concern as she lengthened the gap between them.

'How?' Megan called back, suddenly conscious of the distance she'd created.

'Lean slightly back and say "Whoa!"' Sure enough, the horse slowed down and gradually stopped. Tobias caught up with them. 'You're a natural in the saddle,' he beamed.

'Thank you,' Megan gushed. 'It's so...'

'Invigorating?'

'Yes, what a way to start the day.' Her eyes drunk in all the scenery: a burnt-orange-pink sunrise soaring over smooth, rolling hills, the pale mist hovering, birds elegantly flying in sequence, all sheer perfection taking her breath away.

'I'm glad you enjoyed it.' Tobias' voice was closer than she expected, making her suddenly turn to face him. His eyes gazed into hers and she stared back into the gold flecks mixed with hazel green. He leant forward and brushed away an eyelash on her cheek. 'Come on, let's get back. I'll show you round the Hall,' he said gently.

Megan followed in silence with a fast-beating heart.

Once the horses had been watered and put back inside the stables, Tobias guided Megan round to the front of the Hall. She gazed up at the beautiful, majestic building hoping desperately she could do it justice with her painting.

Tobias sensed her self-doubt. 'Megan, I know you'll do a fantastic job. I've seen your artwork.' He then opened the large, wooden door and steered her inside. A vast hallway greeted her with a stone floor and dark oak panelling. A chandelier glimmered in the centre of an ornate plaster ceiling, showing heraldic symbols of the Cavendish family, their coat of arms depicting a cross and a lion. A solid staircase with intricate carvings ran up the middle of the hallway, which led onto an overlooking balcony. Hanging from the wall was a huge tapestry of a knight wearing a white tunic with a red cross. 'My family had strong connections to the Knights Templar,' Tobias explained, following her eyes.

'Oh, I see,' replied Megan faintly, completely overawed by the splendour of such surroundings.

'I'll show you the great hall.' He ushered her through the first door off the hallway into a long room, which ran the full length of the building. A huge oak table stood in the middle, decorated with silver candelabras, family portraits proudly stared down from the high walls. 'We only use this room for large family occasions.'

That's probably why it's so cold, thought Megan, wincing at the thought of what their energy bills would be.

The next room they entered was the drawing room. This was much smaller and far more homely. Again, family portraits surrounded them, along with smaller landscape pictures. The marble fireplace was lit, with a small crackling fire, giving a warm, cosy feeling. A coffee cup left on the side table and a crumpled newspaper on the Chesterfield sofa were obvious signs that this room was certainly lived in. The library was Megan's favourite room, with its mahogany panelling and endless rows of books. A mobile stepladder was suspended from the highest shelf. The dark wood floor was covered with Persian rugs and the whole space was illuminated by the light streaming through the large stained-glass window at the bottom of the room. The pictures showcased the Cavendish family pedigree through marriage from various earls and possible royalty, judging by the crowns that were worn. Megan longed to ask, but didn't want to appear crass. A dried flower arrangement filled the large, tiled fireplace, inviting Megan to investigate further at the portrait above it. It was of Tobias, recently painted, by the look of it. The likeness was uncanny, with his sparkly green eyes, dark shiny hair, and the signature grin playing round his lips.

'This is brilliant, Tobias!' she gasped in awe, thinking her own effort would be insignificant compared to this.

Sensing her unease again, Tobias moved to stand behind her and put a hand on her shoulder.

'You can do better,' he whispered gently in her ear.

She halted. His breath felt hot, caressing her neck. His hand was still on her shoulder, warm and heavy. Her chest started to pound. Megan was unnerved by the effect he had on her. Not for the first time she wondered just how much of a distraction Tobias would prove to be. To her, painting the Hall was an important commission that may set the course for a new, much-longed-for career. But was it just a game to him?

Chapter 19

With heavy hearts, Gary and Tracy Belcher closed the
door for the last time on their small terraced house.
They hauled the last of the removal boxes that
contained their remaining belongings into their new
Range Rover complete with personal number plate:
'B3LCH'. Tracy wanted to take their pine double bed
and her grandmother's rocking chair, Gary his forty-
two-inch plasma television. But apart from those
things, their clothes, crockery, framed photographs
and cushions, they had basically left the house and its
entire contents to the young couple who had bought
the house, much to their delight.

Feelings were mixed as Gary and Tracy drove
down the motorway to the Cotswolds. The obvious
sadness of saying goodbye was tinged with a sense of
relief. Both Gary and Tracy had witnessed the looks
on friends' faces when learning of their move. After
the initial surprise, the Belchers couldn't help but
detect a foreboding disapproval. Why the need to go?
Were they too good for them now? And more to the
point, who was going to pay for everything? Once
realising the gravy train was about to depart,
resentment set in. Snide remarks were made, making
them feel uncomfortable. In the end Gary and Tracy

had sold their home for a song, desperate to get out. They hardly needed the money and the purchase of the Gate House in Treweham had gone smoothly. Once they'd decided to go ahead with buying the Gate House, it had just been a matter of signing and releasing the money. Oh so simple when compared to the hoops they had had to jump through to get a starter mortgage. Money really did make a difference, they were beginning to learn in many ways.

The one thing they clung to was that they had each other. There was no change to the way they felt, their ideals, aspirations, or what they wanted out of life. Gary and Tracy had always wished for a simple, safe, family life and that's what they were going to get, but in another location. One free from jealousy, assumptions, opinions and, in some cases, hatred.

Tracy had opened an anonymous, hand posted letter containing malicious threats. A demand of £10,000 was to be sent to a PO Box, unless they wanted to come to some harm or, even more terrifying, they wanted their parents to come to some harm. That was the last straw. Two new homes were bought for their parents. Gary and Tracy moved in with Tracy's mum and dad for the last week, before completion of the sale of the house, and emptying it of the last bits and pieces they wanted to take with them. Tracy was relieved that it was a Monday, so Cut Above was closed and she didn't have to suffer

Sharon glaring at her from the shop window, arms crossed, eyes narrowed with scorn. It had all gone terribly wrong. It was time to go. Tracy's eyes filled with tears as they slowly drove away from a happy little home that had such fond memories.

Gary put his hand on her lap. 'Don't cry, Tracy. It's for the best.'

'I know. It's just so sad to be leaving with all this ill feeling.'

Gary sighed. 'That's human nature, Trace.'

Together they drove past the terraced streets, where children played, mums pushed prams and corner shops thrived. They drove past the old cotton mills, now renovated to apartments, through the busy town, bustling with workers, students and traffic spewing exhaust fumes. They drove past the magnificent Town Hall, the market square, the railway station, past the docklands and onto the motorway to a fresh start, a new life.

It literally was a breath of fresh air arriving in Treweham, surrounded by lush, green meadows bursting with wildflowers. A brook bubbled gently and the cooing of a wood pigeon could be heard in the distance. They had collected the keys to the Gate House from the estate offices and had called in at the local pub for a bite to eat. Sitting outside The Templar on wooden benches, they clinked two glasses of Prosecco in celebration to the future.

'Here's to us, Trace.' Gary put his arm round his wife. He could see she was still slightly edgy about the move.

It *had* been overwhelming, considering what they had experienced, he thought: going from being a typical working-class couple in the North-West of England, to winning three million pounds, losing your identity, your friends, your family being threatened, and now relocating alone to a completely new place. Whilst Treweham was charming with its stone cottages and pretty countryside, it wasn't home. Not yet. Gary knew he had to be positive, for Tracy's sake. For both their sakes.

'Do you remember coming here on honeymoon?' he asked, keen to recall the cheery times they had spent in Treweham.

'Yes.' Tracy's face lit up. 'They had a barbecue and all the villagers came. It was lovely, wasn't it?'

'It was. That's us now, Trace, we're two of the villagers.'

'Yes,' she smiled, 'we are.'

'There's another do here tomorrow. Racing on the big screen. One of the jockeys, Dylan Delany, has got some connection to Treweham.'

'Really? Let's go, it'll be fun.'

That's more like it; his old Tracy was back, full of enthusiasm, a bit of bounce. 'Let's,' he replied, squeezing her tight.

Chapter 20

The Templar was heaving. Megan, Finula and Dermot were working flat out behind the bar. On the far side of the wall hung a huge screen, its volume vibrated round the pub, adding to the already high-pitched excitement. Seamus and Tobias sat close by, eager to see Dylan riding Midas Touch, a horse from the Fox's' training yard. Seamus' dad was at Newmarket, overseeing operations, which was precisely why Seamus was in Treweham with Tobias. The last thing Dylan needed was a potential disagreement between father and son, so Seamus had wisely decided to stay at home. Every so often Megan would catch a glimpse of Tobias through the crowd. She watched how his eyes looked intently at the screen, deep in thought as he sipped his brandy. Seamus, too, looked sombre. This was obviously a big deal to him: after all, it was his business, his livelihood.

Finally the signature tune of the afternoon racing programme blasted out from the speakers, to the cheers of the crowd. The pleasant face of the presenter came into focus, welcoming all to the Newmarket races. Soon she was interviewing a retired jockey for his thoughts on the 2000 Guineas winner, having won the prestigious race three times before in the nineties.

'Well, clearly they're all top-class animals to be here, but with the drying ground, I'd have to favour Jo's Comet and Midas Touch.'

This sent the pub wild. Tobias and Seamus allowed themselves tight smiles.

'And, of course, Midas Touch has the assistance of Dylan Delany in the saddle,' replied the presenter with gusto.

'Yes, who rides Newmarket better than Dylan Delany?'

This caused even more cheering and clapping. Flora was sitting right at the front, on a table next to Tobias and Seamus, with two friends from the stables. Her heart was thumping wildly at the thought of seeing her lover on the big screen. No one knew about her and Dylan, even though they had been meeting quite regularly. It was her precious secret. The TV presenter then moved on to Sean Fox, as Midas Touch's trainer. He stood tall and proud. Seamus gave a deep breath, bracing himself for his father's concise, no-nonsense answers. Almost everyone in The Templar had placed a bet on Dylan winning the 2000 Guineas, at good odds too, having known early on he was racing today.

Gary and Tracy, being caught up in the thrill of it all, had decided to put a wager on as well. They sat near the bar and had got chatting to the locals. It was hard not to get swept along with the camaraderie. Everyone was jubilant as the drinks flowed and last-minute bets were placed urgently via mobile phone.

Only Seamus and Tobias appeared serious. Megan wondered how much money Tobias had put on Dylan winning his race. Judging by the way he was acting, a lot. Only once had he smiled and acknowledged her. The 2000 Guineas was scheduled to run after the first two races, allowing anticipation to build. The atmosphere was electric. Applause and cheers announced the end of each race, or groans and ripped tickets thrown in despair. Then the big moment arrived. The 2000 Guineas was next.

The camera zoomed into the parade ring, where the snorting horses were met by their jockeys. It was a hive of activity. The jockeys, trainers and owners were having final discussions. Then the camera closed in on the most famous jockey in the race, Dylan. He was talking to Sean Fox. Gone was the carefree playboy. Instead his expression held absolute attention, utterly focused on the job in hand. He was wearing silks in the owner's colours: claret and gold hoops. His dark curls could just be seen tucked under his cap. Instead of his blue eyes twinkling, they looked piercingly into the close-up of the camera, making every woman watching sigh. Flora thought her chest would burst with pride. Megan watched

Tobias grip his glass as he stared at the screen. He'd been a gambler most of his life and he'd enjoyed a few good wins. But he'd never stood to win ninety grand on one race before. Seamus, too, was as still as a statue, waiting for the race to begin. The horses were mounted and made their way to the starting line. The sun was warm on Dylan's back and his confidence was growing with every stride as he cantered down to the start. He circled Midas Touch behind the stalls as the starter called out the jockeys' names and the handlers began to load them up. Within seconds the starter had pulled the lever and they were off.

Dylan quickly caught hold of Midas Touch's mane as he bolted forward and immediately set into his stride. Once his body had adjusted to the pace, he let go and settled him into the middle of the field as planned. Dylan knew the race would not continue to be run at such speed, so calmed Midas Touch and waited for the pace to slow. Shouts of frustration from The Templar echoed round the bar, the viewers thinking Dylan had lost his stride. Tobias and Seamus thought better; although tense, they knew to trust Dylan's tactics. Horses thundered past Midas Touch as Dylan waited to make his mark. Searching for a gap, he moved his horse into position. Seamus leant forward in his chair, knowing this was the moment. Dylan paced up his speed and passed two horses, causing cheers from the pub. Again Dylan looked ahead and saw a space. Taking advantage of it and his speed he immediately directed Midas Touch to ride through it, overtaking another rider. More shouts blasted out from The Templar. Now they were facing the run to the finish. Dylan felt Midas Touch hit his stride. All he had to do was steer him and they'd be certain to win. The horse directly in front of him began to slow down. Dylan pulled to go round on the outside, when suddenly Jo's Comet appeared from nowhere and knocked him off balance towards the rails. Midas Touch briefly lost momentum and Dylan found himself tightly boxed in, unable to find a gap to manoeuvre.

In the stands Sean Fox gripped his binoculars with rage. 'He's got himself boxed in,' he hissed through gritted teeth. Meanwhile, the bookmakers by the railings smiled. A pale-faced Tobias looked away from the screen with a gulp, as if his last chance had died. The horse in front of Dylan was losing ground so quickly that Jo's Comet had no alternative but to go on, leaving Dylan behind him with space to move, but now lengths off the leader. Dylan gripped hard on the reins and once again Midas Touch was running. The horse galloped as though giving his all but, a furlong from home, Dylan took his whip and gave him one good crack behind the saddle. The response was immediate. In an instant Midas Touch took off, moving up a gear like a high-performance car. With a hundred yards to run Dylan gave him one more crack, and then rode him out with full force. Fifty yards from the post he passed all the horses and won by a length and a half.

'He did it!' Seamus bounced up from his seat and punched the air.

Tobias knocked back his drink, then looked towards Megan behind the bar with a huge beam on his face. Hell, he was handsome, she thought, as her heart fluttered uncontrollably.

The whole pub erupted with whoops of joy, people jumped up and down in delight, and champagne was ordered. Gary and Tracy basked in the atmosphere. It felt so good to be part of this community.

In the midst of this pandemonium Nick appeared at the bar. Finula ignored him, leaving Megan to serve.

'Hi,' he smiled. 'A glass of red, please.' Megan poured and handed him his drink. 'Do you know how Ted is?' he asked, handing over his money.

'I saw him the other day. He's OK, but didn't want to go back to his cottage. He'll have gone into a care home by now.' Megan's face dropped a little, remembering her visit to Ted. 'I must go and see him there.' Nick cupped her chin with this thumb and forefinger.

'Hey, don't worry. Ted'll be fine.'

'A brandy, please, Megan.' Tobias slammed down his glass on the bar and glared at Nick. Megan jumped slightly and took his glass. Nick shrugged, smirked and left.

'There you go.' Megan handed Tobias his drink.

'Thanks. Was he bothering you?' He nodded towards Nick, who was standing talking to a group of people near the door.

'No,' she frowned, 'he was just asking about Ted.'

Tobias didn't look convinced. Then his shoulders relaxed.

'Help me celebrate my winnings, have dinner with me tonight?'

With him looking like that, how could she refuse? Yet she had to.

'I'm sorry, I'll be working here until late tonight.'

'Tomorrow, then?' He wasn't taking no for an answer.

'Yes, but I'll cook dinner. You come to mine.' He was dangerously attractive and she felt safer being around him on her own territory.

'Fine,' he smiled, 'I'll be there.' Then he leant over the bar and kissed her on the lips. A quick, uncomplicated, innocent kiss, which left her dizzy. He took his drink and returned to Seamus.

'I saw that,' whispered Finula in her ear.

'He didn't mean anything by it, he's just excited about Dylan winning the race,' Megan said with ease, making light of it, even though her chest was thundering.

'It was a warning to Nick,' replied Finula. They were distracted by clapping when the screen showed a triumphant Dylan entering the winner's enclosure. The buzz of excitement was palpable as Midas Touch was welcomed back by a cheering crowd, and at the front was Sean Fox. The TV presenter quickly ran to Dylan and lifted her microphone up to him.

'That was a close shave, Dylan!' Dylan gave a lazy smile: back was the assured, confident Romeo.

'All in a day's work. I knew Midas Touch could do it.'

'Well, he certainly did. Congratulations! I take it you'll be celebrating tonight?'

'I think so.' He winked, making the reporter weak at the knees.

Megan smiled to herself watching Dylan on the screen with his self-assured way.

'Now what's making you smile, Megan?' Nick was back at the bar. 'Not that kiss from his lordship, surely?'

'I was smiling at Dylan, actually.' Megan blushed slightly, feeling a touch defensive.

Then Nick leant forward over the bar and said in a low tone, 'Don't be taken in, Megan.'

'Sorry?'

'With Tobias. You look just like his dead girlfriend. He's only after a substitute. You're better than that and deserve so much more.'

Megan stared, dumbfounded. Nick patted her hand and walked away.

Chapter 21

Celebrate he did. Dylan shared a bottle of champagne with the grooms from the training yard, Sean Fox and the owners of Midas Touch. He wouldn't be racing for a few days, so he allowed himself to relax and enjoy the merriment.

Sean Fox slapped him hard on the back. 'Well done, son. I knew you'd do it!' Dylan took his bravado casually, knowing full well the wrath he would have incurred had he not won. Although the atmosphere at Newmarket was buoyant, Dylan couldn't wait to get back to Treweham, to really celebrate with his friends in The Templar. He knew they'd all have been watching, cheering him on, and it warmed him to picture it. For a moment he thought of Flora – would she be there? Imagining her slim, toned body turned him on like a switch. Winning always made him horny, and he was a winner.

'We're heading back to Treweham now. You coming with us?' one of the grooms asked.

'Sure, let's go.' Dylan collected his gear and followed him, glad to be sharing a lift home with the stable team, rather than Sean Fox.

The journey was a pleasant one. They'd tossed a coin to nominate a driver, leaving the rest to pass round hip flasks of whisky. Raucous laughter bellowed from the Land Rover, and they were in high spirits by the time they arrived at The Templar.

It was early evening, and the pub was still packed when Dylan walked through the door. He was greeted by loud whistles and cheers. Finula raised and clapped her hands, her face rapt with joy for him. Dylan came straight over to her and leant over the bar. 'Now surely that deserves a kiss, Finula?'

She threw her head back with a laugh but Dermot intervened in the nick of time.

'No it doesn't, Delany.' Everybody chuckled. Except Flora, who was sitting quietly in a corner, out of sight.

People shook Dylan's hand, slapped his back and bought him drinks, then more drinks. Everyone wanted to speak to him, to be a part of the celebration. Tracy asked for his autograph. He paused, looked straight down her top and said he'd be delighted. Where did she want him to sign? Still Flora sat in the corner. Her friends had left long ago. She had wanted to stay to wait for Dylan to return. Patiently she looked to catch his eye, for him to notice her and come dashing over with open arms. But nobody was aware of her; it was all so busy.

Dylan, however, was aware of a woman with long, blonde hair looking over. Now and then he would glance across to find her staring at him. As the drinks continued to flow his spirits lifted higher. He clocked her again and took in her cleavage, which was spilling out of her low-cut tight red dress. He smiled in her direction, but then a local man distracted him, eager to shake hands with him. A few moments later the blonde made her way over.

'Fancy a drink, Dylan?'

He turned, swaying slightly. Blinking to focus properly, he saw that the tight red dress complimented her curves and showcased her long, shapely legs. He homed in on her chest again. That switch turned on. Suddenly Dylan wanted his bed. He was tired of celebrating; he wanted to lie down.

'I've had enough to drink, thanks,' he replied. 'It's time for bed.' The woman gave a sexy grin.

'Is it really?'

Dylan stared into her face. She had pouting, red lips and inviting eyes.

'Follow me,' he ordered, then took the stairs to his room. The woman tottered on stilettos behind him. Within moments they were both outside room four.

Meanwhile, Flora had witnessed it all. Shaking, she got up and walked straight out of The Templar.

Dylan pulled his conquest inside and locked the door behind him. He grabbed her to him and began to unzip the back of her dress. She feverishly unbuttoned his shirt. The feel of the bare skin of his broad shoulders and back beneath her palms was breath-taking. Dylan yanked off the red dress, leaving her standing in nothing but a lace thong. He took her hands impatiently, pulling them down to his enormous erection. She groped him slowly, then felt for his button and pulled down his jeans and boxer shorts. Unable to hold out any longer, Dylan guided her to the bed. His powerful legs and chest bearing down on her was wildly exciting. When he tore off her underwear and launched himself inside her, she cried out in pleasure, arching her back against him. A raw urge overcame Dylan. He moved his mouth to her breasts, taking each nipple between his teeth and tongue, increasing the pace of his thrusts. She dug her fingers into his buttocks, pulling him further inside her slick heat. Dylan couldn't control himself any longer. He let out a guttural moan and exploded inside her. They both lay panting for several minutes.

Finally Dylan rolled onto his back and stretched out his arms. He was tired, so tired. The room started to spin from the drink and exhaustion. As he closed his eyes he felt a cold, hard grip on his wrist. Then he was out: sleep had taken over.

The next morning Finula was waiting to cook Dylan's breakfast. All the other guests had had theirs and his was the only one left. She'd expected him to be up late after last night's partying, but she needed to get on with preparing the lunches soon. Looking at the clock and frowning, she decided to go up to his room and see if he wanted breakfast in bed.

Tapping at the door she tentatively called, 'Dylan, are you there?' There was a ruffling noise, then a cough.

'Finula, is that you?' he hissed back.

'Yeah, is everything all right?'

'No. Are you alone?'

'Yes. Why?'

'Come in,' he said in hushed tones. Turning the door handle and poking her head round the door, she fought hard not to laugh. There on the bed lay a naked Dylan, covered only by a crumpled linen sheet, handcuffed to the brass headboard. 'It's not funny! The bitch's fastened me to the bloody bed!'

'Oh, Dylan.' Finula doubled over in hysterics. 'Who was it?'

'I dunno! Some woman who I can't remember came on to me.'

Finula wagged a finger at him. 'Well, let this be a lesson to you, Dylan Delany.' Then she started to laugh again.

'Finula, this isn't funny. Please, get me out of this thing,' he whispered urgently. She came to inspect the handcuff, which held Dylan's wrist in a steel grip.

'Where's the key?'

'How the fuck should I know?'

'Wait, hold still.' Finula reached into her hair and took out a hairpin that was helping to hold up a messy bun. An auburn tendril of hair fell across her forehead.

'God, you're sexy,' Dylan's eyes drank in her pretty, freckled face.

'For goodness' sake, Dylan, don't you ever let up?' she asked in exasperation, as she carefully picked the handcuff lock. After a few moments she had managed to unlock it. Rubbing his wrist, he sat up.

'Thanks. Where did you learn that?' he asked with a sly smile.

'Girl Guides, actually, very resourceful. Now, probably best not to mention this to my dad.' The look on his face made her giggle again.

'Definitely not,' he agreed.

Chapter 22

As promised, Tobias was knocking on Megan's cottage door the next evening. Wearing a fitted black open-neck shirt and black jeans, he looked devilishly handsome.

'Hi!' Megan tried to sound breezy, as her heart started to thump at seeing him.

'Hello there.' He handed her a bottle of red wine. It looked extremely expensive to her. Probably came straight from his cellar, she thought. What did the likes of him want with her? Was she a novel distraction? Or did she very conveniently remind him of his lost love? She watched him glancing round the kitchen, taking in the alterations she'd made. The cupboards had been painted with a country-cream chalk paint and she had sewn a pair of floral curtains, which hung prettily in the leaded window. The open shelves on the walls housed multicoloured crockery, giving it a lovely twee, cottage look. Megan had bought an old brass lantern from a car-boot sale, which shone on the Welsh dresser, giving the room a warm, cosy glow. A new rag rug lay on the freshly scrubbed stone floor and she had pulled the small dining table into the centre of the room and lit the candles on it. She hesitated: did it look too romantic? Suddenly she lost her nerve.

As if reading her mind Tobias turned to face her.

'How beautifully snug this is, Megan,' he smiled. 'Let's open the wine.' She handed him a corkscrew and with expertise he extracted the cork. Pouring two generous glasses, he lifted his to propose a toast. 'To your new home.'

Megan grinned and clinked her glass with his. Taking a sip, she was surprised at how delicious she found it. Ripe, juicy plums and cinnamon hit the back of her tongue. It was so smooth and rich she took another sip immediately. Tobias gazed at her. 'You like?'

'Hmm,' she nodded, 'it's lovely.'

'It was the first one I came across in the cellar.' Megan's lips twitched. He really did belong to a different world. 'Something smells good.' Tobias nodded towards the oven.

'Beef casserole with baked potatoes.' Basically something she could just leave in the oven, not being too much of a cook. 'It should be ready. Take a seat.' She couldn't help but notice again how he dwarfed the little kitchen. He must feel cramped in here, she thought, being used to so much space in Treweham Hall.

As Megan busied herself dishing out the meal, Tobias sat at the table observing her. She wore skinny jeans, which showed off her slim legs and perfect, round bottom, and an off-the-shoulder blouse. He admired her graceful neck and noticed a strawberry-shaped birthmark on the dip above her collarbone. He felt a compulsion to lick and taste it. He found her so elegant, so quietly self-assured, qualities he respected in a woman. But he sensed a cool, distant side to her, too, as if she lacked trust in herself, or maybe others. He was experienced enough to know that she enjoyed his company – why else would he be here? He was certain she wouldn't be painting the Hall if she didn't like him, but there was just something missing, a reluctance he couldn't put his finger on. The other day, riding, there was no mistaking the chemistry between them. He'd so wanted to kiss her, but had backed off. He had felt her tense when he touched her and whispered in her ear whilst looking at his portrait. Was that because she didn't trust him, or herself? He didn't want to rush and ruin things, but watching her now, at ease in her own surroundings, he was finding it very difficult.

She turned with the two plates of steaming casserole and put them on the table. 'There you go.'

'This looks lovely. Thanks, Megan.'

After a couple of glasses of wine, they both relaxed into each other's company. They exchanged stories of their childhoods and youth, making each other giggle. Tobias mentioned his younger brother, Sebastian, and how he used Treweham Hall as a base, when not touring with his travelling theatre company as an actor.

'I've seen him in The Templar. He's a friend of Nick's, isn't he, the one with blond hair?'

'Hmm, I'm afraid he is.' Clearly Tobias didn't approve of this friendship.

Changing the subject, Megan commented on an article she had once read about him being a wild child.

He shook his head. 'Don't believe everything you read in the paper. I wasn't half as bad as they made out.' This was actually true; he was worse.

They had soon got through the bottle of wine.

'I've another bottle, but it won't be to your standard,' Megan said over her shoulder, as she stretched up to the shelf to get it. He caught a glimpse of flesh as her blouse rode up and felt something stir inside. After a few more glasses of wine, he reached his hand out to cover hers on the table. There it was again: she'd tensed. Suddenly a dark thought hovered over him like a thunder cloud and made his stomach clench.

'Megan, can I ask you a question?' He looked so grave, she wondered what it was.

'Yes.'

'Has anyone ever physically hurt you?' Just one name, that's all he needed and he'd break the bastard's legs.

'No! Of course not,' she answered immediately, shocked that he should think such a thing. He appeared to lighten up. 'I know I might appear... a little cool at times—'

'Subzero,' he cut in, making her throw her head back and chuckle.

'You're funny, Tobias. You make me laugh,' she smiled.

'You're beautiful, Megan. You make me horny,' he replied with a wicked grin.

Megan's eyes widened, 'Tobias!'

'I'm teasing you,' he lied; he'd never been so aroused. 'I'm sorry, please, carry on,' he smoothed over.

'Well, if I'm *subzero* it's because I've been hurt in the past, but not physically, emotionally.' There was a poignant pause.

'What happened?' Tobias asked softly. His eyes were burning into hers. The wine had loosened her tongue and she told him everything about Adam and his secretary. He sat in silence, taking it all in. When she'd finished, she took a gulp of wine and looked directly at him. 'So now you know.'

'We're not all like him.'

She gave a hard laugh. A spark of uncertainty stung her. It was the comment Nick had made last night in the pub. With Dutch courage she looked straight at him again, almost accusingly.

'Can I ask you a question?'

'Of course.'

'Is it me you find beautiful, or the fact I look like your late fiancée?' The question floored him.

He sat rigid. Narrowing his eyes he asked in a quiet, controlled voice, 'What exactly is that supposed to mean?'

'It's something Nick said, about you kissing me yesterday in The Templar.'

'Did I offend you?' His tone remained stilted.

'No, of course not,' she quickly replied, beginning to feel uneasy. 'He said you kissed me because of who I reminded you of, not for me.' She stood up, wanting to put some distance between them. Why had she opened her mouth? He stood up too, staring into her face. She moved backwards, towards the corner of the kitchen and he stood in front of her, blocking her in.

'So that's what the bastard's been saying, is it?' he rasped with fury.

Megan swiftly tried to calm him. 'I'm sorry, Tobias. I've made you angry.'

'It's not you who's made me angry. Yes, you do look like Carrie did, but *you're not* her. She was taller than you, had a different voice, she was a damn sight warmer than you,' she flinched, 'and she didn't have a strawberry-shaped birthmark above her collarbone.'

Oh, to hell with it, he couldn't resist any longer. He plunged his mouth down and kissed and licked it. Megan gasped, tension was at fever pitch, but she didn't want his lips to stop. She nuzzled her face into his glossy dark hair, loving the fresh pine smell of him. He ran frenzied kisses up her neck and she responded by pulling him closer. Her hands reached inside his shirt and ran over his toned back.

'Megan,' he groaned as his mouth found hers, his tongue explored her lips, then gently probed inside.

Megan's legs buckled as she felt faint with desire. Her body had never responded this way ever. Tobias held her tightly, his lips plundering hers deeply, intensely, taking her breath away. She wanted more of him and her hands cupped the sides of his face, then ran through his dark hair, which felt like silk.

He thrust his pelvis into her, making his erection evident. Then, with an almighty will, he forced himself to stop. His chest was heaving. 'Megan, unless you want me to take you right now over the kitchen table, this must stop.'

Blushing furiously, Megan also calmed herself, 'I'm... sorry... I...'

He dipped his head to face her. 'Don't ever apologise for touching me,' he smiled, still shaking slightly. They hugged each other closely for a moment, drinking in the smell of each other.

Finally Megan spoke. 'Fancy a coffee?' She was desperate to return to the previous light-hearted atmosphere.

'That would be lovely,' Tobias answered with a grin.

Chapter 23

The walk home cleared Tobias' head. Under a moonlit sky, dotted with stars, his mind buzzed with mixed emotions. Megan had awoken something deep within him. Something that had been lying dormant for years. Never had he believed the sensation pounding through his veins would ever return. It both shocked and satisfied him. It was as though he had been whisked back in time to when he was younger and at his happiest. It wasn't disloyalty to Carrie's memory – he'd got over that feeling a long time ago. He always knew at some stage he would have to produce an heir, so hadn't envisaged being alone, but he assumed any future relationship would rate second-best. Tonight he'd been proved very wrong. Now he knew he could build a future with the right person, for the right reason. Adrenaline had coursed through him when she'd asked about Carrie.

He was outraged by Nick Fletcher's meddling. When he'd seen him touch Megan yesterday behind the bar, not once but twice, he'd wanted to tear him apart, especially seeing how uncomfortable she appeared. And just why was Nick snooping at her garden gate the other day when he'd strode past him? How dare he cast aspersions about him? Especially after the way he had acted towards his brother, Sebastian. That thought left a very bitter taste in his mouth. It also strengthened his resolve to protect Megan from any unwanted attention from Fletcher. His need to safeguard her made him understand his father for the first time, and how he must have felt towards his wife. Then it suddenly became clear. In a moment he realised just how he could be close by, watching over Megan. He gave a slow smile and felt a warm, comforting glow inside.

From her bedroom window Megan watched him strolling home down the lane. Tonight had unnerved her. She'd been stunned at her response to his touch; her body still tingled. Pulling the curtains shut, she lay on the bed and stared at the ceiling, trying to make some sense of it all. Think logically, she told herself. He was attractive, charming and he made her laugh. So far, so good. But he was also from another world, lived in a grand house, had a disreputable past, plus a string of glamorous girlfriends. Was *she* just a novel distraction? Could he be trusted? More to the point, could she trust herself? Tomorrow she planned to work on the painting. Had she made the right decision to work so close to Tobias?

*

Flora had learnt a hard lesson in who to trust. The newspaper in front of her told her, in no uncertain terms, just what a love rat Dylan Delany was. A picture of him stared up at her, with his dark curls, twinkling blue eyes and confident smile. The caption read:

Champion Jockey Celebrates

and it was followed by a kiss-and-tell story of how Sadie Stringfellow had been ravaged by the rampant jockey. Tears stung Flora's eyes. What a complete fool she'd been, with her crush on Dylan allowing him use her. The complete bastard!

*

Finula was reading the article, too, while spluttering with laughter. The story even mentioned how Sadie had handcuffed Dylan to the bed, the little minx. The Templar had got a mention, which could be good for business, all publicity being good publicity. Although she wasn't sure her dad would see it that way. Probably best to keep the paper away from him.

*

Dylan sat at his breakfast bar with a strong, black coffee and read all about his 'energetic lovemaking' and 'athletic physique' with a wry smirk. Could have been worse, he thought, could have been called a shit shag. Then another thought entered his head. Flora. Guiltily he gulped his coffee. The girl worshipped him. What had he done to her? She was bound to have read the article. He pictured the way her fresh, innocent face lit up with joy at seeing him. They'd met quite a few times in the stables and as well as the sex, he'd actually got to know her. He found her easy to talk to, not just because he didn't have to make an effort, but she was uncomplicated, honest and had no hidden agenda, unlike the Sadie Stringfellows of this world.

He paused and took another gulp of coffee. The seeds of blame took root and began to gradually grow. He remembered not wanting Flora to be there at The Templar. Why? he asked himself. She would have appreciated what he'd experienced. It wasn't all about winning and celebrating, but the time, sacrifice and preparation it took to get there. He very nearly lost that race. She would know that. Flora understood horses, how unpredictable they could be, and she knew how to handle them. He'd seen how they responded to her gentle yet firm way; she was a natural around them. Flora's routine meant being the first to arrive early in the stables and the last to leave. Her commitment was commendable, especially for one so young. Dylan had often thought she was wasted at Treweham Hall stables and should be working in a racing yard, where her efforts could really be appreciated. On impulse he scrolled through his mobile and rang the local florist, having used them several times before.

'Hi, I need you to send a dozen red roses, please.'

Instantly recognising his voice, the florist replied with humour, 'And who to this time, Dylan?'

'Flora, at Treweham Hall stables. Make sure my name's on them.' Then he added, 'In fact, put "With love from your Dylan".' Did that sound a bit cheesy? Probably, but these young things liked that kind of thing, didn't they?

*

Tobias didn't have time to read the morning's newspapers. He was up very early, busy with his plan, which meant paying old Ted a visit in the nursing home. Ted was pleased to see him. The Cavendish-Blakes had always been good to him over the years and Tobias had often called in to his cottage for a quick visit. Ted considered Tobias to be a gentleman and a credit to the Treweham Hall estate.

'Tobias, good to see you.' Ted, too, was up early and sat in the sun lounge with a tartan rug over his lap. He'd grown accustomed to being looked after and, apart from missing Zac dreadfully, had adapted to his new life well.

'And you too, Ted. How are things?'

'Not bad at all. What brings you here?'

Tobias sat down next to him. 'Ted, it's about your cottage. Are you absolutely sure you don't want to return to it? It's still there if you want it.'

Ted sadly shook his head. 'Thank you, Tobias, but I'm staying put. I feel safer here, if you know what I mean?'

'Of course. I understand. In that case, I'll be taking it over.' Ted's cottage belonged to the Treweham Hall estate. The Cavendish-Blakes had rented it out to Ted years ago as an almshouse.

'To rent out or sell?' Ted was wondering what would happen to his little cottage and whose home it would become.

'To live in,' replied Tobias. Ted's face creased with a knowing smile; he might be old, but he was no fool.

'Megan's a grand lass. Look after her for me, won't you?'

Tobias laughed to himself. Was he that transparent? 'I certainly intend to, Ted.'

Chapter 24

Megan woke with an uneasy feeling that refused to be dispelled. Whilst being excited and eager to paint Treweham Hall, this feeling was matched with slight hesitation at what she had agreed to take on. Not just the task of reflecting the magnificence of such a splendid building, but the inevitable contact with the Cavendish-Blakes. The tour of the Hall had proved to be very interesting. She loved the place, totally steeped in family history, from the décor of the grand rooms to the secret passages and priest holes, to the picturesque lawns and working kitchen gardens. Treweham Hall was a well-oiled machine that seemed to run smoothly, with its small team scurrying in the vast kitchen, washing, chopping and packing all the fruit and vegetables to be distributed to local businesses, and the groundsmen who worked on the estate and also in the greenhouses, vegetable plots and orchards. Megan couldn't help but be impressed.

She had witnessed the easy manner with which Tobias treated them. He clearly had good working relationships with his staff. Finula was right, he didn't lord his position over them, or anyone else. Despite his reputation, he genuinely did appear to be a decent man. Certainly not someone who would drive recklessly, as Nick would have her believe. She pondered over Nick and Tobias and why their opinions of each other were so low; and also why Finula obviously couldn't stand Nick either. Then another quandary entered her head. The letters. She leant to the side of her bed and pulled out the Parma violet tin from under it. There they were, all the letters and photographs of Gran and 'E'. With a shaking hand, she decided to read the rest of them.

17 February 1945

Dearest Gracie,

Let me start off by telling you how much I miss you, and how I long for the day we are together again. Darling, I do love you so. I get a lump in my throat just looking at your picture. I am desperate to get home soon. I am so sick of this war, but it looks like the end is in sight – I hope so.

In your letter you mentioned having attended a wedding. What kind of a wedding do you want, my sweet? Or should we wait until I get home so you can tell me?

I will never forget how I felt that night I left you at the train station. It was then that I was sure, oh so sure.

This is Saturday night and always the loneliest night of the week for me. Oh, Gracie, how I would love to be with you, to have you in my arms, to talk and talk. I wonder what you are doing tonight. I sit and brood over how we are cheated of so many precious moments on account of this terrible war. I am not complaining, darling. I also get a lot of enjoyment dreaming about you and the things we will do when I return.

War news is again looking good. Although the end is in sight the war will be as hard or even harder than before. Everyone over here has given up predicting the date of its end, but hoping it will be over soon.

Will close, darling, hoping all is well with you, and that you are thinking of me tonight.

All my love,

E.

28 March 1945

Your letter was wonderful. The men know that they can ask for almost anything on the days that I receive a letter from you. I can tell I have a letter from you before it gets into my hands because the mail clerk has a big smile when he comes up to me.

The war news is wonderful. It should be over soon. It would be a great gift from God if it would end before Easter Sunday.

I am getting that spring feeling also and long more and more to be with you. Do you ever see me in your dreams? Most every night when I fall off to sleep I live over the times we were together – the things we did – what we said and the many things we should have said… Oh my sweet, how I miss you. All my prayers are to get home in one piece to you.

All my love,

E.

8 April 1945

Dearest Gracie,

Oh Gracie, I am praying for this war to end and for me to get home to you. The way it looks now Hitler is going to fight until the last German. I can't understand how a few men can have such control over a country when the majority know that they are fighting for a lost cause. Such useless loss of life and limb. .

When you receive this letter, we will be working hard to end this miserable war. Remember, my sweet, that I am always thinking of you and that you have all my love.

E.

Tears ran down Megan's face. The last letter 'E' had sent was dated April 1945. Megan calculated that Gran must have been four months pregnant, as her mum had been born the following September. So that was it, Grace had actually been expecting when waving 'E' off to war, standing on the station platform, ignorant of the events due to unfold. 'E' was undoubtedly her grandfather, as the dates made that clear. But why hadn't Gran told her any of this? What about Granddad Michael, the caring, gentle giant that had worshipped her mum? Did her mum know any of this? Megan's stomach clenched. There were so many questions she wanted to ask, so many things that needed explaining. The one resounding certainty echoing in her mind was that Gran had chosen for some reason to share this with her now. Why else leave a tin full of love letters and photographs, the quiet, living evidence of a past life, a family secret that had never been shared? Her gut instincts told her that her mum didn't know, because if she did Megan was sure she'd have told her. Why not? And if Gran had never told her own daughter, why tell her granddaughter? The whole scenario left her with a burning curiosity. Her coming to Treweham had been premeditated; Gran must have known what she was doing when bequeathing Bluebell Cottage to her. She was determined to learn more about the man behind the letters, however hard it was going to be.

Her heart melted, being transported back in time to when a young couple had been cruelly torn apart by a vicious, raging war that dictated they be at opposite sides of the Channel, 'E' fighting for his life and Grace pining for the father of her child. Tears swelled once again when reading 'E's desperate words, 'How about you throw me a rope?' If only. How must Gran have coped when learning of his death?

Megan's thoughts then went back to Granddad Michael, who gallantly stepped into the breach and married an already pregnant Grace. Her heart then warmed, recalling how good they must have been together. Her mum had been the apple of Granddad's eye. Megan was convinced she knew nothing about 'E', or her parentage. So just *why* would Gran want her to know? The same questions kept repeating themselves in her head.

A loud noise interrupted her thoughts. Getting up and drawing back the bedroom curtains, she saw a truck parked outside Ted's cottage. It was unloading a skip. Was Ted's home about to be emptied? A lump rose in her throat. She felt emotional about losing old Ted for a neighbour and cautious as to who would be replacing him.

*

Dylan's mobile rang. 'Bloomers' flashed before him. With a knowing smile he answered. 'Hi.'

'Dylan, I'm afraid Flora from Treweham Hall stables refused the roses.'

'What?' he spat. 'Did she know they were from me?'

'Yes. Do you want to know what she said?'

No he didn't. 'Yes,' he replied.

'Well, to quote her,' there was a pause, he could hear the laughter in the florist's voice, 'she said, tell the bastard to stick his flowers where the sun don't shine.'

'Oh.' He stared into space.

'Looks like you're losing your touch, Dylan,' she giggled down the phone.

'Hmm, we'll see about that.'

Well, he hadn't seen that coming. Deciding to face her, he set off with resolve to Treweham Hall.

Flora had had a busy morning mucking out the stables. Feeling hot, sweaty and tired, the last thing she wanted to see was Dylan making his way across the yard. She hated her traitorous heart for beating so wildly. Did he really think she would forgive him because he'd sent red roses? How stupid did he think she was? Pretty stupid, she thought dully. Look how easily she had fallen under his spell. Well, not any more.

He stood in front of her while she carried on brushing the stable floor. After a few moments he spoke. 'Flora, please, talk to me.'

She stopped and looked him in the eye. 'I think it's you who needs to do the talking.'

'Look, I'm sorry for—'

'Ignoring me in The Templar? Shagging behind my back? Actually no, that wasn't behind my back, I saw everything.' Dylan stopped. So she had been there. His feelings of guilt started to build.

'Flora, I'm sorry. I… I was drunk.' He cringed at how lame he sounded.

'Yes, I saw how drunk you were. I watched everyone buy you drinks, celebrating the money you'd made them. Nobody cared that you could easily have lost that race. I watched you get boxed in by the rails. Your horse lost his balance and you could have been badly injured!' she screamed, tears falling down her face.

Dylan's stomach contracted. He felt sick with shame. He tried to touch her arm, but she flung it away.

'And don't ever touch me again!' she bellowed, making him flinch.

My God, this had gone badly wrong. He didn't know what to say, or do, he just stood frozen. All her words were true. Nobody in The Templar but she would have realised or understood what he had experienced in the race, making all the celebrations seem so shallow in retrospect. Flora was the only one who would have worried about his welfare – and the horse's, for that matter.

Swallowing, he whispered huskily, 'I'm so sorry, Flora.'

She glared at him, then spat, 'Get lost. I mean it, Dylan. Piss off.'

Chapter 25

Megan took a deep breath and set up her director's chair on the front lawn of Treweham Hall. Laying a sheet of watercolour paper on her drawing board, she began to draw a simple outline sketch of the Hall. She wondered how long it must have taken to build, with its vast stone walls, corner turrets and sturdy buttresses. The Gothic stained-glass windows glimmered prettily in the sunlight. She'd forgotten how much she enjoyed sketching and painting, not having done it for so long. Soon she was in her own world, totally absorbed capturing how regal and imposing the magnificent building was.

Megan had half expected to see Tobias at some point, but he was nowhere to be seen. She couldn't make her mind up if she was disappointed or relieved after last night. Maybe he had regrets and was avoiding her? Then, as if on cue, she saw his silver sports car coming up the gravel drive. She watched him park and walk towards her, wearing a playful grin. He looked very much the country squire with his jeans, check shirt and Barbour jacket. 'And how are you this morning?' His eyes danced with mischief. Obviously not avoiding her, and no regrets.

'Fine, thank you, and you?' she answered with as much bravado as she could muster. Then, seeing he was about to look at her drawing, she quickly stopped him. 'No, don't look yet.'

'Oh, why?' He looked disappointed.

'It's too early,' she pressed.

He shrugged. 'OK. Come on, it's lunchtime.'

Megan packed up her things and put them into her car. She'd been sketching for three hours and was glad of a rest. Following Tobias into the back of the Hall, she was once more amazed by the place. They passed through the enormous kitchen, where Tobias ordered sandwiches and tea to be served in the drawing room. It felt surreal to Megan. A few months ago, if someone had predicted her sitting in a stately hall drawing room, sipping tea with a handsome aristocrat, she would have laughed out loud. Yet here she was, sitting next to Tobias on the Chesterfield sofa in front of the marble fireplace, staring at the priceless artwork.

'Thanks,' he said to the housekeeper, who had swiftly delivered salmon and cream cheese sandwiches and a pot of Earl Grey tea. Megan noted every last detail, from the fine bone-china crockery to the way the sandwiches were cut into small triangles. She pictured the doorstep jam butties she regularly made and again her lips twitched.

Tobias was watching her. 'What's making you smile?' He passed her a cup of tea and handed her a plate of sandwiches.

'All this, I suppose.' She glanced around the room. He frowned. 'I mean… well, it's so different from what I'm used to. It's another world to me.'

'It needn't be.' Now she frowned. Tobias continued, 'It's just stone and mortar, like your cottage.' It bothered him that she felt in awe of the Hall. He so wanted her to feel at ease, more at home with the place, not hover on the periphery like an anxious guest. 'With all this grandeur comes the cost and worry of running it.'

Didn't it just. He was beginning to lose sleep over the cost of the Hall.

'Yes, I suppose it must,' Megan replied quietly. She recalled the conversation she had had with Finula about the responsibility Tobias must carry and felt a little humbled. He was right, it was just stone and mortar. The fact he had been born into an aristocratic family with a title and estate was purely chance. Although he lived in a stately hall, it was, to all intents and purposes, still just a home to him. He must tire of people like her judging. He had an obligation to all his staff, too, not to mention the tenants in the village. She looked at him and for once didn't see the playboy, the wild child he so often had been portrayed as, but a man born into a system that dictated honour, duty and commitment. Megan suspected he did worry about money, judging by his demeanour whilst he had been watching Dylan at Newmarket. He must have had a lot riding on that race. All this made her life seem so simple and straightforward. Like Tobias, she had been bequeathed her home, but she didn't have the same pressure of managing it.

He was gazing at her deep in thought. God, she was beautiful. Her forehead had furrowed slightly and her brown almond-shaped eyes held a pensive expression. Her fringe fell into them. He tenderly swept it to one side with his fingers so he could look into her face. For once, she didn't tense, which was progress. 'What are you thinking, Megan?' he softly asked.

'About you, and how hard it must be at times.'

The answer surprised him. 'You mean living here?'

'In a way. It's down to you to keep the whole show ticking over. People rely on you. It must be...'

'It must be what?' He ran the side of his hand down her face. Megan felt that tingling sensation start to return.

'It must be stressful, knowing so much is hinging on you,' she replied, trying to concentrate. His hand cupped her chin, whilst he bent forward and placed a gentle kiss on her lips.

Then he straightened and replied, 'Yes, there is a degree of pressure, but nothing I can't handle. Anyway, I won't be here for the foreseeable future.' He was exaggerating, testing the water to see how she'd react. Her look of alarm answered his question and gave his ego a satisfying boost.

'Where are you going?' she asked sharply.

'I'm renovating a house, thought I'd live in it whilst working there. Get the job done quicker.'

'Oh,' she sounded deflated, making him smile.

'I won't be far away.'

'I see,' she replied flatly. He'd got the reaction he wanted, so came clean.

'It's Ted's cottage. The estate owns it. We rented it to Ted as an almshouse years ago. He was in need of a place to stay and the cottage was free. My father was happy to help him.'

'Really? You mean—'

'We'll be neighbours, Megan,' he replied with a grin. Megan's mouth opened in astonishment. He nudged her chin up to close it. 'Drink up, Megan, your tea's getting cold.'

Chapter 26

'So, do you think we made the right move then?' Gary was sitting back in his favourite recliner, hands behind his head, looking round the spacious lounge.

'Definitely,' replied Tracy. She was lying on the black leather settee. 'It's lovely here and everyone we've met so far seems quite chatty.'

'Yeah, the local's a good pub, isn't it? I know it's full of la-di-da horsy people, but they're actually all right when you get talking to them.'

'I think they find our northern accents a bit funny, though,' Tracy sat up and crossed her legs, 'you know, the way they try and copy us, as if they think it's funny.'

'They probably do. Maybe it's their way of being friendly.'

'Hmm. Lord Cavendish-Blake's never showed his face round here. If it were me, I'd pop round and say hello.'

'Perhaps he's waiting for an invite.' This gave Gary an idea. 'Let's have a house-warming party, invite the whole village. It'd be a great way of getting to know everyone.'

Tracy looked apprehensive. 'I'm not sure about that, Gary. It could be a bit over-facing.'

Careful not to upset her in any way, especially as she had struggled to try to settle, he quickly replied, 'Yeah, see what you mean. How about just a select few?'

'Who?'

'Well, the girls from The Templar seem nice enough.'

'And that jockey, Dylan Delany, was very friendly when I asked for his autograph,' added Tracy with a grin.

'You mean when he was looking down your top,' quibbled Gary.

Tracy giggled. 'He does seem quite a character.'

'What about Lord Cavendish-Blake himself?'

'Yes. I'd be interested to see what he's like. I've only ever seen him fleetingly in his car, on his horse or in the pub. I was sorry we didn't get to meet him the other day.'

'Good, let's do it. I'll arrange the invitations. Two weeks' notice should be enough.'

'I'll arrange the catering. I don't think my hotpot would fit the bill.'

'I do! A Lancashire hotpot, what could be better?' Gary enthused.

*

Dylan pounded the treadmill. He'd clocked up four miles and sweat was pouring from him. He always left the tread mill till last, after the weights and rowing machine, to really blast the rest of his adrenaline. Lately he'd been almost punishing himself, pushing his limits to the very brink. Mentally he was haywire. The guilt Flora had installed in him had embedded and taken root. Every word she had yelled at him had been played and replayed over and over again in his hyperactive mind. Each time made him hate himself a little more.

For someone so young, Flora spoke an awful lot of sense. Flora, probably without knowing it, had made a big impression on him. She'd put his lifestyle into perspective. He'd come to realise how superficial those around him actually were – only singing when you were winning. What about when you lost? Would they still be there, solid as rocks, supporting him? Or would they be like sand, slipping away? He knew where he'd place his bet.

He finished his run and wiped his face with a towel. He needed a long, hot shower and a rest in the sauna. Maybe a good steam would help ease his aching body and mind.

The hot air hit his lungs as he entered the sauna. It was empty, so he sat on the upper ledge, closed his eyes and tried to relax. He heard the door open quietly, then close. After a few minutes he became aware of someone sitting on the bench beneath him. He opened his eyes slightly and saw a blonde head. His heart missed a beat, and for a split second he mistook her for Flora. Wishful thinking, he thought with a sigh and closed his eyes. Moments later he felt a slight tug at the towel that covered his lap. His eyes shot open.

'Hello, Dylan. Remember me?' For a dreaded moment he thought it was that bitch who had sold her story to the paper, then realised it was the girl who worked at the gym as a personal trainer. They'd once got friendly in the sauna before.

'I do.' Hell, what was she called? She pulled his towel completely off him. Dylan felt his libido start to stir. She was able to see the blood surging through his shaft as it pulsed, lifting up towards her in invitation. An invitation she couldn't resist. Her tongue moved slowly, excruciatingly slowly along his length from base to top. Dylan groaned as it dipped and tasted the sensitive tip. Her lips were driving him insane as he gripped the bench with both hands. Unable to take any more he reached out and lifted her, placing her legs spread-eagled across his muscled thighs. She moved slowly against the rigid hardness of his arousal. Her towel slipped. His mouth closed over her exposed breast and sucked hard on the nipple, making her moan in pleasure. She then curled her fingers about him and began to guide him inside her, inch by inch. He grasped her hips, his mouth capturing hers as he began to thrust rhythmically inside her. Desire engulfed him as his thrusts deepened and hardened. He felt her tighten around him as she cried out in pleasure, then the heat of his own release surge down and burst inside her. It had been hot and frenzied. Both recovered composure quickly, rewrapping their towels tightly. Good job, as a minute later another person entered the sauna. Dylan got up to leave.

'Nice meeting you again,' he nodded.

'Yeah, you too,' she furtively smiled back.

Driving home, however, his mood hadn't lifted. If anything he felt worse. More guilt. What was the matter with him? He'd never experienced this before. No one had ever got under his skin the way Flora had. He had to see her, but then he recalled her last chilling words to him. *Get lost, Dylan.* He decided to go for a drink in The Templar instead of heading straight home.

Finula picked up on his frame of mind immediately. 'You all right, Dylan?' she asked, passing him his fresh orange. Since celebrating his win at Newmarket, he hadn't touched a drop of alcohol.

'Not really. I think I'm having a mid-life crisis.'

Finula raised an eyebrow. 'At thirty? I doubt it,' she laughed. Then realising he was serious she

161

stopped. 'What's the matter, Dylan?' she asked in a sincere tone.

Why not tell her? It might do him good to offload. Finula would be discreet, he knew. So he did. He relayed how he had met a girl with whom he had a lot in common, got to know her, like her, then messed up big time.

'I take it she's read the article about your night of passion with Sadie Stringfellow?'

He nodded pitifully. 'She saw us. She was here in the pub. I just hadn't noticed her.'

Finula frowned, wondering who she was. Probably someone who lived, locally if she was here. Then she remembered a blonde girl sitting alone in the corner that evening after her friends had left. It was Flora, who worked in the stables at Treweham Hall.

'It's Flora, isn't it?' Finula asked quietly.

'Yes.' Dylan looked at Finula, and his blue eyes were so sad she actually felt sorry for him.

'Have you tried talking to her?'

'Yes. She won't listen. Told me to piss off.'

'Give it time. She's only young.'

'Flora may only be twenty, but she's the most genuine person I know.'

'Then don't give up, Dylan. Persevere. She'll come round if you're really contrite.'

Chapter 27

Tobias commended his timing. As he was about to move into Ted's cottage, Aunt Celia decided to grace Treweham Hall with her presence. Arriving in the morning, with her luggage piled at the front entrance, wearing a tweed suit and a tight smile, she flounced in, ordered the staff to collect her cases and demanded to see Tobias. Hearing the commotion from his bedroom, Tobias made his way down the stairs.

'I thought you were going to ring me, Aunt Celia.'

'Ah, there you are. Order tea, will you? I'm parched. I decided to get a taxi.'

'Come into my study. I've something to show you.'

Owing to the efficiency of the staff, Tobias and Aunt Celia were soon sitting drinking tea at his desk. He was talking her through the plans for converting the old stable block into a café and gift shop. Since his talk with his mother, Tobias had given the plans for the old stable block plenty of thought. The conversion idea seemed a good one, especially as he had seen similar projects work well.

Celia's beady eyes darted over the foolscap paper containing the drawings. She pushed her tight curly grey hair behind her ears in concentration. Tobias valued her opinion. Celia might be eighty, but she had a sharp mind and was extremely intuitive. He waited for her verdict. She looked at him and shook her head.

'It won't work,' she stated flatly.

'Why not?' Tobias replied, surprised.

'How would you gain access?'

'We'd have to build a pathway at the side of the Hall.'

She looked warily at him, 'And have people traipsing past your home all the time? Can't see your mother buying that.'

He had to admit, it wasn't ideal. In fact it would be quite intrusive. Sighing, he folded the plans away.

'I've got to do something, Celia. We're broke.'

'It's going to take more than coffee and cupcakes to save this place, plus you'd be spending money on the conversion and the staff.'

He nodded in agreement. 'I thought it would be a good way of utilising the old stable block. It's just standing there doing nothing.'

'You need to do something that won't cost you to set it up.' Then she narrowed her eyes, a thought having occurred to her. 'Have you closed any of the rooms off yet?'

'Mother won't hear of it,' he answered dully.

'Good.' He looked up questioningly. 'The answer's staring you in the face. Open up the house—'

'She'd never allow it,' he cut in.

'Listen, this place is huge enough to separate your private quarters from the rest of the rooms. Guided tours could be conducted with the minimum of disruption. Just set your boundaries as to when and where the public can visit. You could even renovate one of the rooms into a tearoom. Damn sight cheaper than converting a stable block.' She sat back and sipped her tea.

The more he considered the idea, the more he liked it. Celia was right, it would be far less costly to open the house up to the public and make a tearoom. A fixed timetable could be implemented. They could even sell merchandise with the coat of arms on, as he had originally thought. It need not be intrusive if limits and confines were adhered to.

'You could be on to something, Celia. But how do I sell this to Mother?'

She huffed, 'Tell her straight. It's either open the Hall, or face ruin. Good God, that woman's been wrapped in cotton wool all her life.' Beatrice was the polar opposite to her much older sister. Celia had practically brought up Beatrice, the baby of the family. She'd witnessed how her parents had doted on their sweet little Bea. She'd watched how her husband had adored her and showered her with gifts; and now she was seeing how her elder son, who had inherited all the consequences of such frivolous spending, was still trying to protect her. It angered her, and that jealous, resentful emotion that had plagued her childhood was starting to rear its ugly head again.

Tobias' mind was buzzing with ideas. It was so obvious now he came to consider it. The rooms he'd wanted to close and cover in dustsheets would be cleaned, polished and showcased. Sharing the family home with the public meant bringing the Hall back to life again; and at minimum cost.

'Do you want me to speak to her?' Celia looked at him directly, arms crossed, lips pursed.

'No... thank you. I'll break it to her. Perhaps that Caribbean cruise won't have to be cancelled after all.'

Celia beamed, making the corners of her eyes crinkle. 'Attaboy.' She patted him on his shoulder. Settling back in her chair she asked, 'Any news from Sebastian?'

'He's touring in Stratford at the moment. We're expecting him home next week.'

Celia nodded, then added, 'I take it your mother still doesn't know he's queer as a coconut?'

'*Celia*, please.'

She shifted in her chair, 'Lovely boy, but it's time he faced his own mother and told her.'

'Why? If you sussed it out, maybe she has.'

'I'm more worldly wise than your mother is. She ought to know. Good job he's the spare and not the heir.' Tobias couldn't stop his lips from twitching. 'Talking of which, isn't it time you started producing?'

'I'm on the case,' he replied drily.

*

That afternoon, after leaving an excited mother and aunt to talk about their Caribbean cruise, Tobias set off to old Ted's cottage. Parking outside, he started to unload his belongings for the next few weeks. He noticed Megan's curtains twitch and smiled to himself. She'd make a terrible secret agent, he laughed, remembering also her hiding behind a tree to spy on him horse riding.

Once he'd packed everything into the spare bedroom, he set about his itinerary armed with his notebook and pen. First he'd rip out the kitchen and replace it with distressed wooden units and a Belfast sink. He decided to keep the pantry; it made excellent storage space and added a quaint touch. The floor tiles needed replacing. French doors instead of the solid wood back door would create light and a sense of space. He unlocked it and stepped outside into the garden. It was lush and colourful, just needed cutting back a little and some pretty garden furniture.

He peered over the garden fence into Megan's garden. He could see her at the kitchen window. She waved and he beckoned her outside.

'All moved in?' She was wearing a red linen dress with a scooped neckline. His eyes homed in on her birthmark again.

'Yes, thanks. Any chance of a cup of tea?'

'I'll pop round with one.' She scurried back inside. Entering Ted's kitchen, Megan was surprised at the smell of damp. 'It's only been empty a few weeks, but it feels like for ever.' She handed him a mug of tea.

'I know, these old stone cottages are quite cold. Once I've got the wood burner and heating installed it'll be a lot better.'

'Sounds like you're going to be busy,' said Megan, blowing on her tea.

'I am, but I'll not rip out the heart and soul of the place. Apart from a new kitchen and bathroom, everything else will be restored like for like. Ted said to keep some of his furniture.'

The old bureau and the half-moon table in the lounge suited the cottage. Megan was touched that Tobias wasn't obliterating Ted's presence. This may no longer be his home, but it must contain many happy memories in the nooks and crannies.

'I must go and visit Ted, take Zac.'

'He'd appreciate that, Megan.'

'Well, I'd better let you get on.'

'Thanks for the tea.' He kissed her on the cheek, then whispered in her ear, 'What time's dinner?'

Megan laughed. 'Would you like to come for dinner, Tobias?'

'Oh, how thoughtful, Megan, I'd love to.'

*

Having spent the rest of the afternoon ripping out the old kitchen units and throwing them in the skip, Tobias decided he'd had enough. He often enjoyed getting stuck into a manual job. Not only did it keep him fit, it released his pent-up energy and stress. Going over the estate accounts again had filled him with utter dread. For once, he had seriously contemplated losing the Hall. The thought crippled him. Coming to Ted's was a break. Covered in sweat and dust, he swept away the rest of the debris into bin liners before taking a much-needed shower. He was looking forward to spending the evening with Megan in her cosy kitchen, rather than enduring a dinner with his mother and aunt banging on about their holiday. That said, Celia had definitely come up trumps with her suggestion of opening up the Hall to the public.

After showering, he towel-dried his hair, put on a clean white shirt and faded denims, which hugged his muscular legs, and set off next door. As he was walking down the pathway he heard a voice. Nick Fletcher was here. Slowing to a stop, he stood to listen.

'I'd like to visit Ted. If you're thinking of going, I could come with you.'

Tobias' hand curled into a fist.

'I was thinking of taking Zac,' replied Megan.

'Yes, he'd love that. So when should we—'

'Evening,' Tobias interrupted. He glared at Nick, who jumped slightly.

'Oh, hello, Tobias. What brings you here?'

'Megan and I are about to have dinner,' he stated.

'R…ight, so…'

'If you don't mind,' Tobias inclined his head towards the pathway, indicating Nick's wanted departure. Megan decided to kneel down and pat Zac to hide her embarrassment. The two men clearly hated each other and she felt caught up in the middle.

'Right, well, in that case I'd better go,' Nick said, looking at Megan for some kind of objection. None was forthcoming. He coughed, 'Er, right, 'bye then, Megan.'

'Bye, Nick,' she replied with a smile.

'Goodbye.' Tobias stared him out. Nick stared back for a few moments then quietly left.

Megan was determined to find out what exactly the history was between the two of them, and between Nick and Finula, for that matter.

Chapter 28

'Hey look at this,' Finula waved a card in her hand.

'What is it?' Megan wiped her hands on the kitchen towel and took it from her. They were busy preparing the breakfasts. 'Gary and Tracy invite you to join their house-warming dinner party at the Gate House,' she read excitedly.

'Look, it's for both of us,' Finula said, pointing to their names at the top.

'I wonder who else is going.'

Finula shrugged. 'Don't know, but can't be that many, it says *dinner* party, not just house-warming party.'

'Hmm, are you going to go?'

'Deffo! It'll be fun. Gary and Tracy seem a really nice, down-to-earth couple.'

'They do,' agreed Megan and decided to look forward to it.

*

Tobias had received his invitation that morning. He had called at the Hall to collect a few more things and his post. He noticed the invitation didn't state plus guest, which left him a little uncertain. Then, feeling he ought to show his face, especially as they had paid over the odds for the Gate House, he decided to go.

*

Dylan opened his invitation. He might as well go. What else was there to do? He'd tried to ring Flora, but she'd barred him from her phone. He put off the idea of going to the gym, in case he bumped into that personal trainer who performed extras in the sauna. Perhaps he should get out and see his friends instead of being cooped up here feeling sorry for himself.

He made his way to Treweham Hall, telling himself it was to catch Tobias, not on the off chance of seeing Flora. Pulling onto the gravel drive, he noticed Tobias' car parked at the front. Dylan rang the front doorbell and was greeted by Henry.

'Good day, Mr Delany.' He ushered him inside and took him to Tobias' study, where Tobias was sorting through his post. Dylan noticed the invitation on his desk.

'You've got one, too?' He pointed towards it.

'Yes, you going?'

'Why not? Nothing better to do.'

'Not busy preparing for Royal Ascot?'

'Should be.'

Tobias looked up. He could see this wasn't the usual Dylan. His spark and charisma had vanished.

Dylan went on to explain. 'I feel like I'm losing it, Tobias, you know, the passion to win. I've come to see it all in a different light.'

'See what exactly?' Tobias put his envelopes down and sat on the corner of his desk.

'Racing. It's a fickle game. You're everybody's friend providing you win and make them money. But *real* friends, well, they don't come easy, do they?'

'Me and Seamus are your friends.'

'I know that, but… what about partners… wives?' he added weakly.

Tobias blinked. 'What do you mean, Dylan?'

'I… I'm lonely, Tobias.' There, he'd said it. He finally admitted it out loud.

Tobias blinked again. 'You're lonely?'

'I want more. I love horses, but I've grown to hate the back-biting, competitive, greedy, money-making side of racing. I mean, look at Sean Fox. Could you take orders from him?'

'No. Seamus has always had a difficult relationship with his father.'

'Not surprising. I've heard the way he orders his staff about in the yard; the man's an absolute ogre. What he doesn't get is that they're there because they love those horses, and want to do the best for them. They don't need him bellowing at them all the time.'

An idea was formulating in Tobias' mind. 'Would you consider setting up your own training yard?'

'Yes, I think I would.' Dylan had half thought of this already, but had dismissed the idea as overambitious. He needed space and plenty of it. 'But where?'

'Here. The old stable block could be improved to your requirements, extended if need be. There's plenty of land. Think about it.'

'I will.' Dylan narrowed his eyes; a plan was formulating in his mind already, one that had ignited a spark in his heart. 'I'd rent the stables and land from you, but want full control of the yard.'

Tobias nodded. 'Fine. Would you not need some form of support, though?'

'I'd want an assistant trainer.' And he knew just the person. For the first time in weeks, his switch was about to turn on.

Chapter 29

Tobias had arranged for a small team of his workers to fit the kitchen and bathroom at Ted's cottage, leaving him more time to concentrate on the rest of the cottage. It was early evening and he was enjoying a brandy. Next door all was quiet as Megan was working at The Templar. He'd so enjoyed having dinner with her. He loved listening to her conversation, peppered with humour, compassion and lots of questions. He found it flattering that she was curious about life in Treweham Hall, not in a crass or envious way, but with genuine interest. She'd told him freely about her childhood and family, especially her gran, entertaining him with stories of her visits to Treweham and how close they had been. He knew the letters she'd discovered had had a profound effect on her and badly wanted to help in any way he could, but how? He felt a real affinity towards Megan, almost as though he had always known her.

He had kissed her long and passionately after their evening together and she had responded. There was no denying the attraction between them, but he was at pains not to push it further just yet. He knew timing was critical, and that he needed Megan's trust.

He was staggered by the actions of her ex-boyfriend. Who in their right mind would jeopardise losing a girl like her?

He looked round the lounge to decide tomorrow's jobs. He'd pull up the carpet and sand and varnish the floorboards. In preparation he moved the half-moon table into the hallway. The old bureau was much heavier to budge. He lifted the front two legs and was dragging it across the floor when the bottom drawer fell open and an address book dropped out. He picked it up and a photograph fluttered from its pages.

Tobias knelt down to examine it. It was an old sepia snapshot. Immediately he recognised the young couple smiling into the camera, sitting by an old tree, with the initials 'G' and 'E' engraved into its trunk. It was Grace and 'E'. Turning the photograph over, Tobias read the inscription on the back. *To my darling Edward, forever yours, Grace. x* Realisation dawned on him. Old Ted was Edward! Grace must have returned to him, years after believing he had been killed in action. He recalled Ted's words to him a few days ago in the nursing home: 'Look after Megan.' Now they made perfect sense. Ted must be Megan's grandfather. Tobias was astonished at his find. Taking a few moments, he pondered over telling Megan. Intuition told him to wait. First he'd go and see Ted.

The next morning, instead of starting on the floorboards, Tobias took the photograph, put it safely in an envelope and made for the nursing home. He found Ted in the sun lounge again. Tobias watched him for a few seconds before approaching him. He saw him differently now, not old Ted, whom his family had helped with the cottage, but a war hero, who had been torn apart from his only love. Ted must have so many stories to share, yet he'd kept his identity a secret from Megan. The whole scenario touched Tobias and made him realise he hadn't been the only one to have lost his first love. There were thousands of people who had suffered like them. Feeling somewhat humbled, he made his way over to Ted.

Ted's face lit up again at seeing him. 'Hello, Tobias. I am honoured to see you again,' he chuckled.

'Hello, Ted.' Tobias sat down next to him.

'Is everything all right, lad? You look damn serious.'

Tobias pulled out the envelope from his pocket and handed Ted the photograph. 'I was moving your bureau and this fell out, Ted.'

Ted took the picture with a shaking hand. His eyes filled as he looked at the young couple smiling up at him.

'Ah, she was a bonny girl, my Grace.'

Tobias waited, watching the emotion on Ted's face. He swallowed before speaking. 'You're Megan's grandfather, aren't you, Ted?'

The old man looked into Tobias' face with such sadness, it took his breath away.

'Technically, yes. But she'll always know Michael as her grandfather and I don't want to ruin that memory. Nor would Grace.'

'But Grace left Megan your letters. She must have wanted her to know.'

Ted nodded sorrowfully. 'Yes, she did in the end. When she knew her time was up.' Ted looked wistfully out of the conservatory window. 'Let me tell you what happened, Tobias. Perhaps then you'll understand.'

Ted had met Grace at a dance in the village hall. She had stood out with her strawberry-blond hair, porcelain complexion and sweet smile. She wore a blue silk dress and had drawn lines down the backs of her legs to imitate the seams of stockings. When he'd asked her to dance, she instantly accepted, being equally smitten with this handsome, dark-haired soldier in uniform. From the moment they had touched an unbreakable connection had been formed. But it *had* proved to be breakable, by a raging, cruel war that had forced them apart. They had always planned to marry, he had proposed by their favourite place in Quercus Woods. Instead of a ring, they had secured their love by carving their initials in an oak tree and agreed to get engaged on his return from the war. They had exchanged letters of hope, love and a constant yearning to be reunited; and they almost were. But one night, when on watch, he had been hit by shrapnel, leaving him unconscious. Eventually waking, he was dazed, confused and had no idea where he was. Struggling to walk, he managed to stagger to a nearby farmhouse. The French family who lived there took pity on the wounded British soldier and gave him shelter. It took months for him to recover and remember all the pieces of his life. The one thing he had was that photograph. That one picture had given him courage and hope to carry on. Then, that fragrance hit him, the smell of Parma violets growing wildly in the farmhouse garden. Immediately he was whisked back to the night of the dance when he had met Grace, and she had smelt of Parma violets.

Almost a year after taking refuge in the French farmhouse, Ted had made his way home, only to find that his Grace had married and had a child. He knew that Grace's little girl was his, and Michael, his best friend, had stepped into the breach, believing he had been killed in action. It was too late; he couldn't intervene. They had all acted with the best of intentions.

But then Michael was killed by the fire in the brewery and Grace was alone again. Ted made his move and contacted her. Their love was still as strong. Grace wanted to be with Ted, but didn't want her daughter upset by the truth. Living next door to each other in Treweham was the ideal solution. The older Grace got, the more unsettled she became by her secret and she wanted Megan, who was the image of her grandfather, to truly know him. It was important to her that Ted was known to their granddaughter. What Megan chose to do with the truth would be a matter for her, but Grace could not die without Ted being acknowledged.

Tobias sat dumb struck. His eyes filled too, listening to Ted's revelation. Finally he spoke.

'Ted, will you explain this to Megan?' Ted hesitated. Tobias added, 'Or should I?'

'Yes. If you would. I… don't want her upset.'

'No, of course. I'm sure she won't be upset, Ted. In fact, I think she'll be delighted she's found you,' he reassured the old man warmly, making his eyes water.

Ted gave a wobbly smile. 'I hope so, Tobias. I hope so.'

Chapter 30

Gary and Tracy sat on their little terrace overlooking the large lawn. Any minute now their guests would be arriving. Tracy was fidgeting with her necklace. 'I should have got caterers,' she said, biting her bottom lip.

'Don't be daft, your hotpot's delicious, they'll love it,' Gary soothed. He knocked back a swig of lager and burped loudly.

'And don't do that in front of them either,' she rasped.

Gary laughed. 'Calm down, Trace. I won't show you up.' He got up and spun round. 'How do I look?' They'd both bought new outfits for the occasion: Gary, blue chinos and a white short-sleeved shirt (which he'd just spilt lager on), and Tracy, a figure-hugging black dress. She'd put her hair up in a high ponytail and trailed ringlets down the sides. A brief sad moment had swept over her whilst doing it, sitting at her dressing table, remembering how Sharon had done something similar for her wedding day. She fleetingly reminisced about the giggles and fizz they'd shared that morning and a profoundly empty feeling had hit her. This made her more determined to enjoy tonight and make new friends.

She was a touch apprehensive about meeting Lord Cavendish-Blake, though inside she told herself not to be. They had paid good money for their house and had every right to be living on his estate. Even so, it was a far cry from the terraced back streets where her old friends would be tonight, living it up in the club, dancing and knocking back the vodka and Red Bull with gusto. She looked down at her cut-glass flute of Prosecco, her hand shaking.

Hearing a car door slam, they both shot up. 'Show time,' Gary said, smiling, then added, 'Relax, Trace. Everything's going to be fine.' Together they walked round the side of the house to greet their first guest. It was Dylan.

'Hiya, mate.' Gary shook his hand.

'Hi, Gary.' Dylan turned to Tracy. 'Looking lovely, Tracy.' He kissed both her cheeks, making her blush slightly. Finula was just walking up the garden path.

'Hi, Finula!' Tracy called, her face looking relaxed for the first time that evening.

'Hello there.' Finula gave her a quick hug and a bottle of wine. 'Hi, Gary,' she nodded, then turned to Dylan. 'Hello, you.' She gave him a knowing grin.

'We're just round the back.' Gary led them all to the seating area on the terrace. After he and Tracy had exchanged a few pleasantries and filled everyone's glasses, Tobias and Megan appeared. They had walked together through the estate and followed the voices in the garden. Tracy was surprised they had arrived together and wondered if they were a couple. They certainly looked comfortable enough together.

'Good evening. Thank you for the invite. I'm Tobias.' Tobias held out a hand to Gary and then Tracy. Tracy shook it, noticing how warm and firm it was: a confident handshake. What else would you expect from a lord? He gave her a charming smile and again she blushed.

'Pleased to meet you,' she replied, then turned to Megan with a beam. 'Glad you could come.'

'I've brought you these.' Megan handed over a colourful posy of flowers, collected from her garden.

'Oh, thanks, Megan. They're lovely.' Tracy went through the patio doors into the kitchen to put them in water and check on the meal.

Gary, Tobias and Megan stood talking together about the plans Gary had for the garden. Tobias was nodding his head rather gravely, looking devastatingly handsome in a green linen shirt, which highlighted his green-hazel eyes. Megan bobbed her head, looking interested in what Gary was saying. She wore a lilac wrapover dress, which complimented her figure well. Dylan couldn't take his eyes off her.

Finula prodded him hard in the side. 'Oy, you, I thought you were supposed to be broken-hearted,' she hissed.

Dylan's eyes widened. 'I am,' he protested.

'Then stop ogling Megan,' she whispered back. 'She's Tobias'.'

Dylan turned to her and frowned. 'News to me,' he replied.

Tracy interrupted, 'Tea's ready everyone!'

As he made his way into the dining area, Tobias cringed inside at the sight before him. For a split second he opened his mouth, then shut it again. What on earth had they done to the place? Gone was the parquet flooring, totally hidden by a thick shag-pile carpet. Gaudy abstract artwork glared from the walls on large canvases. A huge plasma TV blared out from the corner, its surround sound filling the room. A smoked-glass dining table stood in the middle, accompanied by black leather chairs; nothing in keeping with an old English Gate House, steeped in history and character. Everything was totally out of place. Tobias winced at all the time, money and effort he had lovingly put into refurbishing this special place. The clumsy satellite dish plonked (illegally) on the side of the house should have been an indicator of the taste of the Belchers. Did they realise the Gate House was a listed building, or didn't they care?

His mood began to decline. His eyes turned to Megan, who was sitting between himself and Dylan. She outshone all with her natural beauty and she looked a million dollars in that dress. He longed to pull the side tie, push it off her shoulders and let it fall at her feet. He could just about see her strawberry-shaped birthmark, which for some reason always stirred him. Suddenly he didn't want to be here, sitting at this hideous glass table with everyone exchanging small talk, but in his big four-poster bed with a naked Megan wrapped round his hips. The thought made him semi hard and he coughed abruptly. Dylan turned sharply, misinterpreting it as a warning to stop flirting with Megan. He backed off immediately, making Tobias laugh to himself.

'So, mate, are you racing at Royal Ascot?' Gary asked with a mouth full of bread, looking towards Dylan.

'I certainly am,' he replied, taking a sip of his drink. There was a pregnant pause. Usually, the mention of racing would kick-start Dylan into conversation, but tonight it wasn't forthcoming.

Feeling the need to fill the gap, Finula commented on the steaming food being piled onto the plates by Tracy.

'Oh, this smells good, Tracy!'

'Yes, it does,' agreed Megan, wondering what the matter was with Tobias and Dylan, who had suddenly gone quiet. Tobias had been in good spirits on their walk to the Gate House, but now he appeared subdued, deep in thought.

'It's a taste of Lancashire, a good old hotpot,' Tracy told them, spooning it out.

Tobias' forehead creased: *a what?* Megan saw it and shook her head. Surely he must know what a hotpot was? Apparently not, judging by his expression. For some reason this annoyed her, that and his obvious coldness towards Tracy and Gary, who were doing their level best to fit in and make a new start. She found his attitude rather high-handed and didn't care for it one bit. He clearly didn't want to be here and it showed. Earlier, when Gary was outlining his plans for the garden, she had noticed how reserved Tobias had been and frankly had found it embarrassing.

'Here's to a happy home!' chirped Finula, raising her glass. Everyone joined in, though Tobias did so reluctantly. Happy home? They'd completely ruined it, stripping the Gate House of its traditional charm and ambiance. It epitomised the sorry state of affairs, of how broke his family must be to sink to this level. How in God's name did the Belchers acquire just under a million pounds to buy it? He should have vetted the buyers first, before instantly accepting the asking price. Then again, maybe nobody else would have offered the asking price.

'So what brought you to Treweham?' asked Megan, once the conversation had moved on from Lancashire.

'Well, we came here on honeymoon a few years ago and since winning the lottery, we decided to relocate here,' Gary answered. The drink had loosened his tongue.

Tobias' head shot up. Lottery winners, of course! Why hadn't he guessed? Megan caught his eye and gave him a quizzical look, which he returned with a tight smile. She took a deep breath.

'Yeah,' Tracy joined in, cheeks hot with all the steam coming from the casserole dish, 'we're beginning to feel more at home, now that we've got the place as we want. Wouldn't mind a proper gas fire, though. All this messing around with the wood burner, it's a right faff!'

Tobias closed his eyes. He wanted to run away from here, away from the Belchers, who had desecrated his family's heritage. And what plans did Gary have for the garden? A bloody hot tub!

The evening droned on for Tobias. A mixture of being force-fed more and more 'hotpot', washed down with warm, flat Prosecco, and listening to Gary's jokes getting progressively louder and decidedly dirtier, didn't do much for his mood.

He noticed Dylan was unusually quiet, and wondered if he had given the renovation of the old stable block any more thought.

Finally, after all had said good night and thanked Gary and Tracy, he and Megan made their way home. Walking in the cool night air, Tobias reached out for her and gently pulled her into him, with his arm round her shoulders. She tensed a little, reminding him of the Megan he had first known. 'Megan?'

'Yes?'

'Is everything all right?' He sensed a reluctance in her.

She stared straight ahead of her. 'Shouldn't it be?'

Tobias frowned, not knowing what had caused the sudden change in her.

*

Dylan had given Finula a lift back to The Templar. Looking sideways at him, Finula asked, 'Not heard from Flora, then?'

'No.' He drove solemn-faced, staring out at the lane in front of him. Finula didn't know what to say. It was strange having a quiet, sombre Dylan, instead of the usual lovable rogue.

'Sorry.' She couldn't think of anything else to say.

Dylan shrugged. Tomorrow he was going to talk to Seamus, run the idea of setting up his own training yard past him. Seamus had experience and was a true friend, and he trusted him to give an honest opinion.

Dylan thought he couldn't go on like this; a deep sense of discontentment was threatening to suffocate him. Never before had he encountered such a feeling of unfulfillment, yet what had changed? He was still Dylan Delany, Champion Jockey, a winner, but something was missing. His own words to Tobias rang true. He was lonely.

His thoughts perpetually gravitated to Flora. It puzzled him that such a slip of a girl had had such an overpowering effect on him. *Why?* Because she was sincere, he told himself. She was young, innocent and wore her heart on her sleeve. There was no hidden agenda, she simply just wanted him – and she genuinely cared. Flora understood him more than he had appreciated. They were the same: she loved horses like he did and he'd witnessed the bond she had shared with them. She had been right, he could have been badly injured at Newmarket. He recalled the tears streaming down her face, the hurt and anger he had caused. He had to talk to her.

Chapter 31

Megan was making good progress with her painting. She had finished the pencilled outline of the Hall and was placing a dab of watercolour onto the palette plate. She mixed the honey stone paint carefully and began applying it to the paper. She had forgotten how much she enjoyed this, deep in concentration, watching the gentle brush strokes work their magic.

Her thoughts turned to last night and again wondered why Tobias had suddenly become so subdued at Gary and Tracy's. Didn't he like them? It wasn't like him to be superior, but she did get the impression he hadn't taken to them like she and Finula had. Deciding to stretch her legs, she waited for the paint to dry and packed away her chair, painting and brushes and headed towards her car. She had been at Treweham Hall for over two hours and wanted a break. After loading the car and slamming the car boot shut, she turned to see an elderly lady in tweeds with her arms crossed, standing staring at her.

'Hello,' Megan smiled.

The old lady didn't return the smile. Instead she barked out, 'Who are you?'

Megan explained she had come to paint Treweham Hall, feeling slightly prickled by the abruptness of this stranger.

'Tobias has arranged for the Hall to be painted? So much for being stony-broke,' she answered with a degree of conceit.

'I'm not actually charging. It's to return a favour,' chipped back Megan with a slight edge to her voice.

'Is it really?' the old lady chuckled, then turned on her heel and strode back inside.

Of all the cheek! Who on earth was that?

Tobias threw his head back and laughed when Megan called in and told him about the strange meeting later that morning. Seeing him laugh instead of being stony faced was a welcome change since the previous evening. He had finished all the downstairs of Ted's cottage and was now starting on the bedrooms. The kitchen looked wonderful with its fresh wooden units, newly plastered walls and French doors. It amazed Megan how quickly he and his workforce had completed it.

'So you've met Aunt Celia, then?' he said, smiling. Megan loved the way his cheeks dimpled when he laughed. It was a far cry from the sulky, furrowed face of last night. He had just showered and his hair was still damp. She longed to run her fingers through it. He was wearing a black polo shirt, unbuttoned, revealing the dark shadow of hair on his chest, which

Megan's eyes homed in on. He had been busy stripping the bedroom walls all morning and had decided to call it a day. He needed to speak to Megan at some point to tell her about Ted, but couldn't think of how or when. Then inspiration came to him as he recalled Ted's conversation. He had mentioned Quercus Woods being a special place for him and Grace. Tobias thought he would take Megan there with a picnic and tell her the whole story of Ted and Grace. He didn't want to put it off any longer. It didn't feel right that he knew and she didn't. After all, it was her grandfather and grandmother.

'This looks interesting,' Megan pointed towards the wicker basket on the side. He had rung the kitchen staff at the Hall that morning and asked them to prepare a picnic hamper. One of the girls had dropped it off just before Megan called.

'I was just about to phone you. We're going on a picnic,' he said decisively.

'Are we?' Megan looked over the basket, longing to see what was inside – all good stuff if it came from Treweham Hall, no doubt.

'Yes, to Quercus Woods.'

'Ah, Quercus Woods, I used to go there with Gran,' Megan's mind filled with memories of old oak trees dappled with sunlight, bluebells, wild garlic and a bubbling stream.

'Let's go,' Tobias ushered her out of the French doors and checked his back pocket. Yes, the photograph was still there. He drove the short distance to the woods.

'You've thought of everything.' Megan looked him up and down. He was carrying the picnic hamper and a rug from the back seat of his car.

'Always come prepared,' Tobias grinned back. Together they ambled through the oak trees until they both decided on a secluded spot by the stream. Tobias spread out the rug on the mossy ground and they sat huddled side by side, listening to the sound of trickling water.

'Did you enjoy last night?' Megan asked quietly.

Tobias sighed, 'No.'

'Why? Don't you like Gary and Tracy?'

'I don't like what they've done to the Gate House. It made me regret selling it.'

'But did you have any choice?'

Tobias gave a wry smile; she was intuitive enough to know he wouldn't have parted with it unless absolutely necessary. 'No, I didn't, and yes, their money's as good as anyone else's, but to see it like that, with all its vulgar décor, it just…' He paused for a moment and threw a pebble in the stream.

'Tell me,' Megan gently urged.

'The Gate House was supposed to be mine and Carrie's, after we were married. She had such plans for it; we both did. I can't help but think what could have been.' He looked forlornly into the shimmering water. Megan felt like she'd been slapped. A cocktail of emotions poured through her: shock, sympathy, jealousy and an overwhelming gut feeling of helplessness. How could you feel sympathy and jealousy in equal amounts? How could you be envious of a dead woman? As she swallowed the lump in her throat her subconscious told her why: because she had real feelings for Tobias. She watched him staring out aimlessly, wanting to touch his face, the crease above his chin, his strong jaw line, his black, shiny hair that smelt of pine. He looked young and vulnerable, just how Carrie would have seen him, she thought, hating herself for the resentment that was settling inside her. He turned to face her and she gazed into his piercing green eyes, not knowing what to say. He stared back, then gently leant forward and kissed her softly. Megan wanted to hold him, but he quickly turned round and reached for the picnic hamper.

'Right, let's see what's in here then,' he said with a forced brightness. The moment had gone. At least now she understood why he had acted the way he had last night.

'Let's. I'm starving.' Together they unpacked a feast of French bread, cheeses, chutney, olives, tomatoes, sparkling wine and two mini cheesecakes.

'This is absolutely gorgeous,' Megan spoke between mouthfuls. 'You're so lucky having staff to make all this for you.'

Tobias nodded. 'Yes, but it all comes at a price, Megan. I've got to make sure we can afford to pay all the staff.' He was responsible for so much, it overwhelmed him at times.

'I know,' she conceded, stretching her arms, enjoying the sun shining through the tree branches and glimmering in the stream, 'but it's just so different from the way I live.'

'Don't say that.' He ran a finger down her back, making her shiver. 'We're not so different, you and I.'

She turned and smiled at him. She looked so young and happy. The sun had brought out the freckles sprinkling her nose; she was irresistible. Sensing now was the moment, Tobias took out the photograph from his jeans back pocket.

'Megan, I found this in Ted's bureau.' He passed her the picture.

She stared at it and blinked. Frowning, she turned it round and read the back: *To my darling Edward, forever yours, Grace. x* Her eyes were wide with disbelief. 'Ted... Ted's "E" ... he's my grandfather?' Tobias nodded. He put his arms around her and relayed everything: how Ted had told him about meeting Grace, their plans to marry, the letters exchanged during the war, Ted's injury and finally him returning home too late, to a Grace who had had his baby and was married to his best friend. Megan sat in silence and a tear ran down her cheek. Tobias kissed it away.

'Oh, Tobias, that's so sad,' she whispered.

'I know. Ted doesn't want you upset, though. He respects Michael's memory.'

'So nobody else knows apart from us?' That confirmed the suspicions about her mum never knowing.

'No. Only us.'

Megan nodded.

'Here, let's finish this off.' Tobias poured the rest of the sparkling wine into the plastic wine cups. They sat in silence for a few minutes. Tobias respected the time Megan needed to digest everything. He watched her sipping on her wine, staring out at the glistening water. He felt a compulsion to protect her, wanting to wrap his arms around her and never let go. How would he have felt with such a sudden revelation? He knocked back his drink and examined her face, deep in contemplation.

Well, what a picnic, thought Megan. In the space of an hour she had encountered so many emotions it had left her feeling a little shaken up. She took a deep breath. Tobias touched the side of her face. She turned to him and saw the compassion in his eyes.

He did care, she knew he did, and in that split second she knew she wanted him. He read it. Reaching out for her, he pulled her body hard against him. She felt his heart hammering in his chest and wrapped her arms round him, her hands ran inside his polo shirt to feel the soft, warm skin underneath. He groaned and kissed her neck, licking the dip above her collarbone. Then his lips caught hers and his tongue probed gently into her mouth making her breathless. Her hands dug under the waist of his jeans, making him thrust into her, his arousal evident. Slowly he unbuttoned her top. She was lying on the rug, eyes half closed, her skin stung pink with passion and the effect of his touch. He gave a sharp intake of breath at seeing the freckles dusted across the swell of her breasts. He lowered his head to lick and kiss them, as she writhed beneath the caress of his mouth. She pulled at his shirt and he urgently yanked it off. Her eyes took in his broad shoulders and muscular chest; his eyes were dark with desire as he unclasped her white, satin bra to expose two round, firm breasts. He moaned, yearning to suckle them, and as his tongue brushed over her nipples she arched her back, running her hands through his hair. 'Tobias,' she whimpered, grinding further into him. He undid her jeans, tugging them down her thighs, his hand cupped between them, making her gasp. His thumb circled her core, making her jolt in pleasure.

'Megan,' he whispered hoarsely in her ear. She opened her eyes. 'Megan, I haven't got... protection.'

Her heart started to steady, realising what he meant. 'I... oh... right.' She was still dazed.

Tobias leant over her, his eyes heavy with lust. 'We'll have to wait,' he whispered, and kissed her. After a few moments he rolled over onto his side and propped up his head. He picked a frond of cow parsley and traced it over her face. She giggled at its touch.

'I thought you said you always came prepared,' she grinned up at him.

Chapter 32

Dylan put the phone down and pondered. Well, that was a turn-up for the books. He had planned on going to see Seamus today, but his agent had given him food for thought. An advertising agency had contacted his agent, enquiring if he would be interested in starring in their new commercial for aftershave, aptly named 'Racer'. Dylan quite liked the thought of appearing in an advert, and his agent liked it even more when they told him what they would be offering. Dylan's eyes widened at the fee proposed. Money to help him set up his own training yard, he thought. Dylan earned a pretty penny with various companies, wearing a certain watch or suit in interviews, drinking a certain energy drink, being a member of a particular gym, even driving a specified car, but actually appearing in a TV commercial – that was something else. The more he thought of it, the more it appealed to him.

'Don't hang about, Dylan,' his agent had advised down the phone, the excitement and greed in his voice evident. 'They're approaching Lance James too.'

Lance James was the latest Grand Prix winner, not as prominent a figure in the sporting world as Dylan, but even so, he didn't want some racing driver pipping him at the post. What had he to lose? The extra money would be more than useful. The old stable block would take some converting and Tobias wouldn't rent him the land for fresh air. Plus he needed to pay staff, not to mention offer enough to entice Flora to be his assistant trainer. Yes, he would do it. He rang his agent back and within the hour a schedule had been set, for the very next day. Hell, they were keen, thought Dylan, and his agent was beside himself with joy.

'This will really put you on the map, Dylan,' he practically purred down the phone.

'I'm already on the map, Connor,' replied Dylan, rolling his eyes. He could just imagine his fat, little agent rubbing his chubby hands together, pound signs blinging from his beady eyes. Dylan didn't particularly like Connor, but knew he was good at his job. He suspected the prompt schedule was more to do with him than the advertising agency. Connor wasn't going to let an opportunity like this slip through his grasping paws. Within a few hours the contract had been signed, sealed and delivered.

Dylan was to meet with representatives of the advertising agency in London. They had arranged for a car to pick him up from home to take him straight there. Not sure what to wear, he opted for casual jeans and a jumper, assuming they would have clothes for him to wear in the commercial. How wrong he was.

On arriving at the agency, he was greeted by a young girl with long dark hair and large brown eyes, which she fluttered at him. 'Good morning, Mr Delany. Please follow me.' He was led to a large studio with cameras, lights and various people buzzing about with clipboards. A small, bald-headed man wearing purple trousers and a red waistcoat scurried over to him.

'Dylan! Dylan! So good to see you.' Dylan blinked – did he know him? He appeared ever so familiar. 'I'm Richard. Please call me Dickie.' He ushered Dylan onto a white leather sofa at the side of the studio and sat next to him, far too closely. Dylan could smell his breath as he gushed, 'We'll put you in make-up first, then try a few shots for light.' His hands rapidly moved as he spoke. Dylan struggled to keep up with the whole scenario. 'You will look am-az-ing!' Dickie slapped his shoulder with glee.

Dylan closed and opened his eyes. Was this really happening?

'Come, come, this way, lovie.' Dickie then put his hand on his back and practically pushed him into a small, bright room, where apparently, 'Tamsin was going to touch him up'. Dylan assumed he meant make-up, but on seeing Tamsin he was open to offers.

Tamsin smiled widely and held out a large brush. 'Let's apply,' she said cheerily and patted the chair in front of her. 'Make yourself comfortable, Dylan.'

Dylan plonked himself down and winced at the bright bulbs surrounding the huge mirror directly opposite him. Suddenly a massive pair of boobs faced him, nearly taking his eyes out. Tamsin was examining his hair, pulling at it from all angles. 'We'll just freshen this up a bit.' She bent down to look at him. 'I'll give you a good blow.' Dylan stared back, speechless. The next thing Tamsin set about him with a super-strength hair dryer, pushing his curls into place. 'Right now, let's look at skin tone.' She moved closer, giving him a close-up of her cleavage. Dylan struggled to keep a straight face when seeing a cotton wool bud had lodged down there. 'Hmm, let's see…' she moved his face back and forth, 'I'd say medium to dark, wouldn't you?'

'I'm in your hands,' he smiled back.

Unscrewing a white pot, Tamsin delved her fingers inside and started smearing Dylan's face with it.

'Just to give you a bit of colour,' she explained, her chest shoving into him, 'to make you stand out.' Dylan was already starting to stand out. 'Now then, let's get those beautiful blue eyes to shine.' She held a blue eyeliner; Dylan leant back a little. 'Don't be alarmed, I'm just going to gently stroke…' she bent down again; Dylan sat still, 'the insides of your eyes.' He could feel her breath on his face as she lightly swept the pencil along the edge of his eyes. She had beautiful blue eyes, too, and full voluptuous lips. He glanced down her top again. 'Right, face done, now for the body,' she beamed.

'Sorry?'

'We'll need to give you a bit of colour there, too.'

'Pardon?'

'It's a shower scene. You'll be wearing only a towel.' She spoke very matter-of-factly. 'Didn't Dickie mention it?'

'No... he just said I'd look amazing,' Dylan replied faintly. Tamsin gave him the once-over and licked her lips.

'I'm sure you will,' she winked.

Damn Connor, thought Dylan as he stood butt naked, save for a small, blue towel only just managing to cover his modesty. Never any mention of this, he cursed under his breath.

'OK, let's roll, Dylan. So you've just come out of the shower, you make your way into the bedroom, pick up the bottle of aftershave, splash it all over and say...'

'Never be pipped at the post,' quoted Dylan through clenched teeth.

'Oooh, a bit livelier, lovie!' chirped Dickie, clapping his hands, 'and then, you turn to camera three for that all-important close up and say...'

'I always win, wearing Racer,' Dylan supplied.

'That's it!' Dickie clapped his hands again, 'and what do you do for that final shot?'

'Wink,' replied Dylan flatly.

'Magic!' Dickie bellowed.

Tamsin was on hand with her brushes, powders and creams, ready to go at him in between takes. The lights burnt into his skin, making him perspire. Tamsin saw to that too, patting him down with towels and reapplying the toner.

Finally it was over. Dylan had given the performance of his life, for the whole two minutes the advert played for.

'It's a wrap!' yelled Dickie, signalling all to pack up and go. Dylan was back in the make-up room, having Tamsin clean all the caked up foundation off his face. What an ordeal. Never again. The only consolation was the money he'd made for a few hours' work – that, and Tamsin's chest, which had been a welcome comfort.

'You were fantastic, Dylan,' she said, rubbing hard at his face.

'Thanks.'

'Are you heading straight back home?' Her eye caught his and she gave him a sexy smirk.

'Not sure,' he answered, stalling for time.

'I'm meeting a friend later. She's a big fan of yours.'

'Is she?' He could feel something start to stir.

'Yes, she'd love to meet you. Why not join us for dinner?' She winked at him again.

'Well, if you insist.' Maybe it hadn't been too bad a day after all.

Chapter 33

Megan had been painting all morning and had finally finished the watercolour. Although she was pleased with the result, she was still a little hesitant to show it to Tobias. All morning she had been thinking about Ted. It was hard to believe he was her grandfather, yet that was undoubtedly what he was. Megan was left to contemplate whether her mum ought to know the truth, too. Surely she had every right to know her true parentage and, in all honesty, Megan resented having inherited the dilemma.

Tobias had been an absolute rock of support. He had shown nothing but kindness and patience. He had always made his attraction towards her clear, but had never pushed or forced her in any way. Megan's insides tingled at the flashbacks of yesterday's picnic. Even then he had shown constraint, whereas she would have lost herself in his arms. Despite her experience with Adam and all the warnings she'd tried to give herself, it was futile. She was falling for Tobias. He was so handsome, caring, good fun, and her body ached for his. How could she not?

She packed up her things and waited for the painting to dry before placing her picture in a carry case. Today she had walked to the estate rather than

207

take her car. A footpath running from the back of the cottages led to the grounds of Treweham Hall.

She had borrowed a chair from the summerhouse and was returning it when she overheard voices coming from inside. Pausing, she waited before opening the glass door. She recognised one of the voices. It was Nick's.

'What was I supposed to do? You nearly ran into her, for God's sake. You were driving like a lunatic!'

'And why's that?' came a rasped reply. Megan shot to the side of the door out of sight.

'Look, I'm sorry, Seb, please.' Megan froze. She could just about make out the two figures through the gap in the glass door. Nick stood in front of a blond-haired man: she recognised Tobias' brother from the pub.

'You let her believe it was Tobias. How could you?'

'Because I care about you.' Nick's voice grew softer, deeper. Megan's eyes widened when she saw the two men embrace and share a long, tender kiss. Gulping, she dropped the chair on the grass and hurried home.

Nick and Sebastian? Kissing? Her mind spun. But Nick had had a fling with Finula and he'd flirted with her, too... Realisation dawned: he must be bisexual. And it must have been Sebastian driving the car that night, and Nick deliberately led her to believe it was Tobias.

Megan was still in shock later that day when working at The Templar. She was itching to speak to Finula, but they had been so busy behind the bar. Finally a quiet spell descended, and Megan grasped the moment.

'Finula, can I tell you something?'

'Sure, what is it?' Finula was wiping down the bar and collecting glasses.

'I saw Nick and Tobias' brother in the summerhouse at Treweham Hall. They were kissing.'

Finula looked straight at her, opened her mouth to speak and was interrupted by a customer. Damn, thought Megan, wishing their shift would hurry up and finish. She was frantic to learn what Finula knew.

At last it was closing time. Locking the door after the last customer, Finula beckoned Megan over to sit by the inglenook fire.

'Nick and I went out together for a few months last year. It was good in the beginning. He was very attentive, made me feel special. Then came the tell-tale signs.'

'What do you mean?' Megan sat forward slightly.

'I'd notice him looking at other people – men, as well as women. I saw the way he looked at Sebastian. We all suspected Sebastian was gay – not that it mattered. Then I found a magazine in his car. We'd been out for the day, and as he was paying for petrol at the garage I had a nosy inside his glove compartment. A semi-naked man from the front cover of a magazine stared back at me. I quickly put it back.'

'Really?' gasped Megan.

Finula nodded and continued. 'Then it all came to a head one night when Nick got drunk. He got nasty, saying how inhibited I was. I retaliated, so he got nastier. Afterwards he was sorry, but I've never forgotten the things he said.' She shivered in disgust.

'What?' whispered Megan.

'He proposed a threesome,' replied Finula coolly.

'You're joking! The cheeky swine.' Megan was dumbfounded.

'Denied all knowledge the next day when he was sober, but it was the end. I never dated him again.'

'Don't blame you. Does Tobias know about this?'

'Yes. I told him. Not long after Nick and I finished, he started seeing Sebastian, on the hush-hush. Only me and Tobias sussed out what was going on. The relationship's been on and off for months.'

'But Nick's... quite flirty... he's—'

'A bisexual slag,' Finula finished with bitterness in her voice.

Megan found it hard to take in. Who would have thought this sleepy Cotswolds village held such secrets? The next-door neighbour really being her granddad; Sebastian being the driver who nearly killed her; and now the local vet, who preferred ham *and* cheese on his toasties!

Chapter 34

After Dylan had spoken to Seamus, he was resolute: he intended to go ahead with his plans for the training yard. Seamus had been quite surprised by Dylan's proposal at first. However, after listening to his friend and what he had to say about his father, although put as diplomatically as it had been, he could read between the lines. Seamus had also spotted Dylan's buoyant spirit again, something that had been sadly lacking of late. Watching his face light up as he outlined his ideas, he saw the old Dylan return.

'I wish you all the best, mate. Seriously, I admire you.'

'You sure? How do you think your father will react?'

Seamus shook his head. 'Couldn't care less. Listen, Dylan, nobody knows more than me how hard he is to work with. I really don't blame you for starting out on your own.'

'Thanks, mate.' Dylan shook his hand.

He had arranged to see Tobias at Treweham Hall to discuss renovating the old stable block to meet the British Horseracing Authority's requirements. He had to prove to them that the premises and facilities were in full working order to train racehorses. He also had to apply to the BHA for a licence. This involved demonstrating he was fit and proper, with honesty and integrity. He paused when reading this stipulation. That bloody tabloid would hardly help his cause, but he was renowned for his care of horses, unlike some jockeys who had been suspended for overuse of the whip.

Dylan was geared up and excitement ran through his blood, building adrenaline, something he hadn't felt for weeks. More than anything he longed to see Flora, tell her about his plans, ask her to join him in running a top-class training yard, to share his ambition. Was he being corny? So what? He was past caring. It had been six weeks since he had last seen Flora and every day she had haunted his mind.

At Treweham Hall's door he was greeted by Henry, who showed him into Tobias' study.

'Good to see you, Dylan.' Tobias was at his desk, the draft plans for the yard spread out before him. Dylan went straight over to survey them. His eyes narrowed, taking in all the details.

'I need more stables. I want to be training at least ten horses, plus I'd need an office on site.'

Tobias nodded. 'That can be arranged.'

'There's plenty of space, that's the main thing.' He looked out of the window behind Tobias. 'All this land is ideal.'

'It certainly is. Plus with the kudos of the Treweham Hall estate, you shouldn't have too much difficulty in pulling custom your way.'

'You're right there. I've put a few feelers out and it all looks promising. Not sure how Sean Fox will react, though.' Dylan looked wary.

Tobias shrugged. 'Shouldn't have too much of an impact on his yard. It's been established for years. What did Seamus say?'

'Wished me all the best.'

'Good. I've a few contacts that might be interested.'

'Thanks.' There was something he needed to run past Tobias that he'd been delaying. 'Tobias, about my assistant trainer…'

Tobias looked up. 'Yes?'

'I'm going to approach Flora.'

'Flora?'

'She works in your stables,' Dylan answered with a slight edge. Didn't he know his own staff? Especially given the amount of time and commitment she showed.

'Oh, yes, very good with the horses.' Then Tobias frowned. 'But how do you know her?'

'I… I… met her when looking round your stables.'

Tobias smiled wryly. 'I see.' An awkward few seconds passed for Dylan.

'You don't mind, do you?'

'Not if you think she has potential. I can soon find another stable hand.'

'Good. Good. Right then, I'll… I'll put it to her.'

Tobias grinned. 'You do that, Dylan.' Dylan coughed and made a hasty departure. Tobias laughed to himself: still the same old Dylan deep down.

Flora had just finished riding Juke and was unsaddling him. Dylan approached her from behind, making her jump.

'Sorry, Flora, I didn't mean to startle you.' He smiled, looking into her fresh, rosy complexion. How he'd missed her. Her hair had grown slightly, giving it a tousled look, and he longed to brush it away from her face.

'What do you want, Dylan?' she asked flatly, refusing to give him eye contact, but instead carried on tending to the horse.

'A minute of your time,' he answered.

'I'm busy, in case you haven't noticed.'

'Please, Flora,' he pleaded.

Turning to him, she saw his blue eyes filled with hope, which sparked her curiosity. Flora had thought of Dylan often – too often, if she was being honest with herself. Initially she had been heartbroken by his actions, but then pure anger had taken over. Now after six weeks of not seeing him she hated to admit it, but she had actually missed him. Keeping herself busy had helped, and there was always something to do in the stables.

'I can't speak now, Dylan, I'm working.' The corners of Dylan's mouth twitched. That had never bothered her before when they had romped in the hay.

'Of course. Let's have dinner,' he held his hands out in surrender, 'as friends. There's something I'd like to ask you.'

Now she was more than curious. 'OK. Meet me in The Templar at seven.'

'Done.' He held his hand out to shake hers, anything to touch her. She gave him a withering look and ignored it. Turning her back on him, she proceeded to take off the horse's saddle and barged past him into the stables. What a woman, thought Dylan, wanting the evening to arrive quickly.

Later that evening, Flora dressed carefully for dinner. Not wanting to appear keen, yet still sexy was proving to be a difficult task. Finally she plumped for skinny jeans and a red sleeveless top with a neckline low enough to show a glimpse of cleavage, without showcasing too much. She wore her hair down, freshly washed and scrunched dried. Entering The Templar, she saw Dylan at the bar talking to Finula and caught her breath. He looked stunning in his dark suit, which matched his black curls, and a blue shirt the same colour as his eyes. Suddenly she felt underdressed in her jeans.

Turning to see her, Dylan leapt up from the bar stool and greeted her. 'Flora, you look beautiful.' He took her hand and kissed it.

'Don't overdo it, Dylan,' she replied drily, commending herself for such composure.

Finula beamed at the pair of them. 'This way. I've reserved one of our best tables for you.' She led them towards the restaurant area, to a secluded alcove. A table for two was prepared with a lit candle and champagne on ice. Flora was impressed, but refused to show it. 'I'll take your order shortly.' Finula smiled at Flora as she eased her into a chair, then deftly opened the champagne and left them. Dylan poured them each a glass. The bubbles fizzed up Flora's nose, making her splutter. So much for the composure, she cursed herself.

'Flora, I've got a proposition for you.' Dylan stared intently into her eyes, then outlined his plans to open a training yard at Treweham Hall and asked her to be his assistant trainer.

Flora was gobsmacked. She took another gulp of champagne to stall for time. Eventually she spoke. 'But I don't know what being an assistant trainer entails.'

Dylan, anticipating this response, was quick to reply. 'Basically, it would mean being my right-hand man. You would plan the horses' training schedules and be in charge of the stable staff. You've got a way with horses, an instinct. I've seen how they respond to you. You've also got a way with people.' He looked deep into her eyes. 'You care. You're a sincere person and I trust you. The rest you can learn from me.' He sat back and waited for her answer. He sensed her hesitation and added, 'Give it some thought. Promise me you'll at least think about it. And I know it's not about the money, but I am offering a competitive wage.'

He was right, conceded Flora, it wasn't about the money, more about working so closely alongside the man himself. Would she be able to resist those dark, gypsy looks every day? Feeling those piercing ocean-blue eyes burn into her? Seeing those capable hands at work, knowing how they had roamed over her body? 'I'll think about it,' she answered in a cracked voice.

Dylan slowly smiled: he'd done it. The charm had worked. Now all he needed to do was back off a little, give her space and she'd come running.

'Ready to order?' Finula asked, looking at Dylan for some form of sign.

'Yes, I think so,' he smiled.

'Good. What can I get you?'

They both settled on the steak with peppercorn sauce. Flora was beginning to relax; the fizz had eased her butterflies and the food tasted delicious. Dylan chatted constantly, telling her about his aftershave commercial, making her giggle in delight. She had forgotten how much he had entertained her, regaling her with tales from the riding circuit and celebs he had encountered. She in return told him about her family, of her brother going off backpacking at the start of his gap year and her parents buying a campervan to go travelling round Europe.

'So you'll be living alone?'

'Yes, temporarily.' It struck Dylan how mature and able Flora was for her years. He considered what he was like at her age and winced at the comparison. She underestimated herself, he suspected, and was anxious this didn't influence her decision in being his assistant trainer.

'Flora?'

'Hmm?' She looked at him, slightly glazed.

'Say yes.'

'We'll see.' Make him sweat, let him wait, she told herself. She wasn't about to jump to his tune, not like before. Now it was different. She had learnt the hard way.

Chapter 35

'Got everything, Trace?'

'Yeah, think so, let's go.' She put the overnight bags in the boot and slammed it shut, then got into the passenger's side.

They were setting off to visit Tracy's parents in Lancashire. She couldn't wait to see them. It had been a few weeks since both their parents had come to visit them in their new home. Now it was Gary and Tracy's turn to return to Preston. Her emotions were mixed: part of her wanted to go back, and another didn't. Settling down for the journey, Tracy turned to Gary. He was staring straight ahead, focusing on the road.

'How do you feel?'

Gary turned briefly. 'What, going to Preston, you mean?' Tracy nodded. 'Fine. Looking forward to it.'

'Doesn't it bother you, you know, the way we left? I mean, those letters, we never found out who sent them.'

Gary sighed. 'To be honest Tracy, I don't think it was some random stranger. I think it was someone we knew.'

'One of our friends?' asked Tracy in alarm. Then the image of Sharon's scornful face came into her mind. Could it have been her? No, surely she wouldn't have stooped so low. 'Who?'

Gary shrugged. 'Could have been any one of them, judging by their behaviour towards the end. Once we announced we were leaving, I suddenly became aware of just who was actually a true friend.' His eyes clouded over with the memory.

'Do you ever wish we hadn't won the money?'

She had, truth be told. Tracy had been happy with her life: working in the care home, living with Gary in what she thought was a happy community. Winning the lottery had changed everything, but not Gary, thank God.

'No,' he replied with conviction. 'I hated my job. I liked the people, but not having to work those long hours stacking freezers.'

Tracy had no idea he had been that unhappy at work and she started to feel guilty. On reflection, Gary was so much happier now. She smiled to herself, picturing him in the garden the other day, directing where the hot tub was to go like an excited child. That night, after it had been installed, they christened it, sitting amongst the bubbles, drinking wine under a moonlit sky. Tracy had lit candles and they had chatted and giggled until the early hours. It was one of the fondest memories she had had since moving there.

Within a couple of hours, the familiar signs started to appear, uplifting her spirits. Squinting, she could just about make out Blackpool Tower way in the distance to the left of the motorway. Driving further north, they passed the green rolling hills, gradually merging into built-up towns, until they reached the junction taking them into the city of Preston.

'St Walburge's steeple.' Gary pointed out the iconic church, towering above the city skyline. The sun was shining and there wasn't a cloud in the sky.

'Shall we go past our old house?' Tracy looked for Gary's reaction. He paused.

'I don't think so.' He was anxious not to upset Tracy and feared a trip down memory lane may just do that. 'What's the point?' He turned to look at her.

'You're probably right.' She stared out of the side window. Feeling he had deflated her a little, he quickly changed the subject.

'Let's go for chips and eat them in Avenham Park, like we used to. We've plenty of time.'

Her face lit up. 'Let's!'

Chapter 36

'Close your eyes.' Megan held the picture of Treweham Hall behind her back. Tobias did as he was told. 'Ready?'

'Ready.' He opened them and looked at the painting with wonder.

'Megan, it's fantastic!' He genuinely sounded astonished, much to her relief.

'Really?'

'Absolutely.' He took it to examine more closely. 'You really ought to do more of these.'

'I've been thinking of advertising, you know, to take commissions,' she tentatively replied.

'You definitely should. Are you sure I don't owe you anything?'

'Of course I'm sure. You sorted my plastering out, so we're quits.'

'Well,' he put the picture down and put his arms round her, 'in that case, let me treat you.' A cheeky smile played round his lips.

'Hmm, that sounds interesting,' she played along.

'I've booked a box at Royal Ascot. Would you join me? Seamus and his wife, Tatum, will be there, too. I'd like you to meet her. I've also booked a room for the night in a nearby country inn.' Megan hesitated.

They both knew what he was implying. Tobias looked intensely at her. This was a turning point, and they knew it.

'Of course, I'd love to.' Was that relief in his eyes? Megan knew exactly what she was agreeing to. Not only was she being introduced to his close friends as a couple, but they would be spending the night together. A seed of anticipation had been planted inside her, together with a feeling of foreboding. There would be no turning back and if it all went wrong this time, she couldn't run away. Treweham was her home now.

'Do you want to see the cottage now it's finished?' They were standing in Ted's lounge. Megan hadn't seen the upstairs yet.

'Sure.'

Together they went up the creaky stairs. Tobias had put in a new spindle banister, along with a new oatmeal carpet. The bathroom had been retiled white, and the old white suite matched perfectly. The bedrooms had been redecorated and the cast-iron fireplaces restored.

'I don't know how you do it,' said Megan in awe. 'It's fabulous.' Tobias had kept it simple, charming and totally in keeping. 'What's your next project?'

'The tearoom and gift shop in Treweham Hall.' Tobias had told Megan about Aunt Celia's suggestions and she had agreed it was a good idea.

He had contacted the Historic Houses Association and sought advice from them.

'How did your mother take the news of Treweham Hall being opened to the public?'

'She'll live with it. At the moment all she can think about is her cruise.'

'Ah, I see,' laughed Megan, picturing Beatrice and Aunt Celia sipping cocktails on a sun-kissed deck.

'Yes, can't come soon enough. They're driving Sebastian mad.'

'So you've very conveniently managed to stay clear, tucked away in this cottage?'

'Yes, I have,' he openly admitted, making Megan laugh.

Then it suddenly dawned on her. 'As the job's finished now, will I be losing my next-door neighbour?'

He kissed her on the lips. 'You don't get rid of me that easily,' he replied, tapping her nose.

Chapter 37

Later that day, Megan put Zac on his lead and set off for the nursing home. It was just outside Treweham village, so wouldn't take too long to walk, and besides, she needed space and time to think.

So much had happened since arriving in Treweham, and her life had changed in so many ways. Not for the first time she compared it to six months ago when she had been living with her parents in the suburbs and working in a busy office, filled with gossip. She wondered what Adam was doing. Probably what he always did: charming clients, playing football, drinking with his friends and chasing women. How could she have been taken in by him? A vivid memory of his hands up his secretary's skirt made her judder. How many times had he cheated on her, she pondered, then realised it really didn't matter; she just didn't care.

Tobias was all the things Adam wasn't, and she thanked her lucky stars that Gran had given her Bluebell Cottage. Was it fate? Where would she be now without it? Still stuck in a town she had grown tired of with a job she had tired of even more. Treweham village was literally a breath of fresh air. She loved its quaintness and charm. She loved the characters in it; well, most of them. Nick had proved to be a dark horse. Megan still couldn't quite believe all she had heard about him, yet it was true. She had discussed with Tobias her seeing him and Sebastian kissing in the summerhouse. Tobias had verified what she had witnessed, confirming Finula's version of events. However, he also shed more light on the matter. Unbeknown to Finula, Nick apparently had always been seeing Sebastian. His relationship with Finula certainly wasn't exclusive. Megan was appalled when Tobias had revealed this, in confidence.

'So you mean he was seeing them both at the same time, all along?'

'Yes. The man has no scruples. Sebastian's tolerated far too much from Fletcher. It's not that Sebastian's gay that bothers me – I really couldn't care less – but it's his choice of partner.'

'But are they partners? Finula described it as on and off.'

Tobias shrugged. 'The simple answer is, I don't know. All I do know is that every time Sebastian's home, Fletcher's about somewhere.' He wrinkled his face in disgust.

It baffled Megan how someone like Nick could be so blasé with people's feelings. Was he so lacking in empathy? Yet he had shown genuine concern for

Ted, so she couldn't decide. The whole scenario puzzled her.

Taking a deep breath, she walked up the driveway to the care home. Zac was allowed in the gardens, so she had arranged with the staff to meet Ted there. She rang the doorbell and was soon greeted by the receptionist.

'I've come to meet with Ted in the garden,' Megan explained.

'Yes, that's right, he's waiting for you in the back.'

Megan looked down at Zac, who appeared alert, his tail wagging. He must know, she thought. Sure enough, as soon as Zac saw Ted sitting in the deck chair with his tartan rug covering his legs, he pelted at full speed to him. Ted's face lit up, making a lump form in Megan's throat.

'Hello, old boy!' Ted's shaky hand patted an exuberant Zac, who was bouncing up and down. Ted turned to her. 'Hello, Megan.'

'Hello, Ted.' Megan sat in the deck chair next to him. For a moment they both sat still. Then Megan took his hand. 'Thank you for telling Tobias everything. It means so much.' Her eyes began to fill.

'Megan, it's so good to be able to tell the truth after all these years.'

'Yes, it must be,' she swallowed hard. 'Ted, I want you to meet Mum.'

'I have met her, lass, albeit she didn't know who I was.'

'I know, but I do want her to know. I want you both to talk.' She looked at him and waited for his reaction. A single tear ran down his weathered face.

'I'd like that, too,' he said, his voice cracking.

'Ted, how must it have felt, me living next door? What if I hadn't found the letters and photographs?'

Ted shook his head, 'Just having you close by would have been enough.'

Megan let out a sob. 'Ted, my brother, Chris, you have to meet him, too.'

'Yes, I'd like that very much. We've so much ground to cover, haven't we?' He gave a little laugh and rubbed her hand in comfort. The last thing he wanted was to upset anyone. He so wished Grace was here.

'Yes, we have. Thank you, Ted, for being… well, you know,' she wiped away another tear.

'No, Megan, *thank you.*'

Zac jumped up onto Ted's legs and licked his hands, making them both laugh.

'He's obviously missed you,' Megan remarked, patting the black Labrador.

'I've missed him, haven't I, old boy?'

They were given tea and scones and sat in the sunshine for over an hour. Megan told Ted about Tobias' work on the cottage, of which he approved.

'It was good of the Cavendish-Blakes to rent me that cottage, for a peppercorn rent, too. I think they took pity on me. I was the soldier who came back when everybody thought I'd been killed in action.' There was a poignant pause.

'It was lucky that Gran managed to buy the one next door, too, wasn't it?'

'Fate, lass, fate.'

'Yes, Granddad, it was,' agreed Megan.

Chapter 38

A few days later saw Megan sipping champagne in the Royal Enclosure gardens at Ascot. The place was a hive of activity with gentlemen resplendent in morning dress and top hats, and brightly dressed ladies air-kissing each other, narrowly avoiding bumping their wide-brimmed hats. The tinkle of laughter and excitement filled the air. Open-topped motors chugged into the racecourse, strapped with wicker picnic hampers, their drivers sporting dark sunglasses and silk scarves that flowed behind them in the gentle breeze. Megan observed Tobias in his grey morning suit looking devastatingly handsome; her stomach had flipped when she had set eyes upon him earlier. He, too, seemed impressed with what he saw, judging by the wolf whistle he had given her. Megan had agonised over what to wear, especially when researching the dress code on the Royal Ascot website.

Strapless, off the shoulder, halter neck and spaghetti straps are not permitted… midriffs must be covered, fascinators are not permitted… must wear a hat… trouser suits welcome… all straps must be at least one inch or greater… dress length just above the knee or longer…

In the end she had bought a new outfit, a duck-egg-blue short-sleeved dress with intricate embroidery, which rested above the knee. It was accompanied by a matching bolero jacket and bow hat. Well, it wasn't every day you attended a racing meeting with the Queen, was it?

At 2 p.m. the Royal Procession would commence, signalling the start of the Royal Meeting.

'Here, have a top-up.' Tatum poured more fizz into her champagne flute. She had been very easy to talk to and had made Megan feel comfortable since Tobias had introduced them. Clearly she wore the trousers, constantly ordering Seamus around, which he took in good spirit, the two playing off each other and making Megan smile. It was hard to believe the two men stood before her were once dubbed 'the Heir and Fox' hell-raisers.

Tobias caught her grinning to herself. He sidled up to her and whispered in her ear, 'And what's on your mind, Miss Taylor?'

'You and Seamus make me laugh,' she replied. Their easy-going banter was refreshing and adding Tatum to the mix injected an extra boost of fun. The three of them together made a good act, thoroughly entertaining Megan. Tobias grinned and put his arm round her waist, pulling her closer.

'So you're enjoying yourself?' He sounded pleased.

'Yes, of course,' she kissed his cheek, 'and thank you for inviting me.'

'My pleasure.' It certainly would be tonight, he thought with pure lust. Megan looked stunning, not too showy, but understated, classically beautiful, just like the girl herself. She was the one, of that he had no doubt. It was just a matter of convincing her that he was for keeps too. His instincts told him she did feel the same, but none the less, he needed cast-iron certainty that her emotions matched his. Tonight would give him that, one way or another, he quietly counselled himself. He was glad she had fit in seamlessly with Seamus and Tatum. So much so Tatum had soon taken him to one side and instructed him to propose to Megan as soon as possible. Tobias had spluttered on his champagne with mirth. 'If you insist, Tatum,' he replied.

'I most certainly do,' she hissed back.

The four of them made their way to the private box up in the stands to watch the Royal Procession. A buffet awaited them, along with staff ready to serve. It was an intimate setting with uninterrupted views across the racecourse. The whole venue exuded wealth and opulence, placing Megan out of her comfort zone. Tobias, watching her, sensed this and was constantly at pains to make her feel at ease.

'Everything OK?' He refilled her glass with more bubbles.

'Yes, thanks.'

'Look! They're here!' called Tatum out on the balcony. Megan and Tobias joined her and Seamus. Megan watched the four Windsor Greys approach along the famous straight mile, followed by the royal carriages. She stood in awe as the royal party passed by, smiling and waving. This truly was another world. Tobias watched her again, those almond-shaped brown eyes taking everything in, her freckled button nose and those full rose lips he couldn't resist. His heart melted. For the hundredth time he thanked the powers that be for bringing her to him.

*

After the procession the races commenced. Dylan was riding in the first race. His horse was called Gaelic Star. It wasn't the favourite, being quite young and not having run at Royal Ascot before, but Dylan had every confidence in it. So did Sean Fox, who was busy hurling his orders about in the parade ring. Dylan studied Gaelic Star closely. Whilst looking in fine shape with a smooth stride, he noticed an involuntary twitch of his ears and the flick of his tail, which signalled to him that the tumult all around had got to him. His coat was covered with a film of sweat. Suddenly Gaelic Star kicked his back legs, and another handler quickly came to assist in calming him down.

'The horse looks anxious,' Dylan warned Sean Fox.

'That horse is in peak condition. I've done my job, Delany, you do yours,' Fox spat back, nerves getting the better of him. Dylan clenched his jaw and gripped his whip, longing to swipe it across Fox's face. Concentrating, he calmly made his way to the starting line, filled with an inner peace. This was normally where the riders started to feel their nerves kicking in, but Dylan felt nothing, he was just focused. As the horses were finally loaded for the start of the race, Dylan, unlike everyone else, relaxed. It was a gift, the ability to switch off when all around were edged with nervous energy. Whatever happened next was out of his control, to a degree. The gates would open and the runners would thunder down the course. It would all be over in under a minute and a half. His last race at Royal Ascot.

The signal was given, and they were off. Gaelic Star missed the break at the start, leaving him trailing the field. Dylan urged the horse on to cover the ground, but soon found himself stuck behind a wall of horses. It was the worst possible start. Proceeding was difficult. Gaps opened ahead and closed too swiftly for him to make a move. Even so, Gaelic Star was travelling well. He was sharp and powerful and had the ability to win. Positioning him to take advantage of this was proving difficult for Dylan, though. The runners were bunched together round the bend and Dylan was still trapped in the middle. In front a group of three horses blocked his progress. He waited, hoping for a gap to appear. Eventually there was room to get out and go round them. He steered Gaelic Star to the left, giving him a chance to stretch out. The horse relished the challenge, notching up a gear despite his anxiety. He pulled away from the group of horses and set off in pursuit of the two runners ahead. The nearest was three lengths away entering the last furlong and Gaelic Star caught up with him comfortably. Now he was just a length down on the horse in first place, Rainbow's End, and poised to swoop past him. But Dylan could hear his horse gasping for breath, so he lay off his whip, willing Gaelic Star to push just a little further. The horse tried his best, but so did Rainbow's End. The two horses raced neck and neck over the finishing line, making it impossible to ascertain the winner.

'A bloody photo finish!' cursed Sean Fox, his face contorted with fury.

Dylan rode Gaelic Star slowly back down the track, waiting for the winner to be announced. A television commentator hastily approached.

'Another win, Dylan?' Dylan didn't answer, he was still in his zone, waiting for the result. In the distance he could see Sean Fox, pacing up and down like a caged tiger. His body language spoke volumes. Again, Dylan felt his jaw tighten. Then it came.

'The result of the photograph finish. First, number five, Gaelic Star. Second, number seven, Rainbow's End. Third, number two, Midnight Express.' The crowd went wild, yet Dylan felt cold.

Entering the winner's enclosure to deafening applause, Dylan jumped off his horse. The TV presenter tried once more for a response from him.

'Congratulations, Dylan, a close shave!' He ignored her. Sean Fox came bounding over.

'Only just, but a win's a win.' Is that all he could say? The horse was young, inexperienced and had given his all to win. Another jockey would have thrashed him to get past the winning post.

'You're a bastard, Fox. That's the last time I ride for you.' Sean Fox's eyes bulged, his face flushed in anger. Dylan coolly walked away. Every television camera had recorded the post-race drama, and the place was buzzing.

Up in the stands Seamus gave a sly smile: about time someone told him. Good for Dylan. Tatum and

Megan had jumped for joy when Gaelic Star had been announced the winner. Tobias, however, had been studying Dylan. Any doubts he may have had about him backing out of the new training yard were quashed. It was blatantly obvious to him that Dylan's heart was no longer in the thrill of the race. Hearing his comments to Sean Fox further confirmed that. He was relieved. The training yard was going to be a real money-spinner. That and the much-needed grant English Heritage would be supplying to assist in opening Treweham Hall would meet the financial demands. If all went to plan, Tobias could just about turn it around, pulling the estate accounts out of the red.

'More champagne!' cheered Tatum.

'I'll second that,' replied Tobias, filling everyone's glass.

Chapter 39

At the end of the day, Tobias' driver drove them to the country inn. It was early evening when they arrived. The aroma of honeysuckle hovered in the air as they walked hand in hand up the stone steps. The Hollies was a sixteenth-century former coach house, steeped in history. Tobias gave his name at reception simply as Cavendish-Blake. The receptionist's eyebrows rose. 'Ah, Lord Cavendish-Blake, please follow me. I will show you to your room.'

'Could you arrange for the luggage to be brought up, please? My driver is waiting outside.'

'Certainly, sir.'

Megan noticed the way people responded to Tobias, yet he never lorded his position over them. Even now he hadn't given his title. They were taken up a grand staircase, then along an oak-panelled corridor to the end room. Megan suspected it was the best room in the house. She wasn't wrong. Megan took in the elaborately carved four-poster bed, draped with gold velvet. There was an antique dressing table and wardrobe, shelves packed with old, leather-bound books, and a huge Persian rug covered the floorboards. Matching gold velvet curtains hung with tassels framed the large sash window. The en suite was floor-to-ceiling oyster marble with a slipper bath and a ribcage shower.

'You like?' Tobias asked.

'I do. It's wonderful.'

'I'm glad you like it. I've booked dinner in the restaurant for seven thirty.'

'Right, I'd better get ready.' He looked into her eyes. Surely he wasn't going to suggest they shower together, was he? She returned his gaze, the effect of the champagne giving her the courage to do so. A knock at the door interrupted them.

'That'll be the cases.' Tobias answered the door, leaving Megan to slip quietly into the bathroom and lock the door. She undressed and let the fine spray of the shower relax her. Nerves had started to jitter. She wondered if he felt the same.

He'd heard her lock the bathroom door and grinned wickedly to himself. What did she think he'd do? Barge in and ravish her? Hmm, the very thought had made him semi-hard. How he'd wait for tonight he didn't know. The anticipation was killing him. Images of her exquisite body lying on the picnic rug in Quercus Woods had taunted him every night as he longed to touch and taste her again. It was slowly driving him insane. He unpacked his dinner suit and left Megan's case on the bed. Soon she entered the room wearing a bath robe, her hair wrapped in a towel. 'Right, I'll leave you to get ready while I bathe.'

Tobias shut the bathroom door behind him, but didn't bother to lock it. On the off chance Megan wanted to come in and ravish him in the bath, she was most welcome.

Once dressed, Megan looked every inch the elegant lady in her long, slim, fitted black gown. It was sleeveless with a rolled neckline. She had worn her gran's necklace, a single diamond on a silver chain. Her hair was fresh and shiny from the shower and dried smoothly into a sleek bob. She squirted herself with a floral perfume, reminding her of Gran's Parma violets, and she felt a sudden rush of love. After a while Tobias came into the room, wearing only a towel round his hips. 'Forgot this,' he grinned, picking up his dinner suit and strolled back into the bathroom. Megan gulped. What a sight for sore eyes. His body was sensational, with his broad shoulders, muscular, dark chest, slim hips and strong legs. She looked at her reflection in the mirror. After tonight there was no turning back.

They made a striking couple walking into the restaurant. Heads turned as they were shown to their table by the window overlooking the grounds. Megan felt a little self-conscious and was glad they were positioned slightly out of the way from the other diners. She wondered if Tobias had booked this particular table for that reason, which meant he must have stayed here before. Instantly prompting the next question, with whom? Insecurity crept into her psyche like an old enemy, taunting her. Determined not to let it ruin her evening she concentrated on the menu. Despite her nerves, she was quite hungry. Once they'd both ordered a starter and main course, Tobias was given the wine list. His eyes flicked over the extensive names from countries far and wide, which meant absolutely nothing to her, but obviously a great deal to him.

'We'll have the Conterno Cicala 2012, please.'

'Excellent choice, sir,' replied the waiter.

After the waiter had left, Megan said quietly, 'Good job you know your wines. I wouldn't have had a clue.'

'Yes you would. I've ordered the wine I brought when you made dinner the first time.'

Megan smiled at the memory. It seemed a while ago now, probably because a lot had happened since then. Tobias must have been thinking something similar as he enquired about her visit to Ted.

'It went really well, thanks. I asked him to talk to Mum.' Tobias was listening as he poured the wine, which had been quickly brought to the table.

'I take it your mum still has no idea?'

Megan shook her head. 'No, I'm convinced she doesn't know Ted's her real dad.'

'But you think she should know?'

'Yes, I do,' she replied firmly.

Tobias loved the way she knew her own mind and agreed with her, although privately he was dubious as to the outcome.

'If you need me to help in anyway, Megan, I'm here.' His hand covered hers over the table, and it felt warm and reassuring. Megan was touched. He had only ever shown kindness and compassion, a total contrast to what she had read about him on the internet.

Curiosity had got the better of her and she hadn't been able to resist reading the various articles that had been written about him. The most recent one had reported his antics on his thirtieth birthday brawl. However shocking the tabloids portrayed 'the Heir and the Fox' she still couldn't help chuckling.

Tobias once again caught her grinning to herself. 'Now what's going on in that mind of yours, Megan Taylor?'

'Just what I've been reading about your sordid past,' she teased.

'Please don't take it as gospel.' Hell, the last thing he needed at this crucial stage was his past catching up on him.

'I'm not sure I'd want my past archived in the newspapers for all and sundry to pore over.'

'Oh, really?' he ribbed, arching his eyebrow. His hand still held hers, his thumb rubbed the inside of her wrist. She gave him a playful smile, which he found incredibly sexy.

'Hmm, never tumbled out of a nightclub without my trousers, though,' she mused.

'It was Fox's doing,' he retorted, half laughing, 'I was led astray.'

'You both had beautiful women on each arm,' she chided, looking directly at him. He lowered his gaze. For a moment neither of them spoke. Then she asked the question, unable to avoid, she had to know. 'Tobias, you seem to know your way round here – have you stayed before?'

'Yes.' Now he was looking directly at her. She swallowed, they both knew what was coming next.

'Who with?'

'A lady whom I've known a very long time and grown extremely fond of, despite her waywardness.' Megan felt like she'd been punched in the stomach. Her jaw dropped. She pulled her hand away sharply. Tobias grabbed it back. 'Aunt Celia.'

Relief flooded her. 'Seriously, you brought Celia here?'

'Yes,' he laughed, 'I took her to Royal Ascot last year for her eightieth birthday and we stayed here, too. Separate rooms, obviously.' His lips twitched. He'd loved her reaction, her jealousy giving his confidence a boost.

'You enjoy teasing me, don't you?' She looked narrowly at him.

'Yes, I do,' he replied, his eyes dancing with devilment. She couldn't help but laugh; he was incorrigible.

After finishing their meal and the bottle of wine they made their way up the grand staircase. Megan had expected to feel those butterfly nerves fluttering away in the pit of her stomach, but she didn't. Instead she was overcome with a sense of wellbeing, having thoroughly enjoyed being in Tobias' company all day. He made her feel special. As they entered the room he took her in his arms and kissed her, gently at first, then as her hands ran through his hair, the pressure of his lips intensified, plunging further. Megan's hands then slipped under his jacket and pulled him further into her, and she could feel how hard he was already.

'Megan,' he whispered huskily, pulling himself away.

His eyes were dark with passion as he watched her undress and climb into the huge bed. Tobias stripped, leaving his body completely bare. Red-hot desire burnt through her. He was an Adonis. His eyes locked with hers, as he rolled back the covers to reveal her body. He slowly devoured every detail: the round, firm breasts dusted with freckles, curved hips, flat stomach and shapely, long legs. He homed in on the silk triangle of dark hair, inviting him. He dipped his head to kiss both breasts, running his tongue over her hard nipples, then lowered his lips to caress her stomach, then finally his tongue moved down over the intimate parting of her, making Megan cry out in pleasure. He gently probed, relishing the taste of her. Megan grabbed his shoulders.

'Tobias, please,' she pleaded. He ran his face up her body and found her lips. Megan stroked his muscular back, loving the contours of his warm skin. He claimed her mouth again, whilst gently parting her thighs.

'Tell me you want me,' he whispered darkly.

'You know I do,' she begged, wrapping her arms round him.

'Tell me.'

'Tobias, I want you.' This sent him into overdrive. With a groan he placed himself between her soft thighs and edged into her, making her gasp. Slowly he pushed further until he was fully inside her. She clutched his buttocks, then he started to move steadily, deeper and deeper sending her into ecstasy. Tobias pressed harder. He'd waited a long time for this and couldn't control himself any longer. Megan arched her back, he could feel her breasts against his chest. With a guttural cry his body juddered and he erupted like a volcano, only just managing to withdraw. Megan cried out in pleasure, clinging to him. They both lay still for a moment, savouring what had happened. Tobias rolled onto his back, while Megan snuggled into his chest. 'That was amazing,' she murmured.

'I know,' he gruffly replied, kissing her forehead. 'Megan?'

'Yes?'

'Promise you won't read anymore bloody articles about me?'

She laughed. 'I promise.' He nudged her to face him. He looked serious.

'I don't want anything to come between us, do you understand?'

She was touched. 'Don't worry,' she soothed, and gently kissed his lips.

He cursed himself for not using protection, but he'd truly got lost in the moment. What she could do to him was frightening. He was totally bewitched.

Chapter 40

For once Flora was relaxing. She had taken the day off work to see her mum and dad off on their big adventure. The campervan looked full to busting, with a cheery dad at the wheel and an excited mum clutching a map.

'You sure you'll be all right, Flora?' Her mum was starting to fuss again.

'Yes! Now stop worrying and have a blast,' reassured Flora, who by now had had enough of her mum's drama and just wanted them to get going. She was secretly looking forward to having the place to herself, with her brother packed off to South America, too. Her dad beeped his horn twice.

'Righty ho! Off we go!'

Flora leant forward and gave him a kiss. 'Bye, have a wonderful time!'

She waved them off until the campervan was out of sight, then went back into the quiet house, made a coffee and sat in front of the TV, something she hadn't done for ages, she realised. Bliss, perfect bliss. Normally she would be up with the lark, grabbing a quick breakfast before making her way to Treweham Hall stables. There she would spend the day mucking out the stables, exercising, feeding and tending to all the horses' needs. It was strenuous work, which left her exhausted and only fit for a long, hot bath and supper by the time she returned home.

It would be good to have a bit more free time, and she considered Dylan's proposal once again. If she was an assistant trainer she would be able to have more control over her time, not be the constant lackey. Flora loved horses, and would always want to work closely with them, but she rather liked the idea of having a bit more say in the running of a yard. One thing that she would always admire in Dylan was his care of horses. She had watched him riding at Royal Ascot and admired the way he had handled his horse, refusing to whip it to death, like some would. Dylan always put the welfare of his horse first, above all else, and she respected him for that.

She flicked on the TV. Dylan's body, wrapped in a small blue towel stared back at her, jolting her senses. Her eyes widened as she watched him walk into a bedroom with a confident swagger, splash aftershave on his cheeks and say, 'Never be pipped at the post.' Flora's shoulders started to shake with laughter. Then Dylan's blue eyes bored into her. 'I always win, wearing Racer.' He gave her that winning wink, before she collapsed on the sofa in hysterics.

*

Seamus had seen the advert, too. Straight away he had got on the phone to Tobias, spluttering with laughter. Dylan knew to expect the text messages left on his phone. He took them with good humour. The one message he craved, though, wasn't forthcoming. He still hadn't had an answer from Flora. It had been a few days now since he'd seen her, and his application for a licence to run a training yard had been successful. The panel deciding Dylan's submission had been favourable. His reputation for his good care of horses had outshone any unsavoury gossip, plus the plans for the new training yard were thorough and detailed, leaving no room for doubt that the whole project would be run professionally and successfully. He suspected the Treweham Hall name had packed some punch and, if the whispers were true, his actions towards Sean Fox hadn't done him any harm. Sean Fox had made one or two enemies in the racing world and seeing a jockey stand up to him had caused many a satisfied smirk. All Dylan needed now was Flora to agree to be his assistant trainer. He didn't want to pressure her, but then again he needed an answer. His mobile bleeped and he rolled his eyes: another message about the advert. But it was Flora's name that flashed before him. He took a deep breath.

Fancy meeting up?

Did he ever.

Yes, where?

he tapped back immediately.

At home, house empty.

Dylan's heart leaped.

On my way.

Wear Racer.

Ha, bloody ha, he thought, smiling widely.

Within minutes Dylan had driven to Flora's house. He saw her in the side garden putting deck chairs up. 'Hi!' he called.

'I thought we'd sit in the sun.' She waved him over. She looked so young and fresh in her shorts and T-shirt, without a trace of make-up. Her hair was in a ponytail that swished as she walked towards him. 'Would you like a drink?'

'Coffee would be lovely, thanks.' He watched her pert bottom tightly tucked in denim shorts as she made her way into the kitchen. A few minutes later she joined him carrying two mugs of coffee. She handed him one and plonked herself down in a deck chair. She blew on her coffee and took a sip. Dylan examined her, mesmerised. Flora got prettier every time he saw her.

'Loved the advert, by the way,' she chuckled.

'It's tough work, but someone's got to do it.' He met her eyes. They both knew why he was there. It was pointless pretending.

'I've been thinking about your offer.'

'And?'

'I'd like to be your assistant trainer.'

'Flora, that's great!' He went to kiss her, then stopped. She held her hand out, backing him off.

'It's to be a business partnership, strictly professional.'

'Naturally,' he agreed. As if. He'd give her a month before she was back in his arms, begging for more.

'When will the yard be ready?'

'Tobias has started renovating the old stable block, and it should take about a month, all hands on deck. We'll need to kit out the stables. I'd like your help buying all the equipment.' Flora's enthusiasm started to build. She knew it was the right decision. Her only doubts lay in the way of temptation, especially after being reminded of how good Dylan's body was by that commercial. As if reading her thoughts, he edged a little closer, giving her the benefit of his deep blue eyes. 'Let's celebrate. Let me buy you lunch.' He gave her his most seductive smile. She couldn't resist, surely?

'No, thanks.'

He blinked. 'Why not?'

'Not really in the mood. Just feel like chilling.' She sprawled her legs out and stretched her arms as if to prove it.

The little minx, he thought. She wouldn't hold out.

Chapter 41

'Mum, I'd like you to come and visit, on your own.'

'Is everything all right, Megan?' The anxiety in her mum's voice was evident.

'Yes, fine. I'd just like to see you.'

'Right, I'll come tomorrow.' There was a pause. 'You sure you're OK?'

'Yes, honestly.'

Megan had decided on her return from Royal Ascot that she needed to tell her mum everything. On their journey home, she and Tobias had discussed it again at length. He had agreed with her, and it felt reassuring to know he was behind her. She had grown accustomed to his sound judgement and felt totally at ease in his company. The night they had spent together would remain forever etched in her memory, and it had been magical waking up next to him. They had gone down to breakfast hand in hand like it was an everyday occurrence, oblivious to the attention they had attracted, totally lost in each other. Megan hadn't felt so happy in a long time, and neither, it appeared, had Tobias. The only nagging apprehension, which refused to disappear, was the issue of Ted and her mum. She took the Parma violet tin from under her bed where the letters and photographs had been kept. Tomorrow she would show them to her mum. Once the revelation had sunk in, Megan wanted her to visit Ted, but she was nervous about the outcome, knowing how close her mum had been to Granddad Michael. Her mum's world was about to be turned upside down.

The next day her mum's car pulled up outside Megan's cottage late morning. Megan flung open the door to greet her.

'Mum!' It was so good to see her.

'Megan, come here.' She opened her arms and embraced her in a bear hug. 'Now what's all this about?' She looked warily at her daughter.

'Come in.' Megan avoided the question and carried her mother's overnight bag into the hallway. 'I'll put the kettle on,' she called over her shoulder. Her mum took in the freshly decorated surroundings.

'This all looks lovely.' Her eyes darted around the room before joining Megan in the kitchen.

'Thanks. I've brought back some of Finula's shortbread from The Templar.'

'Oh, that looks good. How is work in the pub?' She sat down at the kitchen table.

'Great. I really enjoy working there and the staff are nice, especially Finula and her dad, Dermot.'

'I'm so glad you've settled in love.'

After an hour of drinking tea and catching up, Megan got the tin and placed it in front of her mum. 'What's this?' Her mum frowned, vaguely recognising her mother's favourite perfume.

'I found this in the attic. It was in the middle of the floor. I think I was meant to find it.' Her mum looked up, puzzled. 'I want you to read what's inside it. There are letters, to Gran... and photographs.' Taking the tin, her mum forced off the lid. Megan got up from the table. 'I'm going to leave you alone to read them. I'll be back shortly.' She touched her mum's hand and left. Feeling the need to give her mum some space, she decided to go to The Templar, and as she entered the pub her mood lifted immediately.

'Hi, Megan!' called Finula behind the bar.

'Hi ya.' Megan pulled up a stool and sat opposite her. 'Can I have a cappuccino?'

'Coming up.' As Finula prepared the coffee she glanced over her shoulder with a huge grin. 'So, how was Royal Ascot?'

'Wonderful, thanks.'

'And... the night of passion with Tobias?' she beamed.

'Even better,' Megan replied without a flinch.

'Megan Taylor!' Finula pretended to be shocked and passed her cappuccino over.

Megan laughed and took a sip, then eyed Finula pensively. 'It's about time we found you a nice man, Finula.'

Sighing, Finula agreed. 'I know, but who? Besides, this place takes up most of my time.'

'Hmm, ever thought of internet dating?'

Finula wrinkled her nose. 'Not really. I prefer to meet people in the flesh.'

'A blind date?'

'Do me a favour.'

'A tall, dark stranger needs to walk into this bar—

'

'And I say, "Of all the gin joints, in all the towns, in all the world, you had to walk into mine,"' interrupted Finula, and they both fell about laughing. After a few moments Megan looked at her best friend with real affection.

'Seriously, Fin, you're wasted on your own.' Damn Nick Fletcher. They chatted until Megan looked at her watch and thought she'd given her mum enough time. She finished her coffee, said goodbye to Finula and left.

Megan returned home to find her mum staring into space on the sofa. 'You OK, Mum?' She settled next to her and linked arms.

'I think so.' She was clutching the photograph of Edward in uniform.

'He looks like me, doesn't he?' Megan said gently.

'Undeniably so.' With a steady breath, Megan filled in all the pieces: Ted living next door, Tobias finding Grace's photograph, his visit to Ted in the nursing home and finally Ted's story of the soldier who came home, but too late

'I had no idea,' her mum choked, a tear falling down her face.

'None at all?' Megan still found it incredulous that she'd never even suspected.

'Absolutely not. My dad meant everything to me.' Her shoulders started to shake.

'And his memory still does, Mum. Nothing changes in that respect. Granddad Michael was a wonderful person who loved you and Gran unconditionally. Me and Chris, too.' Megan spoke firmly, fighting back the tears.

'Yes, you're right. Poor Ted, what a life he's had.'

'Mum, I want you to see Ted.'

'Yes, of course,' she gulped. Then turning to face Megan she asked, 'Why didn't she tell me?'

'I don't know, perhaps because you were so close to Granddad. She didn't want to hurt anyone.'

'Then why let you find these?' She pointed to the letters on the side table.

'I think she only decided to reveal the truth when she knew she was dying. Me finding the letters must have seemed the most logical solution. I suspect in her own way she was letting me decide whether or not to tell you. Do you think I made the right decision?'

'I do, but I'm not sure it should have been your responsibility.' There was a steely edge to her voice, one that Megan understood.

Megan arranged for her mum to meet up with Ted at the nursing home the following afternoon. Choosing not to be present, respecting the space the two of them would need, she dropped her mum off at the entrance.

'I'll walk back, Megan.'

'Yes, of course,' she replied, appreciating the time alone her mum needed.

Megan drove home in silent contemplation. She badly wanted to speak to her dad and brother, but then thought perhaps it was better if her mum told them first. She felt a sudden wave of home sickness. Although she'd settled in Treweham, she missed the daily chats she used to have with Chris. She also missed Kate, her friend from the office. They had exchanged text messages regularly, but the topic of Adam was forever lurking in the background. Megan did and didn't want to know what he was up to. It was a strange feeling and Kate obviously wouldn't broach the subject unless asked.

The rest of the afternoon was spent in a bit of a blur, constantly wondering how it was going with Ted and her mum. Should she go over to the nursing home and find out? Just then she heard her mum open the door. She waited with baited breath for her to enter the sitting room. Expecting her to be emotional, she was surprised to find her in quite good spirits.

'Well, that went really well,' her mum smiled.

'I'm glad.'

'What a lovely man. I'm bringing Chris and Dad to meet him.'

'Good. It'll be great to see them,' Megan smiled back.

'Megan, this can't have been easy for you. Thanks, love.' She stretched her arms out and Megan fell into them, hugging her hard.

Chapter 42

The Templar was packed. Megan and Finula were rushed off their feet. Every table was occupied by the tenants in Treweham village, who paid rent to the Cavendish-Blakes' estate, mainly rustic farmers who demanded a constant flow of beer. It was the night of the Landlord's Supper. By tradition, the Lord of Treweham Hall paid for all his tenants' supper once a year and in return they would submit their annual rent. Of course, nowadays it was all done monthly electronically, but some traditions prevailed and this was one tradition Tobias and the village of Treweham were keen to uphold. Megan had laughed when Tobias and Finula had explained the custom, dating back to the medieval times.

'But it's an important event,' pressed Finula. 'There'd be uproar if it didn't take place, plus it's good for the pub.'

Tobias agreed. 'Absolutely, it's worth every penny to keep the tenants happy. Besides, it's a good night, brings the community together.'

It was certainly doing that, thought Megan as she wiped her forehead and pulled yet another pint of ale. Dermot had called upon all his staff to assist with the cooking and serving. Finula and Megan were working flat out behind the bar. Megan could see Tobias sitting centre at the top table, looking very fetching in a navy suit and white shirt, chatting and laughing with nearby farmers. He must have felt her watching him, as he suddenly glanced towards her and smiled, and her stomach flipped again as she quickly smiled back.

Megan's curiosity grew when she saw Sebastian sitting next to Tobias. Judging by their easy manner together it was obvious the brothers were close. Megan tried discreetly to study Sebastian. With his blond hair and a smaller build he looked nothing like his brother. He had the same mischievous grin, though, she noticed, and was a tad dramatic in his demeanour – a real performer, she suspected. His voice certainly carried well as she remembered his clear, sharp tones in the summerhouse.

As if reading her mind, Sebastian made his way to the bar and presented himself. With a wide smile he said, 'Sebastian Cavendish-Blake, at your service.' He bowed.

Megan giggled. 'Pleased to meet you, Sebastian. I'm Megan.' She held her hand out, which he shook firmly.

'Ah, yes, the fair maiden who has stolen the heart of my brother, no less.' He held such presence and spoke with real drama, almost as though he was starring in a Shakespeare play. She assumed his world was the stage and he never really stopped acting.

'What can I get you?'

'A large malt for my lord and master and a pint of your finest for me.'

'Coming up.' Megan saw Nick enter the pub out of the corner of her eye and braced herself. Not really knowing how to react to him, she glanced over at Finula, but Finula hadn't spotted him. Neither had Sebastian, as he took the drinks and made his way back to the top table. Nick sat down alone in the corner. After a few minutes he approached the bar and Megan saw him stumble slightly.

'A large, red wine, please.'

Did she imagine it, or was he slurring his words a touch? Megan poured him a glass.

'Seen Ted?' he asked. Megan's heart dropped: he was obviously keen to exchange pleasantries.

'Yes, I took Zac to see him the other day.'

Nick smiled. 'He'd have enjoyed that. Next time you go let me know.'

Megan didn't answer. She saw Tobias look over, stormy faced, though Sebastian still hadn't seen Nick. He had his back to the bar and was entertaining a small group with animated gestures, causing raucous guffaws. Nick took his wine and returned to his table.

'Have you seen him? He looks pissed to me,' Finula hissed. She had noticed the way Nick had plonked himself down, spilling some of his drink on the table.

'I know,' Megan whispered back, a sense of foreboding washed over her. 'Oh, no, he's coming back,' she said in a hushed tone. Nick's glass was empty. He must have downed in one what was left in it.

'*Fin*-ula,' he drawled, 'always a pleasure to see you.' Finula gave him a look of utter contempt. He turned to Megan, 'Another glass of red, please, Megan.'

'Nick, are you sure?' she quietly asked.

'No. You know what? I'll have a white wine instead.' Then, leaning forward over the bar, he reached out to touch Megan's necklace. 'That's a very pretty necklace.' Megan could smell the alcohol on his breath; he had bloodshot eyes. His hand moved towards the back of her neck and he pulled her towards his face. 'Kiss me, Megan,' he slurred.

'Take your hands off her, Fletcher,' Tobias ordered.

Nick gave a look of exaggerated surprise and released his hold on her.

'Oh, look who it is, Lord Cavendish-Blake himself.'

'Outside, now.' Tobias was taking his jacket off. Megan and Finula exchanged looks of alarm.

'Pardon?' laughed Nick. 'Outside? And will I be needing my duelling pistol, or my sword?' Sebastian, finally noticing Nick's presence, was making his way over.

'Right, you asked for this.' Tobias curled his hand into a hard fist and punched Nick full in the face, making him roll back and fall on the floor. A shocked hush followed. Finula ran to get her dad. Tobias had turned his back to get his jacket when Nick suddenly rose to his feet, grabbed a nearby stool and threw it at him.

'Tobias!' screamed Megan, just in time for him to turn halfway and elbow the stool out of his path, hurtling it onto a table full of glasses. Shards of glass flew everywhere. Tobias lunged at Nick with one final blow, throwing him across the bar, causing more smashed glasses. The pub was silent. Dermot appeared with a frantic Finula.

'I'll pay for all the damage, Dermot.' Tobias wiped the hair from his face.

Dermot nodded sternly.

'Worth every penny,' murmured Finula, looking at Nick slumped across the bar. Sebastian was white with shock; gone was the court jester.

'I'll take him home,' he said, attempting to lift Nick's slouched body.

'Here, you'll need a hand.' Dermot took hold of Nick's arm and wrapped it round his shoulder. Together they managed to get Nick to the door.

'Tobias, are you all right?' Megan rushed to him, not believing what had just happened.

'Nothing I can't handle.' His eyes were like chips of ice as he watched his brother and Dermot fumble Nick out of the pub. Finula had started to sweep up the smashed glasses.

'I'd better help get this cleaned up.'

'I'd better get back to my guests.' Tobias turned on his heel and with absolute composure returned to his table.

*

The next morning Megan woke to hammering on her front door. Glancing out of her bedroom window she couldn't see a car parked outside and wondered who it could be. Quickly pulling on her dressing gown over her pyjamas she scurried downstairs to open the door. There stood Sebastian, looking rather contrite.

'Hello, Megan. May I come in?'

'Yes, of course.' She stepped aside to let him enter the hall.

'Sorry, did I wake you?' He looked at her attire with an apologetic smile.

'No, it's fine. I'll put the kettle on. Come through.' She ushered him into the lounge and pointed to the sofa. 'You sit down. Tea or coffee?'

'Tea would be lovely, thank you.' Megan soon returned with two full tea cups and sat opposite him with a questioning look.

'Megan, I've come to apologise.'

'What for?' she asked surprised.

'For nearly driving into you that night. I'm sorry, I know Nick implied Tobias was driving, but we both know he'd never do such a thing.'

Megan's eyes avoided his for a moment. Then she replied quietly, 'No, he wouldn't.'

'Please believe me, I am very sorry. We'd had a terrible row, me and Nick, and I just lost it. I drove like a mad man. I truly do regret it.'

'Sebastian, it's OK, really.'

'But—'

'No, honestly, don't worry about it.'

'Are you sure?'

'Yes. Perhaps it's best if Tobias wasn't told about this. You know, with—'

'Carrie,' blurted Sebastian. 'Yes, of course. Losing the love of your life to a drunk driver is bad enough.'

Megan drew in a shaky breath. It was hard hearing Tobias had lost the love of his life. What was she? Second best by default? Sebastian was too wrapped up to realise what he had implied. Megan looked at him, so pale and anxious, thin and blond, almost translucent, ghostlike; the complete opposite to his older brother. Yet instead of being offended by his clumsy comments, she felt sorry, almost protective of Sebastian. He appeared hurt and vulnerable somehow. She cursed Nick and the harm he had inflicted on both Sebastian and Finula.

She patted his shoulder. 'Let's forget it ever happened.'

His lips curled into a slow smile. 'You sure?'

'Yes,' she smiled back. Then asked quietly, 'How's Nick?'

He shifted uncomfortably. 'Probably the worse for wear after last night's episode.' There was a short silence. 'That was the last straw.'

'Sorry?'

'Me and him. We were close once, you know.'

'Oh, right...' Megan was unsure just how to react, but Sebastian carried on regardless.

'I'm off, back on the road. I want to put all this behind me once and for all.'

'I see...' she said, even though she didn't. 'Where are you going?'

'To Canterbury. The travelling theatre performs there the day after tomorrow.'

'Ah, well, good luck,' she smiled encouragingly.

'Thank you.' Then he paused and looked at her as if really seeing her for the first time. 'Megan, I think you'll be very good for my brother.'

'Thank you.'

'You're most welcome,' and with that he rose dramatically off the sofa and headed to the front door.

Chapter 43

'Now are you sure you've got everything, ladies?' Tobias couldn't help smiling to himself at his mother and aunt's excitement. They had both been up since the crack of dawn, scurrying around like headless chickens, packing and fussing over last-minute arrangements. Tobias had arranged for a car to take them to Southampton, where they would board the *Jewel of the Ocean*. He was more than ready for them to set sail. With his mother and aunt safely off on their voyage and Sebastian in Canterbury, he had Treweham Hall all to himself, to entertain the lovely Megan. Ted's cottage was now advertised as 'to let', being fully renovated and Tobias had moved out.

'Come to the Hall tomorrow evening. I'll cook dinner,' he had suggested last night at The Templar. Megan had just finished her shift and Tobias had arrived for last orders and to walk her home.

'We both know it won't be you doing the cooking, Tobias,' replied Megan, grinning.

He raised an eyebrow seductively, 'I'll have you know my *coq* au vin is to die for,' he purred.

'Really? And what about dessert?' she batted back.

'Oh, you'll get your just deserts, don't you worry.' He grabbed her by the waist, she put her arms round his neck and together their lips met.

'Have you no homes to go to?' asked Dermot drily as he guided them both out of the pub doors.

As they strolled to Megan's cottage hand in hand Tobias continued, 'Stay over tomorrow night. It'll be just us, with everyone gone now.'

Megan was so tempted, but if she were being completely honest she still felt a little in awe of the place. Tobias wanted her to be more relaxed, to treat his home as her own. This meant her being accustomed to the space and grandeur, plus the team of staff that kept Treweham Hall ticking over like the fine machine it was. He noticed her hesitation.

'Megan, it's my home. I want you to be comfortable in it,' he reasoned.

'I know you do and, yes, it would be lovely to stay over, thank you.' She realised how it must seem to Tobias and really didn't want to cause any offence. Besides, another night with him was what she had been privately craving since Royal Ascot.

To say it was what Tobias had been craving was an understatement. He was at fever pitch to have Megan in his four-poster bed – permanently, if he had his way. He was aware of how possessive of her he had become, hence why he had taken to walking her home after an evening shift in The Templar. The thought of Nick Fletcher sniffing around Megan filled him with rage. He had startled himself at his own reaction when seeing Fletcher touch Megan at the Landlord's Supper. Once again, he understood the lengths his father had gone to in protecting his mother.

'Good. That's settled then.'

*

The following evening, Megan, despite her nerves, was still eager to stay at Treweham Hall with Tobias. She was glad it would be just the two of them the first time she stayed over. Not really sure if dinner would be a formal affair in the great dining hall, or an intimate supper in the drawing room, she found it difficult to decide what to wear. In the end she opted for a simple cream tea dress with a matching fine wool cardigan. She arrived at the Hall and went through the back way, via the kitchen. The staff were familiar with her by now, as she always passed by the kitchen to see them when calling at the Hall. Even Henry, who deep down hadn't approved of Megan initially, had succumbed to her friendly manner. It would have been foolish not to. If his suspicions were proved right, Megan's presence would be a permanent fixture in the not-too-distant future.

'Ah, Miss Taylor, Lord Cavendish-Blake is expecting you in the dining hall.'

'Thanks, Henry. I'll make my own way there.'

'Very good, madam.' He bowed slightly. Megan's lips twitched: was he always this formal?

Walking along the corridor, she glanced upwards to the many portraits staring down at her. The dining-hall door was open, but there was no Tobias inside. She entered the huge room and wondered why he had chosen this ceremonial setting for just the two of them. A long mahogany table ran down the centre of the room, with ten chairs seated each side. A silver candelabra burned brightly in the middle. Two places had been set on the corner towards the top end. Megan giggled, thankful they weren't sitting at opposite ends of this great long table, imagining herself whizzing the salt down to Tobias. Just then he walked in, looking rather dapper in jeans, shirt and a Harris Tweed jacket.

'Sorry, I was just on the phone to Dylan.' He kissed her mouth firmly. Moving towards the drinks cabinet, he poured himself a brandy. 'What can I get you?' he called over his shoulder.

'A gin and tonic, please.' Megan gazed around the room, remembering the first time Tobias had shown her Treweham Hall. A spectacular chandelier hung in the middle of the ceiling, its cut-glass flickering light on the pale silk walls. She looked enquiringly as he handed her drink. 'Why are we dining in here, Tobias?'

'Because it's a dining room,' he replied simply.

'You know what I mean,' she chided. 'Why so formal?'

He sighed. 'Because I want you to get used to all this.' He raised his hands in the air. Megan frowned. 'Look, all I want is you to be yourself, as relaxed here as you would be at your cottage.'

'Bit different, though, isn't it? I don't have staff wandering around the place. Don't you find it a little intrusive?'

'Not really. And talking of staff, I've been thinking.' Megan took a long drink: this sounded ominous. 'After dinner I'll show you the rooms that will be open to the public. The teashop conversion is about to start. I'm renovating a downstairs room. It's big enough to house tables, chairs and a kitchen, plus there'll be a small annex selling souvenirs of Treweham Hall.'

'It all sounds great.' Megan couldn't help but be impressed with Tobias' drive and vision. He was committed to Treweham Hall and she hoped his hard work would pay off. 'How's the training yard coming along?' Yet another project he was dedicated to.

His face lit up with enthusiasm. 'Good. Dylan knows exactly what he wants and I'm more than happy to accommodate. That training yard will be the saving of this place.'

'Really?' Megan was surprised. 'I never knew there was so much money involved.'

'You kidding? We'll aim to get clients from the Far East who'll pay astronomical amounts of money to train a world-class racehorse.'

'You mentioned staff?'

'I did.' He looked straight at her. 'Megan I'd like you to manage the tours and the tearoom, obviously with a small team of staff.'

'Why me?'

'Because I trust you and know you'll do a good job.' Plus he wanted her under his watchful eye, truth be told, not behind a bar in the local pub being ogled at by the punters. He'd seen, on more than one occasion, various men casting lustful glances in her direction and objected to it. This way she would still be earning money, enjoying a rapport with colleagues, but in surroundings that suited him, basically under his own roof. Again, he was conscious of his possessiveness, but couldn't help it. He excused this to himself as being protective of her. Megan was taken aback.

'Oh, thank you… but what about The Templar?'

'I'm sure Dermot can find another barmaid, and you'll still see Finula. The Templar's your local pub.' Megan was pondering the idea when dinner arrived.

Tobias led her to the top of the table. 'Think it over,' he told her, pulling out her chair. And fast, he thought. He aimed to get the whole operation running as soon as possible.

One of the reasons he arranged tonight was for Megan to become familiar with Treweham Hall and all it encompassed. He loved the idea of her working alongside him as well as it removing her from any unwanted attention. If Nick Fletcher dared to touch her again he'd kill him.

After dinner Tobias showed Megan the route of the public tour. He explained with eagerness where the public and private boundaries lay and the information cards that would be displayed in each room, depicting the history and items of artwork they contained. He had been given advice from English Heritage and the Historic Houses Association, who had been more than helpful.

Megan listened with interest, admiring his zeal. Everything he did was done to the max, she concluded. He was always giving his all and his energy was contagious. Suddenly she wanted to be a part of it.

'Tobias, I'll do it,' she stated with conviction.

'Is the right answer,' he replied with a smile. 'Come here, you,' and he hugged her hard. 'And now,' he whispered softly in her ear, 'to bed.'

Megan's heart fluttered uncontrollably as he took her by the hand and led her to his bedroom.

Chapter 44

'This is the life, Trace.' Gary sat back in the hot tub, letting the bubbles flow over his body. Tracy was relaxing on a nearby sun lounger, head behind a magazine. He reached for his lager and took a long swig. Was his wife actually listening to him? She looked very engrossed in what she was reading. Still, she did seem to have settled more.

He had taken to country life quite well, joining a local shoot, which he enjoyed. Gary had proved to be a breath of fresh air to the stuffy lot whose Land Rovers packed with Labradors met together once a month, wearing tweed, Barbours and rather smug smiles. Gary had only tried clay-pigeon shooting, but come autumn he was looking forward to the shoot that would take him out to the woodlands packed with pheasants. Knowing full well he was the joker of the pack, Gary played up to the role and had them all hooting with guffaws. He was actually a very good shot, which for all his gusto had earned him a lot of respect, and, of course, he had money. Gary had learnt to keep his own counsel when it came to background. Whilst proud of his Northern roots, experience had taught him not to disclose how he came about his wealth. Unlike his old friends back home, here they didn't pry. Their curiosity was blatantly obvious, but they would never be so bold or crass as to ask, and for that Gary in turn respected them. In an odd way their differences complemented each other and it worked. They would mock him with his accent and naïvety, whereas he was easily capable of returning the quips, calling them Hooray Henrys who couldn't hit a barn door with a cannon ball. Even Tracy had to stifle a laugh at him in his plus fours. He made a refreshing change; his carefree outlook and jolly disposition made him popular, and he and Tracy were frequently receiving invitations to various dinner parties and charity events.

Tracy had made friends with a few of their wives and had morphed into a lady who lunched. But for her, something was still missing. She longed for an overall sense of purpose. 'I just don't feel like I'm useful any more,' she had commented to Gary. He had tried to appease her by telling her to relax and enjoy their good fortune. But it wasn't in her blood. She had been brought up to work hard, as she had in the nursing home where she had thoroughly enjoyed seeing the fruits of her labour. Tracy often wondered how the residents were, especially Alf. It didn't seem right that all she had to worry about now was what to wear. She had seen her husband adapt to their new lifestyle like a duck to water. He never appeared bored or discontented. He was jovial, forever playing the clown in company; not like her, quiet and watchful on the side lines. What she needed was motivation, a reason for getting up in the morning, other than meeting another 'friend' for lunch, with whom she had very little in common. The article she was reading was giving her food for thought. It talked about volunteers who offered respite in nursing homes, socialising with the elderly, making crafts and enjoying days out in local areas. How rewarding, she thought.

'Can you hear me, Tracy?'

She turned to Gary who was luxuriating in the water. Didn't it bother him, all this nothing to do? Maybe it was different for him; after all, he had hated his job. Couldn't really blame him – she wouldn't have liked lugging around heavy boxes and stacking freezers all day. He'd never complained, though, always cheery.

'Sorry, what did you say?'

'I said, this is the life!'

'Yes.' She smiled weakly. *For you maybe.*

*

'*Bon voyage!*' trilled Beatrice, holding her glass to Celia, who reluctantly clinked it.

'Calm down, Beatrice,' she replied crisply, smothering her sister's happiness. They were sitting out on the deck with a bottle of cava. Beatrice had insisted they celebrate the start of their cruise in style. Celia would have been quite happy with a cup of Earl Grey.

'Have you decided what to wear tonight? We are at the captain's table, after all!' Beatrice squealed in delight.

Celia rolled her eyes, it was always the same with her, gush, gush, gush.

'I was thinking of my new pink taffeta dress. What about you?'

'My old grey suit,' stated Celia flatly.

'Celia! That thing? What about your floral dress, you know the one with the forget-me-nots on it?'

'Hmm, possibly.' There was no forgetting how much Beatrice grated on her nerves. Ever since they were small, little Bea had perpetually stolen the limelight with her effervescent charm. Celia had been the much older sister, the sensible one. Little Bea had blossomed into beautiful Bea, who had the pick of any man she wanted. Celia had remained a spinster. Then Beatrice had married a lord and become a lady, while Celia remained the dutiful daughter. Beatrice had gone on to have two healthy sons who adored their mother. Celia remained alone and childless. Now she was subjected to a retirement community, while her sister still played Lady of the Manor. Life was so cruelly unfair. But Beatrice was all she had, and she loved her nephews. Celia didn't like this resentment eating away at her. She knew she was fortunate to have Tobias' care, knowing how much the home cost. Even so, the unhappy truth was her lonely existence was killing her, slowly sapping her of life. Celia thought this cruise would buck her up, give her a boost, but in reality it was highlighting the stark contrasts yet again between her and Beatrice.

Chapter 45

Dylan was in high spirits. He was driving to Flora's. Together they were going to look at all the equipment needed for the new training yard. The list was endless, from hay nets, water buckets and saddle racks for the stables, to wheelbarrows, shovels and brushes for the yard. Also there was the tack to consider, bridles, reins and training aids, not to mention the grooming kit of clippers, hoof care, fly repellents and first aid. His head was buzzing with ideas, and he was keen to get on and get going. The fact that Flora was alongside him heightened his eagerness.

Flora, too, was keyed up. All night her mind had been racing with the task in hand. She was taking her new position very seriously. Dylan had shown her the plans for the yard and she'd seen first-hand the beginnings of it taking shape. It felt somewhat alien to listen to Dylan and Lord Cavendish-Blake discussing matters in front of her, as if she was their equal. She had to keep reminding herself that she was there on merit, because Dylan considered her worthy, which in itself was all the confidence she needed. Now and then she'd catch Dylan staring at her. She knew he was waiting for her to surrender to him, which made her more determined to keep the relationship strictly on a business level. Though she had to admit, it was hard; and he knew it. The way he'd leant over her when examining the plans, his chest pressed firmly against her back, his thighs touching the edge of her bottom, the way he sat next to her with his arm casually draped across the back of her shoulders... Occasionally his hand would catch her hair and swirl it round his fingers. He knew exactly what tactics to use and Flora hated herself for very nearly succumbing to them. He was too damned attractive for his own good, and hers, for that matter. She fully expected him to try to lure her into his home tonight on some pretext. Well, no, she wouldn't yield. Pre-empting the scenario, Flora had told him that she had to be back in good time, because she had a date.

'A date? Who with?' Dylan tried to sound casual, while inside he was burning.

'No one you know.' Flora, in turn, was at pains to sound equally nonchalant.

'No worries, I'll soon get you back safe and sound.' Like fuck he would. There was no way he was bringing her home early to spend the evening with some other bloke. And just who was he, anyway? Flora, without realising it, had played right into Dylan's hands. Instead of trying to avoid a situation, she had intensified it. Dylan was a born winner, refusing to lose anything or anyone he had decided was his.

He pulled up outside her house. Flora saw him through the window, grabbed her bag and left the house. 'All ready?' he smiled, those blue eyes twinkling with anticipation.

'Certainly am,' she beamed up at him. She looked so young and excited, he wanted to grab hold of her. Nobody had come close to making him act this way. Then it suddenly struck him: was she too young, too naïve for him? She was only twenty, while he was thirty. Was that too old? Then another brooding thought crossed his mind. How old was the guy she was supposed to be meeting tonight? Slamming the car into gear, he gripped the steering wheel and set off.

It took just over two hours to get there. Two large barns were packed to the rafters with every item they could possibly need, and it was hard to know where to start.

'We'll both make lists, then compare. You start here, I'll go next door,' instructed Dylan. He had switched to professional mode instantly.

Flora nodded and set off down the first aisle. Out of the corner of her eye she saw a couple of women turn to look in his direction, obviously recognising him. Dylan didn't notice, even though one of them deliberately crossed his path and smiled. He was clearly on a mission and oblivious to any attention. This surprised Flora, assuming he would never miss an opportunity. After an hour she had completed her list and set off to meet Dylan next door. He was there, assessing saddles. His face held a concentrated, studious look.

This was a side she'd not seen: the serious Dylan. Gone was the blasé playboy. She stood back and watched him some more. Again she saw one or two people double take when passing him, but still he was unaware. Then a little girl with her mum stopped and asked him for his autograph. Crouching down to her level he signed the pony-riding book she had just purchased, making her jump for joy. He ruffled her hair before they both thanked and left him. How sweet, thought Flora, and her heart began to warm, cracking the frozen solid ice protecting it.

Then he saw her, smiled and beckoned her over. 'What you got?' He looked across at the piece of paper with her scribbling on.

'Let's go for a drink.' She pointed towards the small coffee shop in the cobbled courtyard.

'Good idea.' He put his hand on her back and guided her out. It felt so natural, like they were a proper couple. But they weren't, Flora reprimanded herself, they were here on business.

Sitting opposite each other with coffees, Flora showed him her list. It was almost identical to the one Dylan had in his mind. She watched his eyes dart across the paper. Again, he looked intense. It was hard to imagine this was the same man who had appeared in a trashy kiss-and-tell newspaper article. He raised his head to look at her. 'This looks fine: more or less what I had in mind. Good girl.' He immediately cringed: did that sound patronising? Again his thoughts were darkened by the age gap between them.

'So, where are you going tonight?' Was she blushing?

'Er… not sure yet.'

He narrowed his eyes. Was she bluffing? In any event, she wouldn't be back in time, that was for sure.

Feeling scrutinised, Flora quickly changed the subject.

'What about the horse feed?'

'Already sourced that.'

'How many horses are we aiming to train?'

'At least ten, to start with. I've got a few contacts from Tobias, plus I've been approached by someone looking to train two horses.'

'Who?'

'Some businessman whose wife owns the horses. I've arranged to meet them this week.' Flora looked impressed. 'You have been busy.'

'I intend to make a success of this.' He looked straight at her. She could feel herself melting under his piercing blue gaze. Swallowing, she turned away. How was she going to cope working day in, day out with him? He was deliberately applying his charisma and they both knew it.

After another hour of finalising their list, Dylan set off to open an account and complete the order. Flora couldn't resist checking out the country clothing while Dylan was gone. Half an hour later and he returned with a broad smile. 'All done. It'll be delivered next week. Thanks for your help today.' Again his hand found her back and together they walked to his car. Flora looked at her watch. It was three o'clock. She should be back early evening. Dylan turned the key, but the engine wouldn't start. He tried again, still nothing. He turned to her, frowning.

'Why won't it start?' she asked.

'Not sure.' He turned the key once more, but there was no life in the engine. 'I'll have to ring for help.' He looked across at the pub on the roadside. 'Fancy going for a drink till they get here?'

'Yeah, sure.' She got out of the car whilst Dylan made the call on his mobile.

After two large white wines, Flora was beginning to unwind, letting her guard slip a little. She didn't mind Dylan resting his arm along the back of her shoulders as they sat huddled together in a dim, snug alcove. Dylan was on orange juice, but made sure Flora's glass was always full. He loved the way her cheeks flushed rosy with alcohol.

'Let's order something to eat,' he suggested, after hearing her stomach grumble. He went to the bar and collected two menus. Flora was starving and the wine was starting to take effect. They both opted for the steak and ale pie and settled down for another drink. Flora detected yet again one or two people turn to peek at Dylan.

'Don't you ever get sick of it?' She tilted her head to one woman openly staring.

He shrugged. 'I suppose it comes with the territory.'

'Especially if you're wearing Racer,' she giggled. He looked at her and smiled.

'It's good to hear you laugh again.' She stared back and for a moment their eyes locked. 'It's getting late.'

'Sorry?'

'Hadn't you better let him know?' Flora frowned. 'Your date?'

'Ah! Yes.' Fumbling for her phone she scrolled down to the first male name she came to – Ben. Then her hazy, fuddled brain told her to text him.

Sorry can't make tonight. Send, there done it.

Dylan watched carefully. So she hadn't been bluffing. Who the hell was Ben? A minute later there bleeped a response. Quickly hiding it from Dylan's sight, she turned to read the message:

?

But then her brother *would* wonder what she meant. Dylan huffed inwardly, frustrated at not being able to read her message.

'Everything OK?' He tried to sound concerned.

'Fine.'

'Good. I'll just check on the car, they should be here by now. You stay here, finish your drink.' He strolled to his car, reconnected the battery and drove it to the pub to collect Flora.

Chapter 46

'So you're leaving?' Finula asked, crestfallen. Megan's face creased with concern.

'Oh, but I'll still be a regular here at The Templar.' It hurt to see Finula's disappointed expression. 'I'll still help out, when I can,' she tried to appease.

'I doubt you'll have time. Sounds like you'll have your hands full working with Tobias.' Finula gave a sly grin and Megan chuckled.

'He does work at full pelt. He intends to have Treweham Hall opened in two weeks' time. Then there's the old stable block conversion well underway. The guy never stops.'

'Goes like a train, eh?' She gave Megan a nudge, making her blush.

Just on cue, Tobias walked through the pub door carrying a parcel. The two of them quickly smothered their giggles.

'Hi, Fin.' He put the parcel down on the bar and kissed Megan. 'I've a present for you, Miss Taylor.'

Megan's face lit up with surprise. 'For me? What is it?'

'Open it and find out.' Finula pushed the parcel nearer to her, eager to see its contents. Megan ripped open the brown paper to uncover a box. Taking the lid of it, she saw two stacks of postcards, her painting of Treweham Hall printed on them.

'Tobias! It's my painting, look.' She took a postcard out and passed it Finula.

'Cool! Look, they've even got your signature in the corner,' Finula cried.

'Oh, Tobias, they're wonderful.' Megan put her arms round his neck and kissed his cheek. Laughing he put his arm round her waist.

'So you like them, then?'

'I love them!'

'We'll be selling them in the gift shop. They'll make great souvenirs.'

Finula watched them. Her two good friends made a perfect couple. She was so pleased, for each of them; but when would it be her turn? Feeling a little awkward, she made an excuse to leave them alone.

'Megan, I'm going away for a few days.' Tobias suddenly looked quite serious. Her eyes searched his face.

'Why? Where are you going?'

'I'd rather not say at the moment, but I'll explain everything when I get back.'

The feeling of foreboding came creeping back like an old enemy. She withdrew from his hold.

'Megan, please.' He tried to take her hand, but she snatched it away.

'What's going on?' she asked quietly.

'Nothing to worry about, honestly,' he insisted. 'It's just for a few days, then I'll be back.' She looked at him, wounded and confused. It killed him to see her like this. 'Please, trust me.' He pulled her back into his arms and hugged her tightly.

*

Tracy had had a busy morning. Reading that magazine article had fired her imagination and she was on a mission to restore some purpose in her life. She had researched the nearest care homes in the area and volunteered her services, explaining that she had previously worked in a home and had all the necessary checks and paperwork in order. She had also contacted the manager from her former job and had arranged for a reference to be emailed. It felt strange talking to him, almost like another world, and in many ways it was.

'Hi, Tracy, nice to hear from you. How's things?'

How did she answer that? Well, winning millions, living in a Grade II listed house in the Cotswolds and having nothing to do but lunch and shop with other rich women hardly seemed appropriate.

'Fine, thanks, Alan. I'm applying for volunteer work in local care homes and would really appreciate a reference from you.'

'No problem. Good for you. I'm sure you'll be a great asset.' She was truly touched. A lump formed in her throat. In that instant she could easily have run back home, to normality, to where she belonged.

'How's Alf?' Her voice cracked with emotion.

'He passed away, Tracy, two weeks ago.' Tracy closed her eyes. There was a few seconds' silence. Swallowing, she thanked him again and said her goodbyes. Feeling more determined than ever now, she put the phone down and said a prayer for Alf.

*

'Come on, have a dip Celia. The water's fine!' Beatrice was sporting an aqua-blue swimsuit, matching the colour of the cruise liner's swimming pool. It looked wonderfully cool and refreshing against the relentless heat, but Celia refused, propped up in a deck chair reading Agatha Christie in her T-shirt, Bermuda shorts and Jesus sandals. 'It's so revitalising, you should try it!' called Beatrice again, wishing not for the first time that her sister would learn to let go and perk up.

'I said I'm fine as I am, thank you,' came the stilted reply from behind the cover of *And Then There Were None*. If only, thought Celia, wishing, not for the first time, her sister would learn to leave her in peace and calm down.

Her thoughts turned to the first night of the cruise. Beatrice, as usual, had soaked up all the attention thrown her way, chatting and laughing with the captain, who had made such a fuss of her. Well, he would, wouldn't he? It wasn't every evening he'd find himself sitting next to a titled lady. Then the way that brigadier chap had latched on to her, making her giggle like a schoolgirl. Not to mention how that Johnny foreigner, Carlos whatever-his-name was, had her jiving in the middle of the dance floor, making complete fools of themselves. Celia had seen it all, sitting at the dinner table, wearing her floral forget-me-not dress and a deadpan expression.

'She's great fun, your sister, isn't she?' gushed the captain.

'An absolute hoot,' replied Celia drily.

Then her sister couldn't fail but to attract attention playing deck shuffleboard, cheering others on and whooping with delight when she'd won. Typical. Beatrice always won. Celia had immersed herself in the newspaper. However, she did push the boat out one afternoon and attended an origami class, but soon found that tedious and somewhat pointless. Tonight was to be a theme night: 'Murder and Mystery'. Beatrice had chosen to be Lady Macbeth and planned to wear a long floaty dress with a silk cape and tiara. Whereas Celia had plumped for her tweed suit, thick tights and brogues, in an attempt to resemble Miss Marple.

'Oh, that's better!' Beatrice had emerged from the pool and was drying herself off. Droplets of water splashed Celia's book. Tutting, she wiped them away. 'Good book, dear?'

'Everyone gets killed off, one by one,' Celia informed her, her eyes never leaving the page.

'It's being so cheerful that keeps you going, Celia.'

Chapter 47

Dylan surveyed the mansion before pulling into the driveway. Whatever this businessman did, it paid well. It was a new build, flat roofed, with tall angular walls and great sheets of glass for windows. A balcony ran round the top half, giving panoramic views of the rolling countryside surrounding it. He could see the edge of a stable at the back and a swimming pool glistening in the sunshine. What a pad, he thought. More to the point, what potential clients to have. This man's pockets evidently ran deep. Dylan parked his car at the front and knocked on the wide, wooden door, which had a strip of glass running down the middle. He could make out a slim figure of a woman coming towards it. She pulled the heavy door open and smiled.

'Hello, you must be Dylan.'

They say first impressions count. Dylan took one look at the woman before him and sensed money, class and sex appeal. He returned the smile and held his hand out.

'Pleased to meet you, Mrs Tait.'

She shook it and purred, 'Please, call me Samantha.'

He clocked the huge diamond on her hand. Samantha Tait had long, thick dark hair that tumbled in ringlets past her shoulders. She wore a short, coral sundress with spaghetti straps, showcasing an ample cleavage and long legs, which Dylan's eyes homed in on like radar.

'Come through. I was just making coffee.' She led him through a vast open-plan lounge, all white sofas and glass tables, into the kitchen area, which had glossy white units and was clinically clean. A percolator was boiling with fresh-ground coffee. Samantha click-clacked her way over the tiled floor in sequined mules. 'How do you like it?' She stared at him. Dylan paused. 'Your coffee?' she added, with a playful grin. Was she flirting with him?

'Black, no sugar, thanks.'

She turned back to make the drinks. Dylan rested his gaze on her slender figure.

Passing his coffee over she explained, 'I'm afraid my husband's had to go away on business, last minute.' Dylan paused again: would this mean a wasted trip? 'But don't worry, I'm sure we can come to some agreement.' She eyed him up and down, making him a touch uncomfortable. Normally he would relish such an opportunity, but this was different: it was business, not pleasure. Then again, Samantha was extremely attractive and clearly in good shape, judging by her toned body and brown, silky skin. The wedding photographs dotted about the place told him she was much younger than her middle-aged husband. Dylan would put her at early thirties.

'Could I see your horses?' he asked, trying to sound as professional as he could.

'Certainly, this way.' She then led him out of the patio doors to the rear of the house. The garden stretched back for miles. The stables were newly built and housed three horses.

'Cleo I've had for years,' she said, pointing to the end stable. A black horse's head leant out of the door. 'These two we bought last year. We've recently moved from my husband's home town in Ireland,' Samantha continued, showing him inside the stable.

Dylan swiftly looked at the two chestnut horses and grasped immediately what thoroughbreds they were. He wanted to get a deal wrapped up quickly.

'I see. Who trained them?'

'Harvey Molloy.' Dylan nodded. Molloy was an arch rival of Sean Fox.

'They've definitely got potential. I can train them to peak performance,' he stated, facing her. Was that a smile playing round her lips?

'Yes, I believe peak performance is your forte.' Her eyes washed over his body and rested on his crotch. Dylan stood still, staring at her. He definitely wasn't going to make the first move. This was a prospective client, and a rich one at that. Any misunderstandings could prove disastrous. Samantha, however, made things quite clear. She moved closer to him. 'I head-hunted you.' He could feel her breath on his face. Still he remained silent. 'After I read that article, you wetted my appetite. Then that commercial showed me everything I needed to know. I knew you'd fit the bill.' Dylan's eyes shifted down, her breasts nestled big and firm in her dress; hard dark nipples poked against the fabric. She spoke seductively. 'I'd like you to train my horses,' Dylan's head jerked up, 'as long as we can reach an understanding.' Her tongue ran across her lips. Dylan looked at her. So he was going to have to tend to Samantha as well as the horses.

'I hear what you're saying,' he answered.

'Good. Shall we go inside and seal the deal?'

'Let's,' he smiled back.

He followed her back inside. She took him upstairs into her bedroom, where French doors opened out onto the balcony. A hot tub was bubbling away outside on the decking. Next to it was a table with champagne in an ice bucket and two accompanying glasses. She'd orchestrated the whole thing, Dylan realised.

'When is your husband back?' he asked.

'Not till tonight,' she replied. Dylan's shoulders relaxed. 'Let's celebrate with a drink.' She poured them each a glass of champagne. Dylan joined her out on the balcony and admired the view. Green velvet fields of all shades lay out before him. It was stunning.

'It's a beautiful place you've got here,' he remarked, turning to take his glass off her.

'Yes. My husband designed it. He's an architect.' And a very successful one concluded, Dylan.

She threw her head back and downed her champagne. Her eyes levelled with his, challenging. Dylan took a sip of his drink, his gaze never leaving her face. She pushed both straps down over her shoulders and slowly pulled her dress fully down to rest on her ankles. She was totally naked, her bronze, silken body was there for the taking.

'Now your turn, Dylan.'

Dylan gulped and swiftly undressed. Her eyes devoured his muscular, toned torso and jutting erection. She walked to the hot tub and lowered herself onto the ledge of the water. Dylan followed and slid in beside her. Immediately she sat astride him, her breasts pushed hard against his chest. Dylan stroked his hands along her thighs, as her lips plunged onto his. There was no tenderness, just a hard, urgent need. He suspected that middle-aged husband of hers wasn't meeting the necessary requirements. She crushed her hips impatiently against him. He sunk his swollen shaft into her, making her cry out and ride him up and down in a slow motion. His mouth moved to her nipples grazing his face, and she cried out again as he ran his tongue over them, sucking and tugging each one. Her hands ran through his black curls as he suckled her, then her hips moved backwards and forwards with urgency, and he could feel her tighten against his cock.

'I've fantasised about this,' she whispered. Dylan jolted his pelvis up, deeper into her, she dug her nails into his shoulders making him wince in pain. Then he released himself fully into her and she gave a gasp of relief. 'I knew it would be this good,' she said into his ear, delving her tongue inside.

Then there was a loud bang. They both froze.

'Sam! I'm home, sweetheart!' called a voice from downstairs.

'I thought you said he wasn't back till tonight,' rasped Dylan.

'He wasn't supposed to be!' she hissed back. Panic-stricken, she jumped out of the hot tub, gathered his clothes and flung them at Dylan, who had leapt out of the water to catch them. 'Turn left down the hall, take the stairs and go out the back. We'll meet you at the stables.' Dylan shot off. He heard Samantha shout down the hallway, 'Just upstairs, darling. Won't be long!'

Dylan dashed down the stairs, dressed and ran. Catching his breath, he went back into the stables. My God, that was a close shave. He cursed himself for very nearly losing a good client, not to mention risking the wrath of her husband.

A few minutes later they both arrived. The transformation in Samantha was unbelievable. Gone was the sexy sundress; now she wore jeans and a white shirt. Her hair was pinned up in a bun.

'Hello, pleased to meet you, Dylan.'

'And you, too, Mr Tait.' They both shook hands. 'These are beautiful horses you have here.' Dylan avoided Samantha and concentrated on her husband, who looked even older than his photograph in the flesh.

'Yes. I believe you have come to some arrangement with my wife?'

Dylan looked him in the eye and replied with a charming smile, 'Yes, I think we're both happy with the terms and conditions.'

Chapter 48

Tobias drove the rented Citroën 2CV through the country lanes of France. He could see the views of the wild, dramatic coastline and the bay with anchored boats. He was driving to a farmhouse situated near the shores of the Southern Coast of Brittany, where Carrie's parents lived. He had contacted them a few days ago and they had been delighted by his suggested visit. It had been a long time since they had seen him. Carrie's parents had moved to Brittany after the tragedy of losing their elder daughter. Desperate to make a new start, without the constant reminder of her in Treweham village, they had decided to sever all ties and relocate to another country. Lucy, their other daughter, was young enough to adapt and had craved the move as much as her parents had. Looking at the small, rocky shoreline, golden sand and turquoise sea, Tobias could see just why Carrie's mum and dad had chosen this area. The air was warm and salty rushing in through the car window. Tobias remembered the way to the farmhouse.

He'd visited them once before, when they had first moved here. Driving further down the coast, he longed to swim in the shimmering sea and wash away the pent-up anxiety that had been gradually building inside him. Flashbacks of Megan's bewildered face stung him. He hated having to be so secretive, but he had to stay focused and couldn't be distracted. He was doing the honourable thing, what any decent man would do. Once he had explained himself to her she would understand. His mind wandered to the previous night, which they'd spent together at Treweham Hall. It felt so right, having her there, her body entwined with his in his four-poster bed. It was empty without her soft skin touching his; *he* was empty without her.

It bothered him how she had reacted to his going away. He could see the betrayal in her eyes. But it wasn't disloyalty, it was a necessity, his coming here. He needed closure. Real closure. Tobias didn't want his future wedding being plastered all over the newspapers for Carrie's parents to read about. He needed to tell them first of his intention to marry. They deserved to hear it from him.

He had his welcome first sight of the farmhouse, its stone walls covered with wisteria, the pretty property surrounded by criss-crossing coastal paths. He parked the Citroën on the dusty driveway. Immediately Carrie's parents, Anna and Mark, came to greet him. 'Tobias! How lovely to see you.' Anna stretched her arms out to embrace him. Despite the cruel knock life had blown her, she was looking well, thought Tobias. The French country lifestyle clearly suited her, giving her a glowing honeyed complexion and highlights in her hair.

Mark shook his hand firmly. 'Good to see you, son.' He'd always called him that, and it comforted Tobias that he still did.

'Thanks for having me.'

'Not at all! Thank you for making the trip,' replied Anna, fussing him inside. Mark took out his suitcase and followed them into the house.

Tobias looked around him. It was just as he remembered: high ceilings and pebbled walls. A wood burner stood in the centre of the open-plan room and a balcony above led to the bedrooms. The kitchen was large, and a typical farmhouse table stood in the middle surrounded by mismatched wooden chairs.

'Take a seat, Tobias. I'll put the kettle on.'

Tobias noticed a framed photograph of Carrie standing on the sideboard. It had been taken a few days before the accident. He absorbed her smile, her long, dark hair, her brown eyes and button nose. Then the face in the picture transformed into Megan. He quickly shut his eyes.

'I thought I'd cook dinner tonight. There's a wonderful market town nearby that sells the most delicious seafood.'

'That sounds great, thanks, Anna.'

'You must be tired after all that travelling.' She passed him a cup of tea. 'I'll show you to your room.'

That evening, after an exquisite supper of *truite au vin jaune* and *crêpes Suzette*, which he learnt was one of Brittany's traditional meals – trout cooked in wine, and pancakes with orange and liqueur – Tobias decided now was the time. They had drunk two bottles of local red wine and were feeling relaxed.

'I've something to tell you both.' Anna and Mark looked at him smiling, encouraging him to continue. 'I've met someone. Her name's Megan and I intend to marry her.' There, he'd said it. Waiting for their response was torture.

Anna was the first to speak. 'Well, I'm very pleased for you, Tobias. It's about time.'

'Yes, we both want you to be happy, always have,' Mark added.

Tobias let out a sigh. The relief was enormous. Anna got up from the table and took two photographs from the kitchen windowsill. She gave one to Tobias to look at. He took it and smiled. It was of Lucy, Carrie's sister. She made a striking bride, joined by a handsome, dark-haired groom.

'She's grown into a beauty, hasn't she? When did she get married?'

'A year ago, married a local boy.' Then Anna passed him the second photograph. It was of a newborn baby, looking the image of the dark-haired groom. 'This is François, our grandson.'

Tobias beamed. 'Congratulations, you must be very proud,' he said, looking to Anna, then Mark.

Mark nodded. 'We are.'

Then Anna added, putting her hand over Tobias', 'It's time to move on, Tobias. Even we've carved out a life for ourselves. Being here, in France, with Lucy, Jean-Pierre and François. We've all to live our lives the best way we can.'

Tobias' eyes filled, he swallowed and looked down.

'Never feel guilty for finding happiness, son,' Mark spoke quietly.

'Thank you,' gulped Tobias.

Chapter 49

'Flora, the order's arrived.' Dylan was swamped with all the equipment they'd purchased. 'I could do with a hand shifting some of it.' He intended to move as much of it as possible to the new stable yard. Half of the stables were built now, plus his office, so he planned to store most of it there.

'OK. I'm out at the moment. I'll be at yours for six-ish.'

Out where? He felt compelled to demand, and who with? Instead he bit his tongue.

'Right, see you then.' Probably off gallivanting with bloody Ben, he fumed. He kicked a water bucket down his drive in frustration. He'd received two text messages from Samantha. One asking for a date to move the horses, the other wanting to know when they would be meeting up. He was beginning to imagine he'd have his hands full with Samantha, quite literally. The woman was blatantly starved of action and craved as good a ride as her horses. Dylan had started to have second thoughts about the whole thing, but then he remembered just how much her husband was prepared to pay him for training his two thoroughbreds. It wasn't to be sniffed at, plus he was eager to get his stables fully occupied. He'd arranged a provisional date to collect the horses and avoided the second question. Luckily she hadn't pressed him.

Flora had gone into town to the chemists. She had a banging headache and was in dire need of some tablets. Bending over to pick up the packet of paracetamol she saw blackness closing in and came over a little dizzy. Blinking, she steadied herself and paid for them. As she drove home the bright light of the sun shining in her face made her wince in pain. She managed to make it back, just. Once inside, she rushed to the kitchen to pour a glass of water and swallow two tablets. After half an hour she felt marginally better, although a fine film of sweat covered her body. Deciding to skip supper, she went to have a quick shower to freshen up. In the shower her headache came back with vengeance. A nauseating sensation overcame her. She got out of the pounding water that had been battering her head and wrapped herself in a towel. Slowly making her way into the kitchen for another paracetamol, lights started flashing across her eyes. Flora dashed to the sink and only just made it, vomiting the entire contents of her stomach. She was now perspiring and shaking badly. Reaching for her phone on the kitchen table, she managed to press Dylan's number before passing out.

'Flora? Flora, are you there?'

There was no answer. Dylan frowned. Where was she? He looked at his watch. She was late. He picked up his car keys and drove to her house. He rang the front doorbell. No reply. He went round the back and hammered on the back door. Still nothing. He looked through the kitchen window and saw Flora slumped over the table in a towel. 'Flora!' he shouted, rushing back to the door. Turning the handle he realised it was locked. With adrenaline pumping through his veins he pushed hard again and again at the door, but it wouldn't budge. In the end he elbowed the glass partition and put his hand through to unlock the door from inside. He cut his palm slightly turning the key. His heart was thumping wildly. 'Flora!' he cried again rushing to her. He picked her body up from the table. She started to rouse slightly. He manoeuvred her onto the kitchen chair, holding her shoulders.

'Flora, talk to me, it's Dylan,' he spoke urgently. Her skin was red hot. She half opened her eyes. 'Flora, can you hear me?'

'Sick,' she murmured. Dylan hastily fetched the washing up bowl from the sink and placed it before her. She bent her head into it and vomited again. Dylan tried to think straight. His immediate reaction was to ring an ambulance, but as Flora finished throwing up, she seemed to be gaining consciousness. He stood behind her, holding her forehead and shoulders. Slowly she eased herself back into an upright position. 'I… I think I fainted.'

'You did. I saw you out cold over the kitchen table.' Dylan put his arm round her. 'Let's get you into bed, you're shivering.' He carried her up the stairs. Flora was oblivious to the towel slipping further down her body, exposing most of her chest. Dylan tried to concentrate and averted his eyes. 'Which one's your bedroom?'

'First on the left,' she answered faintly. He placed her gently on the unmade bed and carefully covered her with the duvet, again at pains not to run his gaze over her now bare body. He plumped up the two pillows and rested them behind her head.

'How are you feeling now, Flora?' His face was etched with concern.

'Better for throwing up, I think.' She looked so utterly vulnerable, almost like a child. Dylan swallowed hard. He so wanted to look after her.

'Can I get you anything?'

'A drink of water, please.'

'Will do.' He shot off downstairs into the kitchen and hurried back. 'Here, let me help you.' He held the glass to her lips and watched her gulp it back. 'I think you're dehydrated. Drink some more.' She did as she was told, then rested back onto the pillows, bleary eyed. 'Flora, I'm staying here with you tonight.'

Expecting her to object, he was startled when her eyes filled.

'I want…' Her chin wobbled slightly. He stopped and stared at her. If she said Ben he'd be gutted.

'Who do you want, Flora?' he asked quietly.

'My mum,' she whimpered. Kneeling down next to her he stroked back her hair.

'Shall I ring her for you?'

'No,' she finally replied, 'they'd only worry.'

'Sure?'

'Yes. I just need to rest.' Her eyes started to close.

'I'll be right here.' Dylan went into the next bedroom to collect pillows and a duvet. He was going to sleep on the floor next to her. Entering the room he saw a single bed with blue football bedding. Various posters hung from the walls: a New York City skyline, Oasis and Red Hot Chili Peppers. There was a notice board displaying a collage of photographs of a teenage boy with long hair, sporting a hoody, sticking two fingers up at the camera with his mates. Dylan also clocked the sign on the door: 'Ben's Room'. Hmm, interesting, he thought wryly.

He entered Flora's bedroom and laid the pillows and duvet on the floor next to her bed. She was fast asleep. He looked down at her, so pale and angelic, ethereal like. His chest tightened with the image of her slumped over the kitchen table. For a moment he had thought she was dead. The thought made him cold. He bent down to hear her breathing faintly and watched her chest slightly rising and falling. Flora, his feisty, stubborn, angelic creature.

He turned out the light and settled down on the floor. Unable to sleep, his eyes adjusted to the dark and flicked round the room. It was full of horsy paraphernalia: pictures, photos, rosettes, trophies, certificates, all documenting her achievements and love of horses. His room had been the same years ago, when he was her age. The age gap once again troubled him. Was he being selfish wanting someone so young? Would she be better enjoying herself with other twenty-year-olds, instead of holding a responsible position with a thirty-year-old lusting after her?

His phone bleeped in his pocket. Digging it out of his jeans, he saw Samantha's name flash up. Oh no. His eyes widened at the text message.

Hungry for cock.

Jesus, what had he started? He had to think of some way to deter her. Flora stirred.

'Dylan? Is that your phone?' she croaked.

'Yes,' he whispered, 'just some random message from my brother. I think he's pissed.' Two can play at that game, he thought.

'Dylan?'

'Yes?'

'I need the loo.'

'Oh. Right.'

'My nightie's in the top drawer.' He got up and put the bedside light on. Dylan took out her nightshirt and placed it over her head, then helped her to put it on. His hands touched her skin. She had cooled down, thank God. He carried her to the bathroom and assisted her. 'Sorry, I feel so useless,' she spoke weakly. He hoped she wasn't embarrassed.

'Don't be silly, Flora. You're unwell. I'm ringing for the doctor in the morning.'

Flora didn't argue, she was just so glad he was there.

The next morning the doctor examined her. He recommended plenty of fluids and rest, suspecting she had picked up a virus that had been prevalent in the village. Dylan was reassured to hear it, fearing it may have been a far worse scenario, which got him thinking. He was going to set up private medical insurance for Flora. He'd cover the cost – he was her employer now and he ought to make sure she was covered. He watched her again, on the sofa now, tucked up with a hot-water bottle and blanket. Her hair was greasy and ruffled, her complexion translucent white, black shadows surrounded her eyes and Dylan realised at that moment he'd never cared for anyone more.

Chapter 50

Tobias had thoroughly enjoyed his time in Brittany. Having a couple of days to chill out was just the tonic he needed whilst all the work at Treweham Hall was in progress. It was good to spend time with Anna and Mark and see how well they had adapted to their life in France. He was so pleased they were now grandparents. Their happiness endorsed his. Any misgivings he may have had were well and truly gone. Now all he wanted to do was to get back home – home to Megan. He deliberately chose not to contact her whilst away. It didn't seem right whilst he was staying with Carrie's parents. Not only that, he didn't want to have to explain himself over the phone. He had to make her understand face to face. The weather had turned. The red-hot sun had vanished, to be replaced by a black, thunderous sky. The rain started to lash down on his drive to the airport. His impatience to get home grew as, entering the terminal, he learnt his flight had been delayed.

*

Megan woke with a queasy sensation in her stomach. She hadn't been feeling her best over the past few days. Little wonder, she thought, seeing as how Tobias had basically abandoned her. The seeds of resentment had taken root and had gradually started to grow. It was one thing being so cloak-and-dagger and disappearing without an explanation, but to not even get in touch? How dare he treat her like that? One minute he was all over her like a rash, the next he'd done a runner! The more she thought about it, the angrier she became. She momentarily retched, then calmed herself down. It couldn't be doing her any good to get so worked up. But *where* the hell was he? A sinister, menacing thought crept into her overactive mind: *who* was he with? Megan wasn't due to start work at The Templar until late morning, which was just as well, considering how long it took her to compose herself and get ready. The nausea kept hitting her in small waves, slowing her down. When she eventually trundled into The Templar Finula took one look at her and commented on how terrible she looked. 'Thanks,' was all Megan could muster in response.

Mid-afternoon, they both settled at the bar for a coffee break. Megan once more gagged over the cappuccino steaming her face. 'You OK? You've gone awfully pale, Megan?' Finula noticed the bags under her eyes.

'No. I've been feeling sick all morning.'

'I think there's a virus flying round the village. It's probably that.'

'Probably.'

Finula hesitated, then went for it. 'Heard from Tobias yet?'

Megan heaved a sigh and slammed her coffee down. Ignoring the spillage on the bar she rasped, 'Not a damn word. What's he playing at, Fin?' Her eyes sought Finula's face for an answer.

'Oh, Megan, don't worry. I'm sure he's got a perfectly good explanation,' she tried to sooth.

'But not to even contact me?' Megan's voice cracked and tears swelled her eyes. Finula tilted her head to one side. Wasn't this a little out of character for Megan? Was her friend overreacting just a touch? After all, Tobias had only been gone three days ago.

'He'll be back soon.' She patted her shoulder in an attempt to comfort her. 'And the last thing he'll want to come home to is a cry baby,' she softly joked.

Cry baby. Megan froze. It suddenly hit her like a thunderbolt: her period was late. Frantically racking her brain, she calculated it was by about a week. That wasn't something to cause concern, was it? Anyone could be a little late at times. But never her. She'd always been as regular as clockwork.

'What's the matter?' Finula stared at her panic-stricken face.

'Fin, I'm a week late,' she whispered hoarsely.

'Sorry?'

'My period. I'm a week late.' There was an awkward pause.

'But surely you've used precaution?'

'Yes, of course! Well, most of the time,' cried Megan, beginning to feel hysteria rising inside her. 'The sickness... oh my God...' She put her head in her hands. The tears started to fall freely now. Finula jumped off the bar stool and hugged her.

'Shush, Megan, it'll all be all right, I promise. Listen, if it helps, take the rest of the day off.'

'Thanks,' Megan said in a strangled voice, taking deep breaths. She intended to drive into town and buy a pregnancy testing kit.

*

Tobias' plane finally landed at ten o'clock that evening. He was tired, but still desperately anxious to see Megan. The weather was even worse in England with the heavy rain pelting down and the rumble of thunder echoing in the distance. Tobias drove at full speed to get back, whilst the relentless downpour whipped against his windscreen. The car ate up the miles and by twelve thirty he was entering Treweham village. Not even bothering to go home first, he drove straight to Megan's. He leapt out of the car and ran to the front door, hammering on it impatiently. Megan was wide awake. Sleep was impossible. She knew it was Tobias at the door, having spotted him though the bedroom window. Well, tough, he could wait in the rain and all night, for all she cared. The knocking got louder. She delved under her duvet, wanting to shut out the world. Then she heard his voice, it was now coming from outside the back door.

'Open the door, Megan!' He knew she was in. The light in her bedroom had been on. 'Megan!' he blasted.

Cursing under her breath she threw back the covers and marched downstairs into the kitchen.

'Open this door, Megan, or I'll break the bloody thing down.' He could see her through the kitchen window. She could just make out his silhouette in the darkness and pouring rain. Megan believed him. He would break her door down, so reluctantly she opened it. He stood in the doorway, rain dripping off him. He took her breath away; his hair was wet through and his green eyes blazed. Despite her anger, there was no denying how her heart had jumped at the sight of him.

He barged into the kitchen and turned on her. 'Why weren't you answering the door?'

'It's late,' she feebly answered, avoiding his intense stare.

'What's wrong?' His face looked genuinely confused. Megan lost it.

'What's wrong! You've been gone for days, without bothering to contact me and you ask what's wrong!'

Tobias closed his eyes and sighed. His shoulders relaxed. 'Megan, sit down. Let me explain.' He led her to the kitchen table and sat her down. 'I've been in France.'

'France?' Megan's head shot up. 'Why?'

'I went to see Carrie's parents. They moved there after the accident.' Megan stared at him baffled, waiting for him to continue. 'I had to tell them that I've fallen hopelessly in love with the girl next door and intend to marry her. The last thing I wanted was for them to read about our wedding in the paper. They deserve prior notice. I owe them that.'

Megan blinked; her mouth was wide open. Had she just heard him right? Tobias grinned. 'Say something, Megan.'

'But... you never said...'

'*Surely* you must know how I feel about you?' His eyes bored into hers. She had to tell him.

'But... I... I'm...'

Tobias looked searchingly at her. 'You're what? Surprised? Disappointed? Give me a clue.' She could hear the frustration in his voice. Oh God. She just went for it.

'Tobias, I'm pregnant.'

'Pregnant?' Now it was his turn to look shocked. Realisation finally sunk in. He got up and wrapped his arms round her. 'Megan, that's wonderful news,' he whispered in her ear. She pulled back to look at him with tears in her eyes. 'Tell me you're delighted, too.' He searched her face.

'I've only just found out, this afternoon, in fact.'

'Marry me, Megan.' It was more of a command than a proposal.

'Yes, Tobias,' she laughed in between tears, 'I will,' and she threw her arms round him.

They both slept like babies that night, entwined in each other's body, safe in the knowledge all was well, safe in the comfort of their love for each other. All the pent-up emotion they had both experienced had finally released, leaving a heart-warming glow burning inside. They had made tender love, relishing the touch, smell and taste of each other. Afterwards they had held together tightly, never wanting to let go.

In the early hours of the morning Tobias stirred, immediately comforted by the warmth of Megan's body lying next to his. He'd not felt this happy in a long, long time. He gently stroked her stomach, elated, knowing his offspring was growing there. She opened her eyes and smiled at him.

'Thank you,' he said gently.

'For what?'

'Everything,' he answered, and kissed her lovingly.

Chapter 51

It was the last day of the cruise. Tomorrow she would be back in her own room, in her own bed, Celia thought with mixed emotions. Whilst deep down she was a bit of a home bird, this cruise had taught her one or two lessons in life she might otherwise not have learnt. The Murder and Mystery night had not been the dreary, monotonous evening she had fully expected. Instead, to her surprise, she had found herself quite enjoying the varied and intriguing costumes the cruisers had worn, inviting interesting conversation. For once, Beatrice had not been the centre of attention. Everyone had mingled together well, each with a story to tell about who they were impersonating and why. One older gentleman, dressed as Hercule Poirot, tentatively approached Celia. She immediately recognised his character and couldn't help but smile; the first time she had done since boarding the *Jewel of the Ocean*. This encouraged him to ask her, 'It's Miss Marple, isn't it?' Celia chortled and was thrilled someone had actually guessed before having to be told like everyone else.

'It certainly is, Hercule Poirot.' He beamed back and his false moustache almost fell off, making them both giggle like hyenas.

'I notice you've been reading one of my favourite Agatha Christie novels.' Had he really? She hadn't noticed him.

'Yes, it never fails to grip me.'

'Absolutely. Although my all-time favourite is—'

'*The Seven Dials Mystery*,' they both said at the same time, causing more giggles. How did she know he'd have the same favourite as her?

'Yes!' he cheered.

'Christie was a genius,' agreed Celia.

'By the way, my real name is Wilfrid.' He held his hand out.

'Celia,' she replied with a firm shake.

Wilfrid had asked if Celia had ever been to the Agatha Christie Festival which was held in Christie's home town of Torquay, but no, she'd never heard of it.

'Oh, it's wonderful, Celia! Last year a local historian led a dawn walk to Christie's former holiday home, Greenway House and garden. It was magical.' Celia pictured Wilfrid trailing through a splendid, colourful garden wearing a panama; she saw him brushing his fingers over a French-polished desk, overlooking peaceful water, where the lady herself scribbled out the criminal mastermind makings of her intellect. An overwhelming desire to be there with him came over her. It was a strange sensation, not one that she had ever encountered.

As if he could sense her longing he continued, 'Celia, I would love to show you Greenway. You must experience it.' Celia saw Beatrice out of the corner of her eye, laughing with the captain, who was dressed as Dick Barton in a trilby hat and overcoat. Occasionally she would place her hand on his arm as she spoke and he straightened her lopsided tiara affectionately with both hands. The brigadier was standing by, totally surplus to requirements, sipping sherry with a vacant expression. He wore what Celia assumed was his old army uniform, but was clueless as to who he was supposed to be.

'Yes, Wilfrid, I do believe I must.' She *would* go to Torquay. She *would* enjoy wandering round Greenway House with Wilfrid. Why not?

'That's just marvellous!' Wilfrid's face lit up like a Christmas tree in a way that made Celia realise what she'd been missing.

The rest of the evening had gone in a blur. It transpired Wilfrid and Celia had quite a bit in common besides their choice of reading. They both loved classical music, cats and the great outdoors. 'I was Scout Master for almost thirty years,' Wilfrid looked wistfully into the distance, mentally reminiscing many camping ventures.

'I prefer to ramble alone,' Celia told him.

'Don't you just!' chipped in Beatrice, who had suddenly appeared on the scene. Not waiting to be introduced, she plonked herself in front of Wilfrid.

'I'm Lady Macbeth,' she announced rather dramatically with a snort. She was tipsy, again, noted Celia.

Wilfrid looked rather uncomfortable. 'Oh… that's who you are…' he said, not sounding at all interested. Celia's mouth twitched. Beatrice moved on.

'My sister, Beatrice. I'm afraid she's a touch drunk,' she explained.

'How awful for you, Celia,' he replied with concern.

So, all in all, Celia's cruise had ended on a positive note. She and Wilfrid had exchanged contact details, along with the promise to write and arrange a trip to Torquay.

As she was just leaving her cabin, she heard him call her name. 'Celia! Celia!' His cheeks were red from exhaustion and he puffed, out of breath, in his effort to catch her before she left the ship. 'Look, this is for you.' He held out a book. It was *The Seven Dials Mystery* with the original cover. 'Please, it's yours. I bought it years ago. It's a first edition and I take it with me everywhere I go.'

'Wilfrid, I can't possibly…'

He shook his head vehemently. 'I insist. Please. I want you to have it.' She could see his mind was made up. There was no persuading him otherwise.

'Well, thank you so much, Wilfrid. I shall treasure it.' She took the book and held it lovingly to her bosom.

'Write soon?' he asked.

'I will. Promise.'

*

Tracy, too, had had an enjoyable experience. In fact, she'd had a ball. As soon as she had entered the nursing home an overwhelming calmness had descended upon her. She understood how the faint tinge of disinfectant and subdued stillness could discourage some, but to her it was a reminder of an environment she felt most comfortable in. Here she could make a difference; she was relevant. Her bubbly character and willingness had made her popular, not only with the residents, but the staff too. They didn't question her choice to work voluntarily, they just appreciated the help.

Tracy had got chatting to Ted, who informed her where he had lived in Treweham village.

'Oh, those cottages are so cute!' Tracy had cooed. 'So you must know Megan?'

'I do that,' he chuckled to himself.

'What do you think of Lord Cavendish-Blake?' she couldn't resist asking, never having really been able to suss out this dark, brooding character who galloped about his estate.

'Grand chap. His family are salt of the earth.' Tracy nodded, trying to understand how such nice people like Ted, Megan, Finula and Dylan all seemed to like Lord Cavendish-Blake, when to her he cut a rather elusive figure.

'You seem happy enough here, Ted. Don't you ever miss living in your cottage?'

'I miss Zac, my dog, but Megan brings him here to visit.'

'Oh, Zac's lovely!'

'Isn't he just,' replied Ted, smiling.

Tracy had walked home with a spring in her step. For the first time in ages she had felt needed. When she had tried to explain this to Gary at tea time he had looked offended. 'But I need you, Trace,' he told her with a mouthful of bread.

'But it's a different need, Gary. You know, just like your shooting club needs you,' she joked. He smiled, understanding the irony.

'OK, I get it. But does it matter, as long as we're both happy here?'

'Absolutely not.'

Chapter 52

'Dylan, stop fussing, I'm fine!' Flora was beginning to tire of him hovering around her the whole time. It had been two days now since he had found her collapsed over the kitchen table and at last colour was starting to show in her cheeks. She had felt so much better after having soaked in a luxurious hot, bubble bath he had prepared for her. She had declined the offer of his assisting her in it and washing her back. Instead he had patiently waited outside the bathroom, sitting on the top stair, and chatted to her. It was endearing the way he had been so attentive, but as her strength was beginning to return she found him getting under her feet. Flora didn't want to seem ungrateful, realising how lucky she'd been that he'd found her and was looking after her, but he'd turned into a lap dog. Flora hadn't lifted a finger. He was forever there, fetching, carrying, plumping up cushions, making drinks and preparing meals.

He'd surprised her with what a good cook he was. Even though she didn't have much of an appetite, Dylan made sure she ate something nutritious every day.

'You're actually quite domesticated, aren't you?' she remarked as he came through to the lounge carrying a tray with their lunch on.

'I believe in looking after oneself,' he replied, putting the tray down on the coffee table. Flora sat up from lying on the sofa and he handed her a plate of spaghetti carbonara. 'Here, this will build up your strength.'

'Thanks.' She looked at him. 'Dylan, you don't need to sleep on the floor in my room, you know.' His head shot up: was this the green light he'd been waiting for? 'Honestly, you can go back home now. I'll be OK.'

'Not just yet. It would be irresponsible of me to leave you.'

Even though his back was killing him from the hard floor boards, he didn't want to go. He enjoyed being there, around her. She made him laugh. Yesterday they had watched DVDs together, huddled on the sofa drinking Cup-a-Soups. They shared the same sense of humour. At one point when they were watching TV his Racer commercial appeared, making them both howl with laughter. The thought of going home to an empty house was a depressing one. He felt completely himself with Flora. He could relax and just *be*. She didn't hound him (unlike Samantha, who had text him again). She didn't expect anything from him. Truth be told, he needed her, not just her sweet body he had spied on through the bathroom door last night, but all of Flora. She was a kindred spirit, they were so... *in tune.* Then his phone bleeped again.

'Is that yours?' Flora asked between mouthfuls of carbonara.

'Yep.' He tried to sound casual, knowing full well what was waiting for him.

'Hadn't you better get it?'

'Suppose so.' He reached inside his jeans pocket and braced himself.

Still waiting for monster cock.

Dylan closed his eyes. Right, this needed nipping in the bud. He was going to put a stop to it.

'Everything all right?' Flora was watching him.

'Yes, it's my agent. He wants to see me urgently. I'd better eat this and get going. Will you be OK for a few hours?'

'Of course I will.' Dylan hesitated. 'Honestly, I'll be fine,' insisted Flora.

Within the hour Dylan was parking outside the Taits' mansion.

Samantha greeted him immediately, looking seductive in another flimsy dress. He took a deep breath and walked inside the hallway. A Norah Jones

CD was playing in the background; he could see champagne in an ice bucket on the kitchen worktop.

'Relax, Dylan.' She'd crept up behind him and was rubbing his shoulders. 'My husband's in Ireland for the next few days, so we won't be disturbed this time,' she laughed softly in his ear.

Dylan clenched his jaw. Her nails were long, pointed and painted a vile purple colour. His flesh was still recovering from when they had pierced into him. Her hands moved from his shoulders, down his back, to his hips, then slowly wandered round to the front of his waist. She unbuttoned his jeans. Dylan went numb, literally. Those roving hands with the vile purple nails fumbled inside. Still Dylan felt nothing. Zilch. Samantha paused for a moment. Then she started to kiss his neck. He could smell her perfume, its strong, potent aroma making his eyes water. Her lips felt dry and crisp, not full and moist like Flora's. *Flora.* He resisted the urge to fling Samantha off him. He had to play this right. She was a paying client, after all. A lot of money was at stake here. Her tongue curled inside his ear, making him cringe; it was hard and intruding. Again her fingers endeavoured to wrap round him, but he was limp, lifeless. Dylan was concentrating hard, but in all honesty it wasn't difficult. He genuinely did not find Samantha attractive any more. Not in the least. If anything, she now appeared desperate, dishonest and dirty. His skin was beginning to crawl under her touch.

She let out an impatient sigh. 'What's the matter, Dylan? It wasn't like this before.'

He turned to face her. 'I'm sorry. It's a problem I have.'

Her eyes widened, 'A problem?'

'I'm afraid I'm not the man you thought I was.'

'But... but... you're a playboy, a—'

'Hype,' interrupted Dylan.

'Pardon?'

'It's all hype, publicity. The article, the commercial, it's just public relations. I blame my agent.'

'You mean... you're impotent?'

'At times,' he reasoned. After all, he had actually shagged her in the hot tub whilst her husband was downstairs. 'It's not you, Samantha, it's me,' he finished, trying to look as sorrowful as possible. It worked.

'Right, well... perhaps you'd better go,' she mumbled. As he was leaving she called to him, 'And, Dylan!'

'Yes?' He turned to look at her.

'Not a word of this to my husband. Or anyone else, for that matter. Do you understand?'

'Of course.' He closed the door behind him and gave a huge sigh of relief. He drove home with the windows down, the air brushing through his dark curls, the music at full volume and a wide smile on his face. He'd done it! He got the demanding Samantha off his back whilst still keeping her as a client. He felt buoyant, elated as he entered Flora's house. She was asleep in the armchair. A book lay discarded by her lap. Picking it up, he smiled. it was *Black Beauty*. She'd told him it was her childhood favourite. He examined her peaceful face in slumber and marvelled at her fair, smooth complexion, full red lips and pale eyelashes. He bent down and kissed her cheek, he couldn't help it. She stirred a little.

'Shush,' he gently whispered and stroked her hair. He couldn't leave her. He didn't want to go home alone.

That evening he made them a roast chicken dinner with piles of vegetables. 'I'll never eat this, Dylan.' Flora gazed at the plate in front of her. They were sitting at the kitchen table.

'Try. It's all good for you.'

'You sound like my dad,' she laughed. Dylan didn't.

'Do you think I'm old, Flora?'

She laughed again. 'No! At thirty? I was only joking.'

Dylan's eyes narrowed, deep in thought.

'Flora, I've been thinking. Why don't you come back to mine for a few days, just until you're fully recovered?'

'Your house?'

'Yes. At least there I can get a decent night's sleep. Not that I mind sleeping on your bedroom floor,' he quickly added. He could see she was mulling it over. 'You'll have your own room, promise.' His blue eyes twinkled with mischief. Her heartstrings started to pull; he really was a lovable rogue.

'I'm not sure…' She was stalling and they both knew it. Dylan pushed further.

'That way I could get all the equipment sorted.'

'Sorry, Dylan, I've been holding things up, haven't I?'

'Don't be silly, you can't help being ill.'

Feeling slightly guilty Flora relented. 'Yes, I'll come back with you.'

'Good, that's settled then.' Tactics worked; and bollocks to the separate rooms.

Chapter 53

'Tobias it's exquisite,' gasped Megan as she opened the small black velvet box.

'It was my great-grandmother's,' he replied, enjoying her response at the sight of the diamond cluster halo ring set in rose gold. 'Here, let me put it on.' He took the ring from the box and placed it on Megan's finger. A perfect fit.

'So now it's official,' she said, a wave of apprehension hitting her as she contemplated what was to follow. Tobias was to announce their engagement to the press next week, once all their family members were notified. His mother and aunt had been told, as had Sebastian, who all had taken the news with pleasant surprise. Megan's parents were shocked, but had been reassured when realising how happy their daughter evidently was. Tobias and Megan had decided not to mention the pregnancy just yet. Keeping that secret between themselves made it special. Tobias had teased her that the Lord of the Manor would only have married a pregnant bride in days of yore, to ascertain his heir.

Megan had rolled her eyes. 'Charming,' she stated flatly. Then her thoughts turned. 'Tobias, it must have happened the first time. You've always been so careful otherwise.'

He looked her full in the face. The thought had crossed his mind, too.

'These things happen, Megan. It was obviously meant to be.' He didn't regret it. He couldn't. It was all he wanted. 'How are you feeling now?' He scanned her face for some form of assurance.

'Much better. The shock's worn off. It seems the most natural thing in the world now.'

'Good,' he replied, kissing her lips.

Megan wrapped her arms round his neck. Everything felt so right, she couldn't be happier.

Chapter 54

An uneasy intuition started to grow as he passed through the village lanes lined with green foliage. Through the open car window he smelt the winter wheat being cut in the fields. He observed a row of cottages through the windscreen and had a distinct feeling of *déjà vu*. Reading the signpost, it all became clear. Treweham. He was in the village where he and Megan had visited her gran.

'What's the name of the place we're staying again?'

'The Templar,' she answered, squinting, trying to read the sat nav for directions.

Adam's thoughts turned to Megan, making him shift uncomfortably. She had left under a cloud, never returning to the office. Everybody had sussed out why, apart from the senior partners he was answerable to; he'd made sure of that. His fling with Moneypenny hadn't lasted long. Once everyone knew what was going on, their dalliance proved to be more of an embarrassment, a far cry from the daring, exciting liaison it had started as. Plus the fact she had a stropping, six-foot boyfriend the size of a brick outhouse didn't help matters. In the end Kay, Fay or

May (he still couldn't remember) had resigned and a new secretary had taken her place. Jennifer.

Jennifer was quiet and conscientious. She was what he had described as 'reasonably attractive' to his mates, with her short, brown hair and trendy glasses. Jennifer was exceptionally good at her job, which made his life a whole lot easier. It was all very well taking Moneypenny over his desk, behind the filing cabinets and in the stationery store, but even he conceded *some* work had to be done. His new secretary's super efficiency and eagerness to take on more work meant he had more time to himself. Instead of his evening poring over files whilst eating takeaway meals, he watched TV, went out with his mates, played football and enjoyed corporate events laid on by the firm. Jennifer was forever there, in the office tending to his every need. Well, almost every need. At first he thought she might be a lesbian. Why else would she ignore his subtle flirting? The lack of apparent interest increased his. It had been some time since a girl had played hard to get with him. It had been a challenge. Then after three months of sharing the same office, nine to five, five days a week, he had made a breakthrough. It was whilst she had been busy typing away at her computer, squinting at the report of legal acts and legislation in front of her that he had seized the moment.

'Jennifer, have I been overworking you?' Her face looked up from the printed sheets.

'No,' she said simply, and carried on typing.

'You look tired. I blame myself. Jennifer, please stop typing.' The irritation in his voice was enough to make her cease tapping away and give him her full attention. 'Why don't you let me take you out for lunch?' he asked in a softer tone, accompanied with a winning smile.

'Because you never ask me,' she answered matter-of-factly. She had taken the question literally. Adam chewed his bottom lip. He'd never experienced someone quite like her. She was unusual, kind of quirky, the way she looked at things so black and white.

'Well, I'm asking you now.' He cocked his head to one side. Jennifer nodded.

'Then, yes.' She lowered her eyes back to the report and carried on typing. The conversation was apparently over. Jennifer's idiosyncrasy kept Adam on his toes because he never quite knew how to read her. Taking her for granted was out of the question, for he wasn't entirely certain if he had won her over in the first place.

Lunch had been an interesting affair. Entering the Italian restaurant, he had been amazed at how many people she had known, politely nodding and saying hello to various tables. Even the staff had asked if she had wanted her usual tale. Curiosity getting the better of him, Adam enquired of her apparent popularity.

'Daddy's clients,' she supplied, reading the menu.

'What does... Daddy do?'

'Lots of things. Mainly real estate.'

'I see,' Adam replied, his brain ticking into overdrive. Then the penny dropped. Jennifer Goldsmith. She was the daughter of Clifford Goldsmith, business tycoon. Settling into his chair, he smugly surveyed the wine list. Well, this had been worth persevering, hadn't it?

From then on Adam played it carefully. Understanding how Jennifer worked was an art in itself, but one he was determined to conquer. Adam was ambitious, a social climber, and her family, in particular her father, gave a whole new meaning to networking. Rubbing shoulders with Clifford Goldsmith would orbit him into a higher level altogether and he wasn't about to mess up. It wouldn't do his status any harm at the office either, once the senior partners got wind of his connections. So Adam had taken things slowly, gradually building up a relationship which, to everyone's surprise, including his own, had started to gel quite nicely. She was a contrast to his rather vain manner. Her pragmatic approach cut to the chase. Instead of getting jealous when he had flirted with another girl one evening, she'd asked him directly, 'If you'd prefer her company, what are you doing here with me?' The confrontation had slightly embarrassed him, turning his flirtation into something pointless and childish, which in many ways it was. Jennifer had a knack of reaching the point immediately, completely hitting the nail on the head, which he found refreshing in a woman. It was almost like being with his mates, that no-nonsense, tell-it-like-it-is attitude.

Physically, he had another battle on his hands. Jennifer was classy. She wore stylish clothes that very cleverly hinted at what lay beneath. Unlike Moneypenny, who had constantly showcased her trophies, Jennifer only allowed the slightest bit of bare flesh to be exposed, which skilfully left him wanting more. They say the mind is the most powerful sex organ in the body and Adam's was haywire at the moment. Trying to read her signals, if indeed she was sending any, was impossible. One minute he thought he'd cracked it when she'd suggested a drink after work, only to discover it was with a group of them, not the cosy twosome he'd been expecting. She fitted in well with the office, being well liked by the girls in the admin team and also the management. He supposed it was because she was used to the business environment, having worked for her father. Adam was interested as to why she had applied for a position with his firm.

'I need outside experience,' she'd told him, 'somewhere people accept me for who I am, not the boss's daughter.'

'Very wise,' agreed Adam. Secretly he thought she was mad. Why put yourself through it? He'd be happy to be the boss's son-in-law and wallow in all the trappings that brought.

After four months of treading on eggshells and finally meeting the man himself, Clifford Goldsmith, Adam had plucked up the courage and invited Jennifer on a weekend away. He'd collared her one late afternoon, when the office was quiet. 'Jennifer, I think we both deserve a break. Would you like to go away for the weekend?'

'Where to?' Forever practical, he thought. Did it matter as long as he could finally nail her?

'Wherever you like, you decide.'

'Leave it with me.' She put the pile of letters awaiting his signature on his desk, reached for her coat and bid him goodbye. What exactly was that supposed to mean? He shook his head in exasperation. The following morning an itinerary, map and leaflet of an old country pub in the Cotswolds greeted him on his desk. Browsing through the material he was impressed with, not only her usual efficiency, but her choice of venue: *A place to unwind and relax in a rustic, country setting, with inglenook fires, traditional food and a cosy, friendly atmosphere.* This was hitting the spot, Jennifer had come up trumps again.

'What do you think?' She'd been watching him perusing her handiwork.

'Perfect,' he smiled.

'We leave at 8.30 a.m. sharp on Saturday, arriving at approximately 11a.m.'

'Sounds good.' He stifled a laugh.

'I'll drive. I'm a safer driver than you.'

Adam stared at her – was she joking? The serious face staring back told him she wasn't. Big surprise.

'Be ready,' she finished curtly.

That told him, didn't it? Hell, what would she be like in the sack? he wondered, and not for the first time. It was a strange kind of arousal, a bit like fantasising over a teacher. He had to stifle another laugh.

So, here they were, about to check into The Templar, in the village of Treweham. 'We've booked a room for tonight,' Adam told a red-headed girl behind the bar, 'in the name of—'

'Goldsmith,' interrupted Jennifer with force.

'Ah, yes, here we are.' The girl ticked the name on the reservation list and handed him the key to the room. 'Upstairs, it's the first on the right,' she smiled.

Adam carried his and Jennifer's case up the stairs. Opening the door he looked inside and stopped in his tracks. Twin beds. Typical.

Chapter 55

'It's gorgeous!' Finula admired the ring as Megan held out her left hand.

'I know,' she grinned back. It was Megan's last day working at The Templar and she and Finula were in the kitchen. Although she'd miss working alongside her best friend, she couldn't help but be excited at what lay ahead of her. Treweham Hall was now ready to be opened to the public. The tearoom was fully complete. It had a chic, classic finish with its pale silver-grey walls, white ornate coving and centrepiece chandelier. White linen tablecloths covered the tables, and each one had fresh flowers in a cut-glass vase. All the teapots, crockery and cake stands were fine white bone china and classical music was to be played softy in the background. The gift shop was fully stocked with Treweham Hall memorabilia, including the postcards of Megan's painting, plus pictures had been made and were now available too. It was amazing, as Megan kept telling Tobias when he had shown her the finished project.

She couldn't wait to start working at Treweham Hall, much to Tobias' appreciation. He was pleased she didn't find the place so intimidating any more.

After all, as he was fond of reminding her, it was going to be her home, too.

Megan had gradually accustomed herself to the fact that Treweham Hall was indeed about to be her home. It felt surreal. She had tried her utmost to remember all the history about her new family-to-be, as part of her duty as a tour guide. She had practised her spiel, touring the rooms with Tobias.

'Welcome to Treweham Hall, home of the Cavendish-Blakes since the early fifteenth century.'

'Sixteenth century,' corrected Tobias.

'Sorry, sixteenth century. Treweham Hall is set in a three-hundred-acre estate—'

'Three thousand.'

'Sorry, three-thousand-acre estate. The Cavendish-Blakes had strong connections to the Knights Templar from 1129.'

'Good,' nodded Tobias with a grin.

'We are currently in what was originally the Billiard Room. Note the pretty light in the ceiling, which illuminated the billiard table. We will now move into the Principal Bedroom.'

'Sounds interesting,' Tobias raised an eyebrow.

'Shush, I'm concentrating.'

'Sorry.' Megan ushered Tobias to the next room.

'This room started out as the bridal suite of Sir James and Lady Cavendish-Blake in the sixteenth century. The four-poster bed has accommodated many royal visitors, including Edward, Prince of Wales and Wallis Simpson.' She paused. 'Is that actually true?'

'It can be,' he replied drily.

'Moving on to the Music Room ...' She brushed past him, and he pinched her bottom.

'No fondling the staff, please, my lord,' she threw over her shoulder.

'Is that not my prerogative?' he teased, following behind her.

Ignoring him she continued, 'Here the Music Room boasts an impressive Steinway piano. Feel free to have a tinkle,' she added with a giggle.

'No tinkling allowed,' he replied, folding his arms.

'Now for the Chapel. Please follow me.' Tobias did as he was told. 'The family chapel features a late eighteenth-century Gillow altar front and is in regular use for family occasions, mainly christening and weddings.'

'The next one being ours.' Tobias stood in front of her and pulled her into him. She smiled up and he kissed her slowly and thoroughly. Megan's heart still fluttered uncontrollably when he touched her. Her hands ran through his dark, shiny hair, loving the texture. Finally they pulled apart.

'How was I?'

'Sensational.'

'Tobias, when should we set the date?'

'Right now. Let's get married next month. We'll marry here in the Chapel and have the reception in the Great Hall. It won't take too much arranging.'

'Don't you ever slow down?' she laughed.

'Get used to it, Lady Cavendish-Blake-to-be.' He held her again, once more thanking his lucky stars.

Finula was still in awe of the ring. 'I'm so happy for you both,' she said, bringing Megan back from her thoughts of the changes awaiting her.

'Thanks, Fin.' Then, mentally shaking herself, Megan asked, 'So, just two breakfasts to serve?'

'Yes. Just the couple from last night.' She slid the bacon and eggs onto the plates and handed them to Megan.

Walking through into the restaurant area, Megan caught sight of the back of a head she recognised instantly. She halted. Surely, it couldn't be? But that self-assured demeanour spoke volumes. She observed him pour his orange juice, flick open the morning's newspaper and check his watch. Who was he waiting for? Then in she came, a pretty girl with glasses. Immediately he stood up when she joined him at the table. Still the same old charmer, she thought ironically. Instead of showing reluctance, Megan walked confidently, shoulders back, her head held high. Who needed a rat like Adam? She had Tobias Cavendish-Blake.

With a breezy smile she approached the table. 'Two full English breakfasts.' Adam's eyes met hers. He spluttered on his orange, splashing the white tablecloth.

'Oh dear, oh dear,' she soothed sarcastically.

'Megan?' he choked.

'The very same.' She placed the two plates down.

'Do you two know each other?' asked the girl with a quizzical expression.

'We did, unfortunately,' retorted Megan, and turned on her heel and flounced off.

Dashing into the kitchen, she couldn't wait to tell Finula. 'Fin, it's Adam in there!' she hissed.

'Adam?'

'You know, the ex who I caught with his hands up—'

'His secretary's skirt,' finished Finula. 'Well, well, well.'

After a rather uncomfortable breakfast Adam and Jennifer packed and made their way down to check out. Megan made sure she was about, next to Finula at the bar.

'Enjoy your stay, sir?' asked Finula.

'Yes, thanks.' He looked sideways at Megan and swallowed. He couldn't fail to notice the diamond ring she was practically displaying as she wiped the bar. 'Who's the lucky man?' He attempted to lighten the atmosphere.

'Lord Cavendish-Blake,' supplied Finula. Adam's mouth opened wide in disbelief.

'Close your mouth, Adam, it's not a good look,' said Megan smiling sweetly, then asked innocently, 'How's your secretary, the one I caught you groping in your office?'

Jennifer, who had had quite enough, picked up her case and told him sharply, 'I'm off. Make your own way home.'

Chapter 56

Flora sat on the bed and scanned the room. It was the complete opposite to hers, being very tidy and minimal, with bare cream walls and dark patterned bedding. It was next door to Dylan's room, joined by a bathroom with two Jack-and-Jill doors. She could hear him in the shower whilst she unpacked the few clothes she'd brought with her. Flora was definitely on the mend, but still a little weak and tired. Despite her initial reservations she was glad to be here in Dylan's home. Secretly she had been dreading him leaving, still not feeling confident enough to be left alone, but hating the thought of Dylan being with her under sufferance, or obligation. Here he had his own space and a comfortable bed, not the hardness of her bedroom floor. Flora wondered how she would have coped without him, then instantly stopped herself. She mustn't get needy or attached. He was her employer now.

He knocked on her door, then poked his head round. His dark curls were wet, as was the dark chest sticking out from behind the door. 'All done, bathroom's free.' He noticed Flora's eyes home in on his bare torso. He stood there a moment longer, giving her the full benefit.

'Er... right, thanks,' she blinked, and turned away blushing.

Dylan smirked to himself. Plenty more where that came from. He was going to make it very difficult for Flora to resist him.

'Do you want me to run you a bath?' He stepped further into her room and stood there in nothing but a towel. Flora couldn't tear her eyes away from his body. She had almost forgotten how well toned he was. His regular visits to the gym and good diet most definitely paid off. Suddenly images of the Racer commercial flashed into her mind and she started to giggle.

Not really wanting or expecting this response Dylan asked rather defensively, 'What's so funny?'

'You, dressed like that in a towel.' Then she imitated his deep voice, 'Never be pipped at the post. I always win wearing Racer,' then winked.

'Oh, very funny, Flora,' he answered with a half-smiling, half-challenging look. 'Any more of that and I'll tickle you.' He remembered exactly where her soft spot was, under her arms. She started to giggle again at him. 'Right, you asked for this.' He jumped onto the bed and began tickling her mercilessly.

'Dylan, stop!' She laughed and wriggled on the bed underneath him.

'No way.' He knelt over her, his hands snatching at her body, making her hysterical. Finally he

355

relented. Tears poured down her cheeks, her chest was panting up and down. 'Surrender?' he asked, staring into her face.

'Never,' she replied, staring back.

'Right, here we go again.' He grabbed under her arms.

'No! I surrender,' she cried.

'That's better.' He stopped and looked into her eyes, then dipped his head momentarily. Flora froze. Was he going to kiss her? She closed her eyes. Nothing happened. She opened them to find Dylan climbing off her. 'Let's get moving. There's lots to do.'

Flora took a deep breath and reminded herself why she was there, as his employee.

Half an hour later they were in Dylan's large garage surrounded by all the stock they had ordered. He passed her a clipboard with the invoice and the order. Whilst he checked each item had been delivered, Flora ticked it off the list. After an hour and all the items had been accounted for, they started to load what they could into Dylan's Jeep and trailer. Flora carried the smaller, lighter items, leaving the heavier, bulkier ones for Dylan to heave about. She marvelled at his strength, watching his muscular shoulders and arms at work. He clocked her staring at him and smirked again to himself. He was a patient man; he'd bide his time. She was looking pretty damn cute too, in her skinny jeans displaying her sexy curves and thin, strappy top which her nipples poked against. The sexual tension between the two of them was evident, and they both could sense it rising.

'You look tired, Flora.' He was concerned, hoping he hadn't overworked her. They'd finally finished loading most of the stock.

'I'm fine,' she lied, obviously not convincingly, though, as Dylan put his arm round her shoulders.

'Come on, it's lunchtime.' He led her back into the house. 'You sit at the breakfast bar and I'll make us a sandwich.'

Flora was glad to rest her legs. She glanced round. It was a typical man's kitchen, she thought, with its glossy black units and granite worktops. The walls were white tiled. He seemed to have every gadget under the sun, from the complicated-looking silver coffee machine to the chrome blender. It was a far cry from the farmhouse-style kitchen at home, with its wooden doors and open shelves packed with mismatched crockery.

'What are you thinking?' He watched her eyes dart around the room.

'Just how clinically clean and tidy your house it. It's very masculine, isn't it?'

'You saying it needs a woman's touch?' He arched an eyebrow.

'No!' she quickly replied, not wanting to cause offence.

He shrugged. 'I'm open to offers,' he smiled.

Flora blushed and looked down. She was so easy to rib and easy to read. An open book – that was her charm he had come to understand. Flora had an honest, simple way about her he couldn't help but warm to. She'd make a wonderful mum. His thought pattern alarmed him. Never had he ever considered this with any other woman. He cast another look at her whilst busy making the sandwiches, propped up on the stool, elbows on the breakfast bar looking so innocent, yet still a touch pasty-faced. Perhaps she'd done too much this morning, fetching and carrying. He cursed himself for not taking better care of her.

'Do you fancy looking at the stable yard this afternoon? It's almost finished.'

Her face lit up. 'Yes! I'd love to see it.' Then she asked, 'Have you advertised for the stable staff yet?'

'Don't need to. Three of Sean Fox's staff have asked me for jobs.'

'Really? Won't he mind?'

'Tough if he does. I don't blame them for jumping ship, the way he treats them.'

Flora looked worried. 'Are they older than me?'

'It doesn't matter how old they are. You're the assistant trainer, Flora, remember that,' he told her firmly. He so wanted to inject some confidence in her, if only she knew how good she was.

After lunch Flora fell asleep on Dylan's enormous leather settee. He didn't want to wake her; obviously she was exhausted. Instead of going to the stable yard, he put a lamb joint in the oven and caught up with his paperwork. He'd been paid for the commercial, which would set him up nicely for at least a year. His agent mentioned a publisher making enquiries about proposing someone to write his biography, which Dylan was dubious about, but may consider in time. Tobias' solicitor had drawn up a contract for the lease of the stables, which needed signing, various sponsors had approached him to wear their clothes and watches, and two more prospective owners had made enquiries about the training yard. Things were looking good. A British Horseracing Authority inspector was to visit the yard in a week, so that had to take priority. Flora began to rouse, and she watched him sitting at his bureau in the corner of the lounge, deep in concentration. A framed photograph of three young boys stood on the top of the bureau. She got up and walked towards it, making him jump.

'Sorry,' she said, taking the picture, 'didn't mean to startle you.' Flora examined the photo. 'Who are they?' she asked.

'Me and my brothers, taken on holiday years ago.'

'How old were you?'

He pointed to the boy in the middle. 'That's me aged seven. Michael, the eldest, was nine and Liam four.'

'Was it Liam who texted the other night drunk?'

'Sorry?'

'You said it was your brother who had texted?'

'Ah, yes.'

Flora smiled at the little boy with dark curls and a cheeky grin. Nothing had changed. 'Feeling better?' he asked, anxious that he had overworked her.

'Yes, thanks. Something smells good.' How would she cope on her own, chiselling ready-made meals from the freezer in future?

'Lamb.'

'Lovely. Thanks, Dylan.' She meant it. Despite what had happened in the past, she sincerely appreciated the way he was looking after her.

After dinner Flora asked if he had any more photos of him as a child. The framed picture of him and his brothers had intrigued her. He took out a couple of albums from a bookcase and together they browsed through them on the settee, laughing together at the antics caught on camera. Flora felt like she was beginning to know yet another side to Dylan. It was evident that family mattered to him and that he had a close relationship with his brothers. There was always a horse about, Dylan riding, or competing and winning a trophy, very much like her. They had finished a bottle of wine and were totally relaxed, leaning into each other. Flora loved the warmth of his body against hers. He was such a comfort. Never had she been so torn.

'It's late, we better get some sleep.' Dylan closed the photo albums and helped Flora to her feet. 'You go up. I'll make us a hot chocolate.'

'Thanks.' Flora suddenly craved a comfortable bed and a hot chocolate under the covers. She climbed the stairs and made her way into the bedroom, undressed, slipped on her silky nightshirt and tumbled into bed. There was a knock at the door.

'Come in.' Dylan held two cups, he passed her one and sat on the bed. He turned the bedside light on, giving the room a cosy, warm glow. 'Thanks for looking after me, Dylan.'

He gazed at her for a moment, then hesitated. She looked searchingly at him: what was he going to say? After a few moments he spoke quietly.

'Flora, I don't want you to go.'

What did he mean? Stunned, she remained silent.

He coughed awkwardly. 'I... I want you to stay.' She stared at him speechless. He unbuttoned his shirt, revealing that dark, muscular chest she had so admired. Then he unbuttoned his jeans and slid them off. He wasn't wearing anything under them.

Flora stared at his naked body and gulped. She put her cup down on the bedside cabinet. He gently slid in next to her. His skin was soft and warm against hers. It would be all too easy to sink into his arms and let him devour her but she stilled. 'What is it, Flora?' he asked softly.

'I can't. Sorry.'

He waited. What did he expect after the way he had treated her?

'Would it help if I told you how deeply ashamed I am of the way I behaved towards you, and promise never to hurt you again?'

'It might,' she replied in a small voice.

'Let me hold you, Flora, please.' She slid onto his chest and he wrapped his arms tightly round her. He kissed her forehead. 'Just sleep, here with me,' he whispered. And she did, in a peaceful, heavenly slumber.

Chapter 57

'So, here's to the grand opening.' Finula clinked her glass with Megan's.

'I can't believe it's actually happening. It's mayhem up at the Hall.' Megan took a huge gulp of her non-alcoholic wine. She was at fever pitch. All day she'd been putting the last-minute touches to the rooms, making sure everything was in place. The tearoom was to be staffed by a team she had selected from the kitchen who were happy to assist. Sebastian had returned home like the prodigal son and announced he would act as a tour guide, much to the relief of Megan, who was glad of the support.

Meanwhile Tobias was with Dylan, overseeing the last stages of the stable yard. Tobias had shown it to Megan, Sebastian, Beatrice and Celia, and all were impressed by the building and the facilities he and Dylan had created. As were the several racehorse owners who had come to look round. Megan noticed that Tobias seemed more relaxed, as far as finances were concerned. He was convinced the stable yard promised to be the saving of Treweham Hall.

Sebastian also seemed a little more tranquil. Having time away from Treweham village, and Nick, had given him space to think. He had discussed his future with Tobias and had decided to rent a house in Stratford-upon-Avon, as he had landed a role at the Royal Shakespeare Theatre. He wanted distance away from Nick. Tobias couldn't agree more with Sebastian's plans.

Even Celia was on form since returning from her cruise. She had congratulated Megan on the engagement to her 'remarkable nephew' and admired her ring. The transformation in her was incredible, when Megan compared this bright-eyed, sharp lady to the cantankerous old bag in tweed of a few months ago. Celia had invited Wilfrid to attend the wedding as her guest. Wilfrid had been over the moon at the invitation and even more so when he read where the wedding was taking place. *He* was to be a guest of Lord Cavendish-Blake and stay at Treweham Hall? My goodness.

Beatrice was in raptures over the plans for the wedding. Although Tobias and Megan had insisted it was to be a small, intimate affair, she had other ideas. Beatrice didn't do small. Treweham Hall didn't do small, either. She would ensure that her son and heir's wedding would be the spectacular occasion it should be. Blow the expense, this was as much her day as theirs.

Megan had picked her wedding dress and had asked Finula to be bridesmaid. Now they were sitting in Megan's lounge sipping a well-earned glass of sparkling non-alcoholic wine.

'What time do you open tomorrow?'

'Ten o'clock in the morning. I'm stopping at the Hall tonight to make sure I'm up and ready for blast off.'

'Don't be nervous! Enjoy.'

'I know, and I will, it's just getting the first day over with.'

'Well, I'll have a coffee and cake in the tearoom when I've finished my shift at the pub.'

'Thanks. I'm so pleased Sebastian's going to be there. The public will love him.'

'They will. I can just imagine him.'

'Talking of which, have you seen anything of Nick since the Landlord's Supper?'

'You mean since Tobias gave him a good thrashing?' laughed Finula. 'No, he's kept a very low profile. Rumour has it he's seeing some millionaire's wife.'

*

The next morning Treweham Hall was a hive of activity, with every member of staff busy about his or her duties. Megan was dressed in a navy-blue trouser suit with a 'tour guide' badge pinned to the collar. Tobias couldn't help but smile at now nervous she was. He ducked his head to read her badge. 'You're a little more than a tour guide, Megan.'

'What? Do you think it should say "chief tour guide"?'

'No. I was thinking that as the future Lady Cavendish-Blake, carrying the future heir to the Treweham Hall estate, you shouldn't need any name badge.'

Megan looked down at it and hesitated. 'I haven't time to discuss this now,' she flapped.

'Listen,' he said in a serious tone, 'don't overdo it. I've given Henry strict orders to be close by, Sebastian will do the bulk of the tours and the kitchen staff know what they're doing. You are there to oversee.' He kissed her hard on the lips. 'Got it?'

'And where will you be?' she asked, folding her arms.

'The BHA inspector is coming today to look at the stable yard. Once they've given their approval, I can hand the whole thing over to Dylan and I'm all yours.' He hugged her into him. 'I know it's manic at the moment, but it'll soon be over, back to normal,' he reassured into her ear.

Normal? thought Megan. What was normal nowadays?

*

'Good morning, ladies, gentlemen and children, and welcome to Treweham Hall.' Sebastian gave a dramatic bow, making the party of people chuckle. He was dressed in a sixteenth-century costume, complete with tights, breeches, a padded overshirt with a ruff and a large felt hat with a feather. Megan's nerves began to settle. He was brilliant, a real performer with such charisma everyone warmed to him immediately. His idea of dressing up was genius and really added to the whole experience. 'May I introduce my glamorous assistant, Miss Megan Taylor, the future Lady Cavendish-Blake.' He stood aside to reveal a rather cautious Megan, who gave the most confident smile she could muster. 'Clock the rocks,' he said in a stage whisper, pointing to Megan's engagement ring. Oohs and aahs echoed round the crowd, turning Megan bright pink.

'*Sebastian!*' she hissed under her breath.

'Let me start by showing you the Billiard Room. This way, if you please.' Sebastian led the party off down the corridor. Megan smiled to herself as she watched his feather hat high above everyone's heads. Instead of following them she decided to check on the tearoom. Tobias had been right; the kitchen staff knew exactly what they were doing. The place was running like clockwork.

'Hi, Megan!' one of the girls called over. 'Sit down and have a cup of tea.'

'Do you know what? I think I will.' She sat down at a small table by the window overlooking the grounds. She could just about see the new stable block in the distance to the left. She imagined Tobias and Dylan working diligently to impress the inspector.

Megan was looking forward to spending more time with Tobias. He'd been so caught up with one project or another, she couldn't wait to be on honeymoon, destination unknown. Typically, Tobias had taken care of that, too. She marvelled at what he could achieve: Ted's cottage, this tearoom, the stables. He was a real grafter, not the high-and-mighty lord she had supposed when first arriving in Treweham.

Tobias and Megan were to take over the south wing of Treweham Hall for their private rooms. Megan was to have a big input into the décor, and this wasn't something Tobias would take over, he assured her. Knowing this had calmed Megan. She quite liked the idea of putting her stamp on the old rooms, really being able to turn them into her home. She also liked the idea of their private rooms not being manned by Henry, who would remain in the current quarters, tending to Beatrice and Sebastian, when he was home. Tobias had mentioned a nanny for the future, but Megan refused point-blank. The differences in their upbringing had reared its head once or twice, but each had compromised, apart from Tobias when he had absolutely insisted Megan see the family's private doctor throughout her pregnancy and not the local village one. He could be quite domineering, she had come to learn, but then she was obstinate, too, as he had pointed out. Together they had blended as a couple and now Megan couldn't envisage life without him. It was that simple: he was her everything. She'd even learnt to love his eccentric family; his drama-queen brother, his overindulged mother and his crabby old aunt. She wondered what their child would be like and gently stroked her bump. Her thoughts were interrupted by Sebastian's loud, confident voice.

'And that, ladies, gentlemen and children, concludes our tour. May I suggest light refreshments in the tearoom? Thank you and good day.' A round of applause followed, making Megan smile again. Go, Sebastian, ever the player.

Out of the corner of her eye she saw Finula enter the tearoom. Soon she was sitting next to her with tea and a cream scone.

'How's it going?' she asked, looking round the room.

'Great. Sebastian's a star.'

'I know. I just caught the end of his tour. By the way, I've picked by bridesmaid's dress.'

'Oh, good. What colour?'

'A kind of bronze-brown. Is that OK?' She looked hopeful at Megan.

'Of course. With your colouring it'll look amazing.'

'Don't worry, I won't upstage the bride.' She nudged her playfully.

'Thanks for that, Fin,' replied Megan drily. 'Still no sign of that tall, dark stranger entering your gin joint, then?'

'Nah, not yet,' Finula replied, munching on her scone. Pity, thought Megan, wishing her friend could enjoy the same happiness she had.

Chapter 58

Opening the envelope, Gary read the invitation and called out to his wife. 'Tracy! Look at this!' Tracy scurried over and read the cream card edged with gold.

'"Lord Cavendish-Blake and Miss Taylor invite you to their wedding..." Blimey, Gary, I didn't expect to be invited to that.'

'Why not?' he replied indignantly. 'We are neighbours.'

'Yeah, but...' Her mind was already spinning with what to wear. Fancy her going to an aristocratic wedding – who would have thought? She pictured Sharon's spiteful scowl and a degree of uncertainty shoved its way in. Gary picked up on it immediately.

'Hey, don't worry. We'll have a ball, Trace. It was fine when they came here, wasn't it?'

'I suppose so.'

'You like Megan, and Finula is bound to be there, too.'

'Yes. You're right.'

He put his arm round her shoulders. 'Come on, let's go into town and buy new outfits. We don't want to let the side down, do we?'

All day they looked, and whilst Gary was soon fitted up with a slim-fit charcoal suit, Tracy just couldn't find what she wanted. All the dresses had been the wrong colour, the wrong shape, too fussy, too boring, didn't feel comfortable, didn't look special, and Gary's patience was wearing thin.

'Surely there must be something you like, Trace? We've been in every shop!' He was exasperated. 'You'll have to look on-line.'

'No. I need to try it on. There must be somewhere else I can look,' she persisted. Then she saw it. *The* dress, staring at her in the shop window. 'That's it!' she pointed. Gary turned in the direction of her finger.

'Oxfam!'

'Yes,' she laughed, 'so what?'

Shaking his head, he crossed the road, following Tracy, who had quickly run inside the shop. By the time he had entered and plonked down his shopping bags, she was in the changing room. Moments later she pulled back the curtain and his jaw dropped. She was right. It really was perfect. The fabric was silky with a silver-green background and bright floral pattern. It was sleeveless with a dipped neckline, slim fitting, tapering in at the waist and it fell just above the knee. It could have been made for her. He swallowed.

'You look gorgeous, Tracy,' he said gruffly, swiftly looking round to make sure nobody was listening.

'Ah, thanks, Gary,' she chirped, swaying round in front of the mirror. Then, turning to him she said, with as straight a face as possible, 'Can we afford it?'

Chapter 59

Flora could hardly contain herself as Dylan drove his Jeep to the new training yard. He looked sideways at her and grinned.

'You excited?'

'Too right. I can't wait to see it.' She fidgeted in the passenger seat, itching to get out and explore her new place of work. They went through the new side entrance nearest to the stables, instead of having to pass along the main drive. And there it was.

Flora's eyes widened. 'Dylan, it's fabulous!'

'I know,' he answered rather smugly. As far as racehorse training yards went, it was the very latest in design. A circular track had been made with rails running alongside in the field next to the yard, and an all-weather woodchip gallop for faster work on the horses ran along the far stretch. The stables could accommodate up to thirty horses. Dylan clearly intended to grow his yard into a thriving business.

Flora's hands flew to her face. 'Oh my God...' She couldn't take it all in. Dylan delighted in seeing the effect it had on her and showing it all off gave him a real buzz. 'The BHA officer passed it with flying colours.'

'I'm not surprised. You'd have to be mad not to want your horse here.'

Dylan nodded in agreement.

'We've shown a few owners around and it looks promising. Hopefully in a few years we'll be working at full capacity.'

'We'll need more staff.' She looked directly at him.

'I know, and we'll get them, don't worry.'

Flora set off for the stables to see the horses that had arrived earlier that day. It had been almost two weeks since she'd ridden and she was anxious to get back in the saddle. Dylan had kept her away until Samantha's horses had been safely delivered, on the off chance Samantha may put in an appearance. The last thing he needed at this sensitive stage was the likes of Samantha putting a spanner in the works. Flora was just on the verge of trusting him again. He had loved her living with him and for the first time in a long while had felt fully content. The thought of her leaving filled him with unease. 'I'll tack up and ride,' she said with gusto.

'You'll do no such thing,' he reproached. Flora had only just fully recovered. He could see she was still a little weak. 'Maybe next week and then only for an hour a day.'

'Stop fussing. I'm fine.' She pushed the stable door open and went inside. 'They're beautiful. What are they called?' She gazed at their shiny, chestnut coats and thick black manes.

'Zero Libido and Femme Fatale are their registered names,' Dylan almost choked on the irony, 'otherwise known as Libby and Femme.'

Flora stroked Libby's flanks, which were deep and wide, ultimate breeding stock. Dylan watched Flora examine the horses; she was a true professional. One or two people had raised an eyebrow at him choosing Flora for an assistant trainer, but he was absolutely certain she had the ability.

As if in proof, she took out a piece of paper from her coat pocket. 'I've drawn up a daily routine for us.' She handed it to Dylan who read it with interest.

5.30 a.m. feed horses, check for heat/swelling in legs.

Muck out stables.

Tack up horses, mount and exercise – exercises for each individual horse to be discussed.

Discuss racing plans with owners and speak to agents regarding jockey bookings.

Late afternoon exercise.

5 p.m. feed and check horses.

8 p.m. check yard and check all horses are content for evening.

What a woman! He couldn't have done a more thorough job himself. 'Excellent.' Flora smiled with relief.

'I think each horse should have one rest day a week.'

'I agree. I'm arranging a full blood analysis of each horse, too.'

'How often?'

'Twice a year.'

The two were on the same wavelength. Dylan didn't doubt they'd make a good partnership. 'Come through to the office. There's the yard staff to meet.' Flora braced herself: this was the only part she'd been reluctant about. Taking a steady breath, she stepped into the office with Dylan behind her. Two girls and a boy who looked to be of a similar age to her stood up to greet them.

'Sit down, please,' Flora said, quickly joining them in the seated area where two settees faced each other. A coffee table stood in the middle with various horse and racing magazines on.

'This is Abbey, Mel and Josh,' Dylan introduced, 'and this is the assistant trainer, Flora.' Flora shook hands with them all. Keen to get going, Flora showed them her draft daily roster. They all looked happy with the arrangements.

'Of course it's flexible,' she was eager to point out.

'It all looks fine to me,' Josh said, smiling widely straight into Flora's eyes. His eyes then travelled lower to her cleavage, then back up to her face. Dylan caught the moment, however brief, and stared him out coolly. Coughing, Josh quickly turned to the two girls, 'What do you say?'

'Yes, it's great,' they trilled, clearly as excited to be there as Flora was. It must seem like heaven compared to Sean Fox's regime, thought Dylan.

After sharing a coffee and a chat, Dylan asked Flora to show the girls Libby and Femme and prepare the stables for the rest of the horses being delivered, leaving him alone with Josh.

'Just one thing,' Dylan sat opposite Josh, 'if you want to keep working here, then stay away from Flora.' His eyes pierced into him like chips of ice. Josh blushed and shifted awkwardly.

'Ah, I see. You and she are…'

'Absolutely,' stated Dylan forcefully, leaving no room for any misunderstanding.

Flora, Abbey and Mel gelled well together mucking out the stables and arranging the hay and water for the new horses arriving. Flora's love of horses meant she would always be happy working in stables, but she knew giving orders instead of taking them would take some adjusting to. She yearned to saddle up and gallop through the fields, despite Dylan's advice.

'Don't even think about it,' he warned behind her, catching her reaching for a saddle in the tack room. She jumped at the sound of his voice.

'Trust you to be there,' she laughed.

'Seriously, Flora, I'll ride with you next week. Just wait a few more days. Remember, these are extremely valuable horses.'

'OK, OK,' she conceded with disappointment.

'Come on, I need to see Tobias.' He guided her out into the yard and together they walked up to Treweham Hall.

Flora had only been inside the Hall once before when looking at the plans for the training yard. Its sheer opulence filled her with awe.

Megan came dashing down the passageway. 'Dylan, while you're here, let me give you this.' She handed him a cream envelope. 'Invitation to the wedding.' She beamed at Flora. 'Tobias is in his study, go through.' She ushered them in. Tobias was sitting at his desk working on his computer.

'Come in, Dylan. Flora, what do you think then?' He was, of course, referring to the yard.

'Amazing,' she gushed. Dylan put his arms round her shoulders.

'I'm sure we'll be very happy there, won't we?' Those striking blue eyes twinkled roguishly.

'I'm sure we will,' she answered.

Chapter 60

It was the night before the wedding. The whole of Treweham village was on high alert. The press had started to set up outside the Hall, and The Templar was heaving. As predicted, the media was keen to snap 'the Heir and the Fox' on such a momentous day. It was big news that Lord Cavendish-Blake was finally getting married after years of hellraising. His old chum Seamus was fulfilling his duty as best man. Megan was overwhelmed by the attention, choosing to stay behind closed doors until the next morning when the horse and carriage, with Dylan at the reins, was to collect her. She was determined to remain calm and enjoy the whole experience, however threatening it was. Her mum, dad and brother were staying at The Templar. Kate, her old work friend, was driving up that night, too. She hadn't been able to get the day off work, so would be booking into The Templar much later. Tonight would be Megan's last night in the cottage. Her mum and Finula were to spend the evening with her, tucked away from prying eyes and flashing cameras.

Megan couldn't fail to see the articles and coverage that the impending wedding had attracted. Tobias' history had once more been dragged up and splashed over the papers for all and sundry to read. Megan cringed at the tabloids' headlines:

Playboy Lord Finally Weds

Lord Cavendish-Blake-the-Rake to Marry

She was beginning to comprehend what Tobias had had to tolerate, fully understanding his need to visit and prepare Carrie's parents in France. Tobias knew exactly what to expect. He foresaw the reporters, with their cameras and microphones, intruding on the village, pestering the locals, desperate for any quick shot of him or Megan they could muster. Megan had been distressed initially, until Tobias had ramped up the security surrounding the Hall and her cottage. For the moment all was quiet.

The Templar was anything but quiet. Finula was breathless behind the bar, serving the jam-packed crowd. Luckily her dad had called in extra staff so she would be able to call in at Megan's later. Finula didn't want a late night, wanting to look her best as bridesmaid to Megan – and for all the press, she thought, daunted. There were so many faces tonight she didn't recognise. This kind of wedding brought out all sorts of people, not just the starstruck and inquisitive, but neighbouring villagers, journalists and reporters. Treweham was no stranger to media coverage with the likes of Tobias, Seamus and Dylan here, but this surpassed anything they had previously experienced. Finula hoped Megan was coping. She saw a tall, dark man enter the pub carrying a camera. Another news reporter, no doubt, she thought. He made his way to the bar. He spoke in a soft Irish accent and instantly Finula knew his origin to be Roscommon, the same county in Ireland as her dad came from. He ordered a Guinness, which Dermot served, then chatted briefly, obviously remarking on their shared home turf. Finula strained to hear what they were saying, but couldn't for the noise of the pub. Then she saw her dad hand over a room key. The man must be staying over.

'Who's that?' she asked when at last there was a quiet moment. 'Another reporter?'

'No. He's a producer. Nothing to do with the wedding.'

'A producer?' Finula was intrigued. 'What kind of producer?'

'Ask him yourself,' Dermot tilted his head to the man who had reappeared at the bar and had evidently overheard Finula asking about him. She looked embarrassed; he smirked and raised an eyebrow. Finula blushed slightly and started to serve another customer.

*

Megan's mum had discreetly left The Templar early and sneaked off to her daughter's cottage. What a commotion. She never would have expected this for her daughter's wedding. What with a lord for a future son-in-law, Treweham Hall Megan's new home and now the media at full pelt, it was all a rum do. The main thing was that Megan was happy, which she undoubtedly was, thank goodness. Gone was the sad, empty girl who had been totally walked over by that wretched Adam. Then the poor girl had had to contend with the bombshell her grandmother had kindly dropped on her. Now she had to face the press and all the hullabaloo that entailed. Walking briskly against the chill in the air, she quickly made it to Bluebell Cottage. It was dusk, the early autumn nights had started to draw in. Knocking on the back door, she saw Megan sitting at the kitchen table with just a lamp on.

Megan saw her mum at the window and let her in. 'Did anyone follow you?' she asked.

'No, don't worry, love, no one saw me.'

'I feel like a prisoner in my own home.'

'I know, Megan, but once the wedding's over, it'll be fine.' She looked at the kitchen table and noticed the Parma violet tin with the letters and photographs in it.

'I've just been reading the letters again,' explained Megan.

Her mum nodded. 'Let's light the fire in the lounge and put the kettle on. It's nippy out there.'

Megan laughed. 'That's just what Gran would have said.' Suddenly they were both filled with emotion.

'She would,' agreed her mum, and reached out for a hug. Together they embraced, tears tumbling down their faces.

'I miss her so much,' Megan choked.

'I know, so do I,' replied her mum, hugging her hard.

A knock at the door made them both jump. It was Finula.

'Come in!' called Megan.

Finula looked very bright eyed and excited. 'Hi!' She plonked down a bottle of wine. 'Crack this open.' Then, looking at Megan's stomach, she quickly added, 'For me and your mum, not you.'

'Finula's right, love, you save yourself for tomorrow, keep a clear head.'

Megan nodded and looked at Finula, and the two exchanged knowing smiles.

*

Tobias was almost at breaking point. He knew full well how the media operated and had put plans in place to cover all eventualities. His main concern was Megan and how she was managing the complete invasion in privacy. It was different for him, he'd grown up with it, learning to expect the lengths they went to to get a story. It had been a while since he'd been in the spotlight, but now he was about to take centre stage again. He cursed his position and how it had affected him at every stage in his life. Even when he had lost his fiancée the gutter press hadn't relented. Bastards. He had called in extra security, contacted the police for assistance, and had hired a bodyguard to follow Megan and keep watch by her cottage. He only hoped this pressure wasn't affecting her health, or their baby's. The sooner they were away on honeymoon the better. He knew Megan thought him a control freak and was being secretive about where they were going, but truth be told he didn't want it leaking in case they were followed. Megan might let it slip to Finula, and then the whole of Treweham would more than likely know. Better to keep it to himself. He knocked back a brandy.

Seamus, Tatum and the girls were staying at the Hall, and they'd been a welcome distraction, with Beatrice and Celia entertaining them with tales from their cruise. Sebastian was in good humour, too, acting the fool with the girls, who had been giddy with laughter. Tobias and Seamus had kept an eye out, closing all the curtains and giving strict instructions to the staff to be extra vigilant. Now they were in his study and the TV was on. Tobias glanced towards it on hearing his name.

'Lord Tobias Cavendish-Blake, the notorious wild child, is to marry Megan Taylor, a local girl from the leafy village of Treweham tomorrow…' Pictures of him then flashed across the screen, some from his early days with Seamus, surrounded by glamorous women.

Seamus stood next to him and knocked back his brandy, too. 'They don't ever let up, do they?' Then the inevitable came, making Tobias' stomach contract.

'Tobias was engaged ten years ago to Carrie Palmer, who was tragically killed by a drunk driver…' Then images of Carrie filled the screen. Tobias drew in a ragged breath and clutched his glass. There was even a shot of her gravestone. Seamus picked up the remote control and switched the television off.

'You don't need this, mate.' He poured him another brandy and Tobias took it with a trembling hand. 'It'll be over this time tomorrow. You and Megan will be married and away from it all. Just concentrate on the life ahead of you, Tobias.'

'I know, you're right.' He channelled his thoughts on Megan and his unborn child, which immediately calmed him. He pictured Seamus, Tatum and their happy little family. This would be him, too, at last. 'Come on, let's join the others.' Seamus slapped his back. 'Tomorrow will be fine, trust me.'

'Thanks, Seamus.'

*

Megan, her mum and Finula had enjoyed their girls' night in. Fortunately they hadn't watched the TV so Megan was unaware of the extent of the coverage being plastered all over the evening news. Kate had texted to say she had arrived safely and was going straight to bed. She had arranged to see Megan first thing in the morning.

It was late by the time Megan's mum and Finula left, after checking the coast was clear. Next door in Ted's old cottage was a bodyguard keeping close watch. It was all a little unnerving. Megan was actually starting to like the idea of being tucked up safely in the fortress of Treweham Hall along with Tobias and his quirky family.

It was half-past midnight when the phone rang. Staring at it, she paused before answering. Then, recognising the number displayed, she picked it up. 'Hi.'

'Hi. You OK?' He sounded concerned.

'Yes, of course. Are you?'

'Yes. Had a good evening?'

'We did, thanks, and you?'

'Hmm, Megan, have you seen the news?' he anxiously asked. Megan knew exactly what he was getting at and had deliberately avoided putting on the TV.

'No.'

'Good.'

'Tobias, it wouldn't make any difference, you know, no matter what's said about you.'

He sighed down the phone. 'I love you, Megan.'

'And I love you, Tobias. See you in the morning. I'll be the one in the white dress.'

He laughed. 'And I'll be the happiest man alive.'

*

Finula rushed through the back door of The Templar. She could hear voices in the bar. Frowning, she poked her head round the door to see her dad talking to the producer chap, who caught sight of her and called out, 'Fancy a nightcap?'

She edged back hesitantly, but then Dermot turned round.

'Ah, Finula, come and meet Marcus.' Entering the bar, she took in this stranger's handsome face. He had a dishevelled, swarthy look about him with stubble and dark hair. His eyes were green with amber flecks, reminding her of someone but she couldn't quite place who. He held out his hand and she shook it.

'Hello there.'

'Hi.' He held her hand a fraction longer than expected. She looked at him and he stared back. 'Well, better get some sleep, big day tomorrow,' she gabbled, suddenly a touch self-conscious. 'Good night.'

'Night, Princess,' her dad called.

Finula climbed the stairs and fell into bed, a warm glow flickered inside her.

Chapter 61

It was daybreak. A rosy sunrise glowed through the valley, just as it had many months ago when Tobias had galloped through the early morning mist in despair. Now he was the happiest and most content he had ever been. Drawing back the heavy curtains, he surveyed the grounds before him. The staff were busy carrying out wicker chairs and tables, ready for the guests to sip champagne on the lawn, before entering the Great Hall for the wedding breakfast. He chuckled at seeing his mother fuss, pointing and flapping at everyone. She was in her element. Celia was on standby, trying her utmost to calm Beatrice down. A knock at his door interrupted his thoughts. Turning, he saw Henry enter the bedroom with his dark grey pinstriped, morning suit, pristine white shirt and silver-grey tie.

'Your attire, sir.' Henry hung it on the wardrobe door.

'Thank you, Henry.' Henry bowed slightly and left the room, leaving Tobias to gaze out of the window at the commotion.

Sebastian was the next distraction, singing at the top of his voice about Tobias getting married in the morning and how the bells were 'gonna chime'!

Tobias laughed and threw a pillow at him. 'Be quiet, you fool.'

'So,' Sebastian rubbed his hands together, 'how are we feeling? Nervous? Excited? Still amazed you've bagged a girl like Megan?'

'All of the above,' Tobias laughed again.

'Seriously, bro,' Sebastian looked sincerely at Tobias, 'I'm pleased for you.'

'Thanks, Sebastian, and one day I'll be saying the same to you.' The two brothers embraced.

'Right, I'll leave you to bathe and dress. Then, show time!' Sebastian jazzed his hands.

Tobias rolled his eyes. 'Go on, out of here.'

*

Megan was remarkably calm. A tranquil peace surrounded her as she ate a breakfast of egg and bacon. To her surprise she was hungry and easily managed a full plate. She had expected to wake a nervous wreck, but the steady, calming influence of her mother and Finula the previous evening had steered her. She peeped out of the curtains to see more reporters lined up by the row of cottages, patiently waiting for the first glimpse of her. It all felt so surreal. Dylan would be here in two hours. Then she saw Kate scurrying up the lane. She smiled, having missed her old chum. Opening her front door, she quickly ushered her inside and embraced her.

'Kate, it's so good to see you!'

'You, too! I can't believe this is happening! Have you seen outside?'

Megan nodded. 'I know, it's mad, isn't it?'

'Sorry I couldn't come round last night. I was knackered from the drive.'

'Don't worry, I understand. How come you couldn't get the day off work? Nothing to do with Adam, was it?' The thought had crossed her mind that he was peevish enough to put a spanner in the works if he could.

Kate giggled. 'No. He's gone, sacked. Thought I'd save that gem of information for you.'

Megan's eye's widened. 'Why? What's happened?'

'Well, apparently his secretary – not you-know-who, another one, called Jennifer – reported him for indecent behaviour!'

'No! You're kidding!'

'About time, I say,' replied Kate with a firm nod.

Well, well, well, Adam had finally got his just deserts, thought Megan with satisfaction. She still found it hard to believe she had ever been taken in by him.

After a coffee and a catch-up, Megan took a long warm bubble bath and relaxed, taking deep breaths in contemplation, while Kate was busy getting ready in the spare bedroom. After drying off, Megan rubbed in her favourite body lotion, which smelt of freesias, then carefully dried her hair into a smooth bob. Kate applied her make-up delicately, to keep that natural look Megan wanted. Now for the dress. Carefully Kate helped her into it. It was the epitome of vintage-inspired femininity, with its scalloped Bardot neckline. The ivory silk fell to a chapel train, creating an elegant and timeless fit. Megan looked every bit the demure and romantic bride. She tentatively put on the diamond tiara Beatrice had given her and fixed it in place. All done. Not too shabby, she told her reflection.

'Oh, Megan, you look gorgeous,' whispered Kate.

'Thanks, Kate. You'd better dash.'

'Will do.' Kate collected her bag and made her way to Treweham Hall, choosing to walk along the back footpath, out of sight, as directed.

Megan heard a stir outside. Looking out of the window, she saw Dylan's horses and carriage in the distance trotting up the track. She took a steady breath and pulled her shoulders back. Time to go.

Finula was in the carriage along with Megan's dad, waving and smiling at the crowd. She was quite enjoying the attention, unlike Mr Taylor, who looked rather startled and uncomfortable.

Finula had woken in a similar mood to the bride, composed. When she had walked down the stairs of the pub her dad had clapped her. 'You look amazing, Finula,' he bellowed with pride. Megan's mum, dad and brother all agreed, as they sat at a nearby table. She did indeed look amazing in her bridesmaid dress, a bronze, chiffon number. It was sleeveless, with one shoulder, and its soft pleats ran down her figure and rested on the ankle. She turned to the side at hearing a wolf whistle. Marcus was sitting at a table eating breakfast. He had his camera with him.

'Mind if I take a picture?' He directed the question to Dermot, which made Finula smile to herself.

'Be my guest,' replied Dermot.

Marcus got up from the table and stood in front of her. She could feel herself blushing again. 'There we go,' he spoke from behind the lens, 'and another for good measure.' He clicked the button, sending flashes across the room. 'All done,' he smiled. Finula lowered her eyes.

'Dylan's here!' called Dermot. Finula quickly went to the door to meet him. Dylan was looking immaculate in his riding suit. Finula squinted to read the sign on the back of the carriage, expecting it to say, 'Getting Married'. It didn't. It read, 'Delany's Racing Yard'. Finula pointed to it and started to giggle.

'Shush,' hissed Dylan, 'Tobias will kill me.' Well, he couldn't miss this opportunity, could he? Megan's dad hopped into the carriage next to Finula, looking terribly self-conscious. His wife and son stood by, waving and laughing.

'Let's go!' Dylan threw over his shoulder, and cracked his whip, forcing the two of them forward. Finula was astonished at the number of people lining the pathways. At last Dylan turned the carriage into Megan's lane and gently drew the horses to a halt outside Bluebell Cottage. There she was, looking as radiant as expected. Megan's dad climbed down to walk his daughter up the garden path and into the carriage. Flashes, cheers and applause came from the gathered spectators, and Megan gave them a captivating smile.

'Megan, you look beautiful,' her dad whispered, barely containing his pride.

Soon Dylan had driven the carriage through the village to arrive at Treweham Hall. Security men stood at each side of the huge, cast-iron gates, ready to lock them shut once the carriage was inside. Once they were secured, everybody gave a sigh of relief.

Dylan turned to his passengers.

'Now let the wedding begin.' He stepped down from the driver's seat and was quickly joined by Flora, who helped him steady the horses.

'How did they do?' she asked Dylan.

'Well, Megan and Finula are fine, but the father's terrified.'

'I meant the horses,' laughed Flora.

Dylan shook his head. 'Ever the horsewoman, eh?' he laughed, and kissed her full on the mouth. Unbeknown to him, a reporter who was still hanging around the gates cheekily snapped them with his camera. Once Dylan and Flora had handed the horses over to the grooms, they sped into the Hall and made for the chapel, leaving Finula to fuss and make sure Megan's dress was in place. Then, with Megan's father leading his daughter, they slowly walked down the marble-floored hallway, up the sweeping staircase, and along the corridor to the chapel entrance. Organ music was playing and the chapel was full of scented lilies. Shafts of sunlight illuminated the stained-glass windows.

Megan saw the back of Tobias, standing next to Seamus on the front row. Her chest started to pound. Seamus turned and gave her a grin. He whispered something in Tobias' ear. Sebastian turned round, too, and blew her a kiss, causing ripples of laughter. Ever the showman, thought Megan with affection.

Gradually she and her father walked down the aisle to meet Tobias. He finally faced her and his heart missed a beat. My God, was there ever a more stunning bride? His green eyes blazed with passion as they locked with Megan's like radar.

The ceremony was both emotional and joyful. Sebastian gave a reading of the Wedding at Cana and afterwards made an anecdote of the wine never running out at Treweham Hall, causing more titters from the congregation. Once the priest had announced them man and wife, a huge applause sounded from the pews and the chapel bell chimed.

Walking back down the aisle, arm in arm with his bride, Tobias bent his head and whispered, 'Love you, Lady Cavendish-Blake.' Megan looked into his handsome face and smiled. Never had she been so happy.

Finally relaxing, everyone made their way for champagne on the lawn. The very last of the summer's rays decided to shine and the air was filled with the clinking of glasses, laughter and a string quartet playing quietly in the background. Dylan and Flora, both relieved the horses had behaved themselves without dumping manure anywhere, glugged back the champagne thankfully.

'Have I told you how pretty you look today, Flora?' he asked, lazily looking her up and down. He could pick her up and roger her senseless in the stables right now, given the chance.

'You scrub up well yourself, Dylan,' she chipped back with a wink.

'Celia, isn't that the famous jockey?' murmured Wilfrid, who was totally starstruck with the whole affair. As soon as he had stepped foot inside Treweham Hall he couldn't take it all in. The place was splendid, all had made him welcome and Celia was as formidable as he remembered.

'Yes. Dylan Delany. An insufferable rogue,' answered Celia directly.

Finula was chatting to Gary and Tracy. 'Love that dress, Tracy,' she complimented. Gary gave a snort. Tracy nudged him hard.

'Thanks, Fin,' she quickly smoothed over.

'I had something very similar once.' Finula cocked her head to one side, sizing it up.

Ted was there, in his best suit, sitting with Megan's mum and brother. They were all deep in conversation. Megan looked on and smiled. She was going to invite Chris to stay in Bluebell Cottage, and really give him chance to get to know Ted. Plus she'd missed having her brother around. Kate seemed to be getting along with him nicely, she noticed.

'They've a lot of catching up to do,' Tobias remarked, handing her a glass of champagne. 'To us,' he toasted, raising his glass.

'To us,' she replied and kissed his lips.

Kate sidled up and congratulated them. 'You didn't tell me what a dish your brother is,' she whispered, making Tobias laugh.

'Is he?' Megan replied in surprise.

'Er… yeah,' Kate replied, rolling her eyes.

Wilfrid tentatively approached them and Tobias immediately made him feel comfortable.

'Wilfrid, meet my wife, Megan.' It felt so good calling her that. Wilfrid shook hands with Megan.

'Congratulations to you both. May I say what an absolute pleasure it is to be here.'

'Not at all, Wilfrid, thank you for coming,' replied Megan. What an enchanting couple, Wilfrid thought, in fact, what an enchanting place. He was still taking it all in.

'There you are,' interrupted Celia, making him jump. Then, turning to the small group, she announced that dinner was shortly to be served. Sure enough a gong was sounded and Henry was politely ushering everyone to the Great Hall for the wedding breakfast.

Once everyone was seated, Tobias rose at the top table, and a hush descended.

'Ladies, gentlemen and munchkins,' he winked towards Seamus' little girls, who giggled in delight, 'may I take this opportunity in thanking you all for sharing my and Megan's special day. I won't be making a further speech—'

'Thank God,' interrupted Sebastian, making everyone chuckle. Tobias smiled.

'– but will leave that job in the capable hands of my best man and best friend, Seamus.' All clapped and cheered. Seamus pushed his copper fringe back, hoping he'd meet their expectations. Tatum rested her hand on his lap for comfort. 'In the meantime, let's enjoy!' The Great Hall was filled with applause.

After a wonderful meal of watercress soup, beef wellington and summerfruit pudding, and whilst the guests sipped coffee and nibbled minted chocolate, Seamus stood up and spoke. His speech was peppered with humour, telling tales from his and Tobias' childhood and early teens, to later describing how their friendship had grown and strengthened with the trials of life. He was witty, tactful and gracious, giving testament to a good, lifelong friend. Megan's eyes filled with emotion. 'So, may I end my speech with a toast. To my best mate, Tobias, and his beautiful bride. To Tobias and Megan,' he raised his glass.

'To Tobias and Megan!' they all cheered.

As the sun shone down and the music played, as the laughter continued and the champagne flowed, as friendships formed and love grew, outside the gates of Treweham Hall, in the churchyard nearby, a spirit finally found solace. Only now could she rest in peace.

Acknowledgements

Researching for this book meant spending days wandering round old halls and ancestral homes, visiting quintessential villages and sipping wine in quaint, country inns, all the things I love doing!

I'd like to thanks my husband, Alex, for introducing me to the wonderful world of racing and patiently explaining all the goings-on at the exciting race meetings I tagged along to.

I honour and pay respect to all those soldiers who sacrificed their lives in the World Wars. Their heartfelt messages of love I read on various websites gave me inspiration for 'E's' letters.

Finally, I give huge thanks to Caroline Ridding, Publisher of Aria Fiction, for spotting me, and to Sarah Ritherdon and Yvonne Holland for their wise words and guidance in editing my book.

Sasha x

About Sasha Morgan

SASHA MORGAN lives in a rural, coastal village in Lancashire with her husband and Labrador dog. She has always written stories from a very young age and finds her fictional world so much more exciting than the real one.

Find me on Twitter
https://twitter.com/HjStafford

Become an Aria Addict

Aria is the new digital-first fiction imprint from Head of Zeus.

It's Aria's ambition to discover and publish tomorrow's superstars, targeting fiction addicts and readers keen to discover new and exciting authors.

Aria will publish a variety of genres under the commercial fiction umbrella such as women's fiction, crime, thrillers, historical fiction, saga and erotica.

So, whether you're a budding writer looking for a publisher or an avid reader looking for something to escape with – Aria will have something for you.

Get in touch: aria@headofzeus.com

Become an Aria Addict
http://ariafiction.com/newsletter/subscribe

Find us on Twitter
https://twitter.com/Aria_Fiction

Printed in Great Britain
by Amazon